A 'COP FOR CRIMINAL

STEAL
— THE —
GOLD

JACK GATLAND

Hooded Man
MEDIA
UNAPOLOGETIC & PRODUCTION & PUBLICATION

Published by Hooded Man Media
Cover photo by Paul Thomas Gooney

First Edition: November 2022

PRAISE FOR JACK GATLAND

'This is one of those books that will keep you up past your bedtime, as each chapter lures you into reading just one more.'

'This book was excellent! A great plot which kept you guessing until the end.'

'Couldn't put it down, fast paced with twists and turns.'

'The story was captivating, good plot, twists you never saw and really likeable characters. Can't wait for the next one!'

'I got sucked into this book from the very first page, thoroughly enjoyed it, can't wait for the next one.'

'Totally addictive. Thoroughly recommend.'

'Moves at a fast pace and carries you along with it.'

'Just couldn't put this book down, from the first page to the last one it kept you wondering what would happen next.'

There's a new Detective Inspector in town...

Before Ellie Reckless, there was DI Declan Walsh!

Read an EXCLUSIVE PREQUEL, completely free to anyone who joins the Jack Gatland VIP Reader's Club!

Join at www.subscribepage.com/jackgatland

Also by Jack Gatland

For Mum, who inspired me to write.

For Tracy, who inspires me to write.

CONTENTS

1

DELIVERY DIE-VER

It was a cold, wet Wednesday night when Paulo Moretti died.

It'd started so well, too. His job for the week had been to take a van from the main Lumetta Oils pound at around five in the morning and ferry a shipment of extra-virgin olive oil across the Channel the same evening. It was a long journey, made longer since the red tape of Brexit had caused so many backlogs for companies shipping into the United Kingdom, but the cost for the olive oil had also gone up, and that was being paid for by the buyers.

So, in a way, the extra money needed for this was already covered.

To be frank, Paulo also knew the shipment wasn't about the olive oil, even though that was what he had in the back of his Mercedes long-based Sprinter Van; he'd had to check it over before taking the keys for it, and they'd made a big song and dance about what was in it for their own records. And Mama Lumetta had Zoom'd in from London as they did this, unable to attend in person, but eager to make sure the job was done to the fullest extent. As ever, she'd treated him like dirt, but Paulo expected that.

Paulo had *always* expected that.

But it wouldn't be this way for long because Paulo had a plan, and soon, very soon, in fact, Mama Lumetta would bow to *him* for a change. After the events of the previous week, this was likely the last delivery like this, and he knew he could make more than double his usual amount when he arrived at the last location.

The Lumetta Oils warehouse was in Cortona, Italy, and from there it was a fifteen-hour, nine-hundred-mile drive to Calais. It was way more than he was legally supposed to do in a day, but at the same time there was a necessity for the security of the stock – or at least a *particular selection* – and even though he'd passed in and out of several countries along his route, it was Calais where the first of his Customs problems would occur. The French officers paused him, checked his papers, examined the contents of the van to make sure they equated with what the order bills said, and eventually, after several long minutes leading into hours – delays which caused him to miss his ferry – they let him through. You would have thought they wouldn't care that much about what was leaving their country, caring more what was coming into it, and this was possibly correct, as Paulo had felt they were just bored, and argumentative that day, but he didn't want to cause any issues, especially with *this* cargo.

Finally, Paulo had pulled the van to a stop in his car-park bay on the next ferry leaving, and had taken the hour and half crossing time to grab a snack before he arrived at the other end. He knew the ferry would arrive late; it was almost the last of the day for a reason, and this meant he wouldn't be pulling onto British tarmac until at least eleven at night. And then, with the Customs checks and red tape that end as well, there was every chance he wouldn't be getting out of the Customs area until gone midnight.

Paulo didn't mind this; he'd been used to spending the night in his lorry, but that was a bigger vehicle, with a bed area in the back of the driver's cabin. Here, he'd have to bed down in the back of the van, next to the pallets of olive oil. However, after twenty-four hours of travel, he didn't think it'd be a problem falling asleep.

He had an inflatable bed and a sleeping bag with him, but he'd realised with a string of expletives as he left Calais that he'd forgotten to bring a pillow. He'd have to use his jacket as an alternative, although it was quite thin. There was a chance he could take some of the extra bubble wrap in the van and make a makeshift pillow out of it, perhaps cover it with the jacket to make it softer, and Paulo had accepted his fate with a smile.

It could have been worse. He could have been sleeping with his wife tonight.

By the time the ferry reached the UK, Paulo was already working out his pillow-making plan. He'd stop at the service station just outside of Dover on the M20; it was a truck stop for a lot of lorries returning to Europe, and he knew it well. He could grab some (very late) dinner there, text Matteo to let him know he was through, and then he could grab some sleep before leaving early the next morning for his three stops. On returning, he'd take it easy, likely spend Friday just outside of Geneva, before arriving home Saturday afternoon. It was a long week of driving, but very well worth it, if he had to be honest. And, if he did the morning deliveries quick enough, it gave him around four- or five-hours' free time, in which he could park up his van, catch his half-brother for a coffee, and visit the British Museum.

Paulo loved the British Museum. He loved all museums, to be honest, but he enjoyed this the most. And his regular trips meant he could take his time as he went through the areas, not rush like the surrounding tourists. In three visits so far, he'd only seen half of the museum, and he was eager to start the Roman Empire section, for obvious reasons.

And then the van in front was moving on, and Paulo followed. He was even whistling by this point, a song he'd learnt as a child. Pulling up in a Customs bay, Paulo climbed out, grabbing a clear A4 folder as he did so, passing it across to the first of two guards that walked over to him.

'Evening, Paulo,' the first said. He was old, in his late fifties and had been working here for as long as Paulo had been travelling through, which was easily two decades. 'Smaller truck than usual?'

'Beauty in small packages, Mister Watson,' Paulo smiled, his accent strong as the guard opened up the plastic folder, passing some sheets to his colleague.

'I told you, I'm Brian,' the guard smiled. 'My dad is Mister Watson.'

'Your dad's a prick,' the other guard, a younger, fitter looking man with short blond hair, smiled. Paulo felt a twinge of fear at his words, as he didn't know this man. Something had changed, and he wasn't sure what it was.

'Don't mind Jimmy, he's my younger cousin,' Brian the guard replied as Jimmy the guard flicked through the order sheets. 'Can he have a look?'

'Of course,' Paulo smiled widely, walking to the back of the Sprinter Van.

'How does this drive?' Jimmy asked as he followed Paulo around to the back. 'I'm thinking of doing one of these up, you know, going all van life.'

'Van life?' Paulo frowned. 'Live on the road, in your van?'

'Yeah.'

Paolo shook his head at this, opening the back doors.

'We call that gypsy,' he said.

Jimmy went to reply, but stopped as he looked into the van's rear storage area. The entirety of it was filled with pallets of one-litre bottles of olive oil, all in glass bottles. Each pallet was around fifteen bottles wide, by the same deep, and there were three towers of pallets lined up in front of them.

'Jesus,' Jimmy stated. 'Do we have to check these? How many bottles are there?'

'There are two hundred and twenty-five bottles on each pallet level,' Paulo explained, the number coming from years of bringing the same stock over, pointing at a pallet. 'Fifteen by fifteen.'

He clambered into the back of the van.

'This is a pallet of nine hundred, as is the second,' he said, tapping a column of four pallets. 'This is warehouse in Maidstone. That one is a food wholesaler in Thurrock.'

He pointed at the third rear pallet. This had an extra row on top, and the label was slightly different, showing 2021 as the year of olive oil creation rather than 2022.

'This is one thousand, one hundred and twenty-four bottles, for wholesaler in East London,' he smiled. 'Addresses and names are on paperwork. I just drive truck.'

'Surely this isn't worth the hassle, though?' Jimmy

frowned. 'The cost of driving it here, paying Customs, driving it to the wholesaler, nine hundred bottles is what, a grand?'

'They sell each bottle for five pound,' Paulo tapped his nose. 'Customer sells each bottle for nine pound. Healthy profit made.'

Jimmy nodded, looking at his sheets of paper. With almost three thousand bottles weighing down the van, there was almost *fifteen grand's* worth of stock there.

'Sounds like it's good stuff,' he said.

'Try some,' Paulo reached down beside the middle pallet and pulled out a fresh bottle, with 2022 on the side. 'Here.'

'Oh, no, I couldn't,' Jimmy waved his hand, noticing Brian walking around to the back, watching him. 'It's not right.'

'Oh, it's very right,' Paul waved back, forcing the bottle on him. 'I have three spares, so if one bottle breaks, I can keep totals.'

He winked.

'Whoops! One bottle break.'

He reached back, passing out another bottle, this one with 2021 on it, presenting it more carefully to Brian, and Jimmy realised this was why his older cousin had walked to the back at this point.

'For you,' he said.

'I get a couple from him every time he passes through,' Brian shrugged at Jimmy, already pocketing away the bottle as he spoke. 'It's nice stuff. Try it.'

He looked back at Paulo expectantly.

'I usually get two, though?' he spoke softly as, forced by peer pressure, Jimmy twisted the metal cap off and dabbed the end on his finger.

'Yeah, that's nice,' he said. 'But I don't know—'

'You broke the seal,' Brian patted his cousin on the back. 'You can't give it back now.'

He looked back at Paulo, still waiting.

'Only one today, I can't afford any more "breakages" on this trip,' Paulo shrugged. 'But you'll still get the same benefits from it, Mister Watson.'

'Brian,' the older guard reminded Paulo, as he considered this for a moment. And then, taking the paperwork from his bemused cousin, Brian waved ahead.

'Stamp him through!' he shouted. 'Until the next time, Paulo.'

'Absolutely, Mister Wats—I mean, Brian,' Paulo's smile didn't waver. He went to walk away, but Brian spoke again, stopping him.

'You sleep at the truck park on the M20, don't you?' he asked.

'How would you know this?'

'Calculated guess. It's gone midnight, you've been driving all day, you need to sleep, next stop is Maidstone, and it's a fair drive.'

'What of it?' Paulo frowned. 'Am I not allowed to do so anymore?'

'Not at all, just a friendly warning,' Brian replied. 'I'd suggest not sleeping there tonight. There's been some truck break-ins, some valuable stock taken, and a couple of EU Nationals have been attacked. Police are still looking into it, but it looks like they go for the smaller vans. Easier to get into.'

Paulo nodded at this, smiling thankfully. Luckily for him, Brian knew the score. And if he suggested staying away, then Paulo would do just that.

'I will keep driving then,' he said, turning back to his van and walking to the driver's door.

The last thing he wanted was to lose the contents of this vehicle.

For that would be more than his life was worth.

IT WAS ALMOST ONE IN THE MORNING BY THE TIME PAULO HIT the M20, and by then the relentless British rain had started. It was only a drizzle, but it was enough to make the roads slippery, and the lorries were slowing down as they drove along it.

The road had been the A20 from Dover, but now there were blue signs with "M" on them, which made Paulo laugh, as it was still the two-lane A-road it'd been a hundred metres behind him, and it wouldn't be any different until the next junction when it became a proper, three-lane road. And, from there, he'd follow for another junction until he reached the truck stop he usually overnighted at.

But not tonight. Not with this cargo.

It wasn't far, only another half an hour before he'd arrive at his new destination for the night, a service station near Maidstone; however, this changed as he approached junction eight. There weren't many other cars on the motorway at this time of night, mainly commercial traffic and lorries, but they were all slowing down, as a series of cones appeared on the fast lane.

Paulo checked his sat nav, connected to the screen through his phone and CarPlay, and groaned. The M20 west, between junctions eight and nine, was closed, with traffic being diverted onto the A20, which currently ran alongside the motorway. In fact, the sat nav, obviously being alerted on the app's cloud of this closure, had already altered the route, taking Paulo off at this junction, and going the route suggested. It was only an extra mile, maybe five minutes more at this time of night, so Paulo shrugged, kissed his St Christopher's medallion and leant back into his seat, as it was still going to be another ten minutes for the current traffic to get off the motorway, what with all three lanes merging.

It might be quiet, but it was still busy enough to cause a slight delay.

He followed the traffic as it moved onto the A20, and over the next fifteen minutes watched as the road became a single-lane carriageway through small Kentish towns, heading away from Ashford down long, winding streets with barely any light. However, as he approached Leeds Castle, the sat nav flashed up a fresh change for him; ahead there'd been a three-car smash, and because of this, the road was currently closed. Instead, he would now turn right up Hospital Road, and follow the country lanes around Hollingbourne, before reconnecting with the A20 on the other side of the accident. Another ten minutes added, but better than the alternative.

As he turned into Hospital Road though, effectively nothing more than a single-lane country track through wood-lands, yawning as he did so, he noticed that the other cars, the ones both directly in front and behind him, had continued on. He assumed the lorries had taken one look at the road he'd turned onto and decided they'd rather wait it out than get trapped on a narrow turn, but was surprised the smaller cars didn't follow, that nobody else's sat nav led them the same way.

Still, the road ahead was lit up, only another mile and a half had been added to the journey, as Paulo shook his head to wake himself up and leant forwards, turning his light on to full beam as he carefully drove along the country lane. There was every chance he wouldn't see another soul here, but if someone the other side of the blockage and travelling the other direction had been given the same sat nav advice, there could be a standoff on these single-lane roads at any moment.

He'd just driven under the M20 underpass, following the winding path as it stopped being a dirt track and returned to being a conventional tarmac road, when he saw the cars waiting.

There were three SUVs, all black Range Rovers, two of which were blocking the road. Looking past them, Paulo could see a roadworks barrier about fifty metres further, with amber lights flashing on it. Anyone coming the other way would be told the road was closed, most likely.

Only someone coming from the south would find themselves here.

Only someone like Paulo.

There was a side road, gated, with two metal barriers now moved aside, and the men, masked and in black jackets, waved their guns at him to follow it. Feeling nervous now, Paulo nodded at them, turning onto the side road, noting the Range Rovers were already following him, the road now reopening to the public, as if he'd never been there.

The route he drove down was nothing more than a track, and likely led to a power station that catered to the train tracks to the left of him, but Paulo didn't care anymore. He knew why they were here and what they wanted. All he had to decide was how he could get out of this alive.

There was a fourth car facing him; it looked like a Tesla, or something along those lines, and the headlights were on full beam, shining directly at him. They flashed twice, and Paulo took this as an order to stop the van and get out. Taking a deep breath, he climbed out of the driver's side, arms in the air.

'I have seen nothing,' he exclaimed, for all the armed men to hear. 'I saw none of you. I just want to live.'

'You think she'll let you live after this?' a male voice spoke from behind the lights of the Tesla, and Paulo stretched to listen to it. There was the slightest hint of an accent, but he couldn't make out if he knew it from anywhere. 'She's been looking for a reason to remove you for years.'

'It's just olive oil,' Paulo replied, trying to make out he didn't hear the truth. 'Why would anyone kill over olive oil?'

'Paulo, Paulo, Paulo ...' the voice tutted as a silhouetted figure moved in front of the lights. 'How can you lie with a straight face?'

'I'm not lying!' Paulo pleaded, tears of fear streaming down his face. 'I know nothing!'

'If that's the case, why give the Custom Officers different bottles?' the man asked, and even though he couldn't see the man's face, Paulo knew he was smiling. 'Should I take only the 2022 bottles? What about the 2021 vintage?'

Paulo's heart sank as he listened to the words. The man knew he'd bribed the Customs Officers. And in this moment, he knew what he'd bribed them, in particular Brian, with.

'I just want to live,' he whispered.

'Mama Lumetta won't allow that, after she sees what she's lost,' the man walked over, raising Paulo's tear-smeared face with a hand, pulling him, with this action, to his feet. 'She'll even let Tommaso do it.'

And then, right at that moment, Paulo saw the man in

front of him, and knew for an absolute fact he would not survive this.

'I'll make it quick,' the man said. 'Just open the door, let us empty the van and I'll let you drift off.'

Nodding, and with his legs trembling, Paulo walked to the right-hand side door of the Sprinter Van, placing the key in and pulling it to the side, revealing the larger of the pallets, the 2021 vintage these men wanted. But then, before anyone could stop him, Paulo leaped into the van, pushing his way behind the pallet, pulling a bottle from the top and grabbing a crowbar from the corner of the space.

'I will not die quietly!' he shouted. 'Let me live or I'll break these! I'll break them all!'

To emphasise the point, he tapped the glass bottle.

'I know how much each of these is worth!'

tap tap tap.

'I'll smash them all!'

tap tap tap.

'You won't make a single—'

Paulo didn't finish his words, as the man quietly raised his gun and shot the bottle, the bullet deflecting upwards and catching Paulo in the neck, passing through and striking the left-hand driver's window behind him, Paulo's eyes widening in shock as he realised that not only would he never be seeing the Roman Empire exhibit at the British Museum, but that he would never see anything ever again.

And, as Paulo Moretti slumped to the floor, blood pumping violently from his throat, the man looked at his subordinates, already opening the boots of the Range Rovers.

'Take everything, but the 2021 goes first,' he said. 'I want those taken straight to the Vaults, yes?'

As the men opened the back of the Sprinter Van, he

looked back at the body of Paulo, crumpled in the van's corner. Clambering into the space himself, he crouched over the body, making the sign of the cross, as if giving a quiet, personal prayer to the departed driver. And then, this done, he pulled on a glove and took the remains of the shattered bottle in his other hand, being careful not to touch the jagged shards on the top. There was likely to be half a litre's worth of liquid still in the remnants of the shattered container, and with it in his hand, he looked over to one of his bodyguards, now helping the other men in pulling aside the 2022 vintage pallets.

'Empty one of those and fill it with this,' he said, carefully passing it over to the bodyguard. 'There's still thousands in there and I won't lose another penny if I don't have to.'

The bodyguard looked at Paulo and paled.

'You killed him!' he whispered. 'I didn't know there'd be killing.'

'Self-defence,' the man replied. 'Are you okay with that? With the money you're making here?'

Swallowing nervously, the bodyguard nodded, already emptying a fresh bottle, pouring the olive oil out of the back door before taking the shattered item and carefully decanting it into the complete bottle, using some wrapping as a makeshift funnel. He winced as he did this, cutting into the palm of his hand from a shard of the bottle as he poured, but he didn't worry about the blood affecting the product.

After all, the driver's blood was also mixed into it, and his boss hadn't seemed to mind.

And, with the remains now finished, and the broken bottle tossed out of the van and into the foliage to the side of the track, the bodyguard took a sharpie from his pocket and changed the "2022" on the new bottle to "2021" in case someone was to mistake it.

'What do we do with the van and the body when we're done?' he asked, pulling out a tissue and wadding it onto his palm to allow the cut to clot, but the man was already walking back to his car, climbing into the driver's seat.

'Burn everything,' the man commanded before he started the engine and, leaving his men to it, drove away from the abandoned Mercedes Sprinter Van, the hijacked stock, and the body of Paulo Moretti.

2

DOG TRAINING

AFTER SEVERAL MONTHS OF LIVING AWAY FROM MILLIE, ELLIE Reckless now found that returning to the life of a dog owner was actually quite difficult.

She'd been fighting her ex, Nathan, for custody of the five-year-old golden brown Cocker Spaniel for a few months now, and then a few weeks earlier, after a rather hectic case, Nathan had appeared out of nowhere with Millie in hand, telling Ellie that she could have the dog back.

The spiteful prick had however kept all her items, toys and food, so Ellie had to burn a favour to gain some supplies until she could buy Millie some more permanent items, but now, almost two months later, Millie was living better than Ellie herself was.

The first couple of weeks had also been simple; there was some fallout over the Danny Flynn case, and the police were all over the team as they tried to work out not only what had happened but also how a rag-tag group of independent contractors solved a multiple-homicide case before the police on the case did. Ellie had smiled innocently, allowing the police to make their own enquiries, never once suggesting that perhaps, just perhaps, *she was better than they were.*

Especially DS Kate Delgado, the backstabbing bitch.

She had taken a couple of weeks off to recover from the case – she'd received a rather vicious head trauma during it thanks to a car accident – so she took a few days to rest up, and by that she meant a few days to play with Millie, remind her who Ellie was, and give her as many treats and belly rubs as she wanted. Which, considering she was a Cocker Spaniel and governed by her stomach, was a lot.

And then over the last few weeks she'd returned to her "official" office in the *Finders Corporation*, a chrome-and-glass building in the middle of the City of London, just south of Farringdon. One of the better insurance investigators in the City, the bulk of Ellie's work was desk-based while her team of miscreants investigated various cases of insurance fraud, and she could bring Millie with her, setting up a new bed area in the office corner.

Millie had a lot of beds, it seemed.

But today, two months after Millie had returned into Ellie's life, they sat in Ellie's *other* office, *Caesar's Diner*, a small breakfast café amidst the City of London, and also just south of Farringdon Station. It was less than a block away from the Finders offices, and emulated a fifties diner: the floor was a checkerboard black and white design, the walls tiled white. There were tables in the middle and along the side were large, opulent red-leather booths, easily wide enough for six or seven people to sit and eat in. On the wall were fifties advertising posters for milkshakes, burgers and soft drinks, and on each table was a small jukebox, where for a 20p piece you could change the fifties song to *another* fifties song.

It was a typical city diner, and its clientele were often rich, hungry and nostalgic.

This was Ellie's office. Or, rather, a red-leather booth at the back corner of the diner, where Ellie and her team would sit when planning out the more "unofficial" cases they took on, was her office.

Ellie currently sat at the booth with Millie boosted onto the seat beside her. In her mid-to-late-thirties, her dark-brown, almost black hair was shoulder-length and curly, and currently in a bunch but with the possibility of completely collapsing out of that at any moment, she was wearing a cheap grey suit, and a pale blue, open necked and collared blouse, her trousers ending with grey *Converse* 'ox' trainers she wore on her feet. As she waited for the others to arrive, Ellie sat back in the seat, considering her last few months.

When she started at Finders, it was because Robert Lewis had brought her on, vouching to his new employers that ex-DI Elisa Reckless would be an asset to the company, and more importantly, was *not* the woman the press had painted her out to be: a corrupt police officer who'd not only had an affair with a police informant, but had also killed him, either deliberately or through her drunken, accidental actions.

It had been Robert who'd defended her against these charges during the lengthy and public court case, but although a jury cleared her of the murder, she was still damned by bad press and opinions, ones which cost her a marriage, and a job.

In fairness, the marriage was doomed anyway, as she *had* been having an affair with the informant, Bryan Noyce, even though they'd recently chosen to break off the relationship before both marriages were damaged.

I know I said it'd be a clean break, but Casey's everything to me. I need to keep joint custody.

I'm sorry, Ellie. I can't do this. I'll lose my son.

Ellie took a deep breath as the memory overcame her for a moment. The last time she'd seen Bryan, their words had been in anger. They'd fought, she'd struck him, bloodying his nose, and staining her jacket with droplets of blood. And then, later that evening he was dead, killed by Nicky Simpson, or at least on his orders, anyway.

The problem was, she couldn't *prove* this. And that blood on her jacket had been a smoking gun against her in the murder enquiry, while Nicky Simpson walked away, innocent of any accusations or charges.

This was the other reason she took the role with Finders, agreeing to work for Robert; he'd allowed her a second, more unconventional income stream. *Favours*. Working for the people who couldn't travel the more regular routes when an item was stolen, possibly because the item had also been stolen in the first place. In this she effectively became a "cop for criminals". She'd solve your problem, for a favour, to be used at any point in her choosing.

Ellie knew that if she could bank enough of these favours, she would eventually find a magic bullet, something to kick off a domino effect of favours, each one leading her to the answers she needed. She could prove her innocence once and for all, as the court case, although giving her the win, had never declared her innocent of all charges, as there were too many muddied elements of the story. There had been too many unanswered questions, ones that she also wanted cleared. She knew someone in the force – someone likely working for Simpson – had tried to have her blamed for things she never did, for example, forcing her to eventually quit the force as it had become untenable to stay.

Those favours would not only take down Simpson's empire but also expose the police mole.

But Ellie wouldn't be telling the police about the latter.

Ellie would find out who betrayed her, who set her up and ruined her life—and go *biblical* on them.

'You can't have that in here,' Sandra, the waitress, brought Ellie out of her thoughts, pointing at Millie. 'It's unhygienic.'

'*That* is a girl, and her name is Millie,' Ellie sighed, picking up her empty mug and waggling it at Sandra. 'And we do this every time. Ali said I could bring her in over a month back, and he's fine with it.'

At the mention of Ali, Sandra's face tightened.

'But it ... but *she* barks,' she muttered. 'Scares the customers off.'

'She barked once, and that's because a Pomeranian barked at her first.'

'Her bark was louder.'

'You're just pissed because Millie barked at your mate's dog,' Ellie smiled. 'Ali said I could have her in.'

'Only because he owed you a favour.'

'Indeed,' Ellie waggled the mug while nodding at Millie, currently panting happily with her tongue out, as she watched Sandra with what could only be described as love and optimism for the possible arrival of sausages. 'And this was the favour I asked for. Refill of tea, please.'

Taking one last irritated look at Millie, watching her with what looked to be a doggie smile on her face, Sandra walked off. Ellie was about to pick up her phone and check for any messages when the door to the diner opened, and Ramsey Allen, the team's retrieval specialist – or, rather, the team's resident *thief* – walked in. Resplendent in a herring-bone three-piece suit over a white Eton shirt and bronze striped tie, his grey, almost white hair cut short, a moustache his only facial hair, and a silver-tipped walking cane in his hand, Ramsey, in his mid-sixties looked like a director of one of the nearby finance companies. In fact, on several occasions, customers had started their meetings talking to Ramsey rather than Ellie, believing him to be her boss.

Of course, once he spoke, his accent a peculiar mix of upper-class and East End barrow boy, all bets were off.

'Good lord,' he exclaimed, making a song and dance of turning around the diner, checking all the booths. 'Can it be that I have beaten the incorrigible Tinker Jones to a diner meeting?'

'You're the first, yeah,' Ellie replied. 'Well done. Have a medal. Now sit down and order some food.'

Ramsey stared at Millie, now standing up on the booth's seat and wagging her tail at him.

'You mean sit next to that?' he hissed.

'Or the other side, I don't really care,' Ellie forced a thin-lipped smile. 'But I'm getting sick of having her called "it" and "that" today.'

Ramsey sat in the booth, reluctantly allowing Millie to excitedly sniff his cheek.

'It's just that she gets dog spittle on my suits,' he bemoaned as she licked his chin, but Ellie could see by his lack of pushing the dog away he wasn't that concerned. And, once Millie had checked him over and returned to her seat, Ramsey waved at Sandra for a menu.

'A number three,' he said, checking it quickly. 'And a strong coffee.'

'Three?' Ellie frowned. 'I thought you were working your way through the menu?'

'I am,' Ramsey said, and a slight hint of uncomfortableness was now audible in his voice. 'I mean, that is, I've lapped. I'm starting again.'

'But you were in the forties last time we met,' Ellie checked the menu beside her, tapping on the laminated page. 'That's a good ten meals short of ...'

She trailed off as realisation took hold.

'You've *cheated* on me,' she hissed. 'You've been coming here without me.'

Ramsey scratched the back of his neck.

'I like the place,' he said apologetically. 'Not my fault you weren't on some of the jobs. You've been away from the company a fair bit over the last few weeks, what with the dog, and getting better, and all the usual things that happen over a summer.'

'But we don't use this diner for normal jobs,' Ellie replied.

'*You* might not, but me, Tinker and the child don't have swanky offices,' Ramsey sniffed, now returning to his usual haughty self. 'So, we make do with what we have. In that case, here.'

Ellie shook off her irritation, leaning back as she observed Ramsey.

'How's Casey doing?' she asked, picking up on his use of "the boy". 'I heard he worked out the last case for you?'

At this, Ramsey shrugged.

'He's okay,' he replied noncommittally. 'I mean, he helped a little. A modicum of assistance.'

Ellie waited.

'Okay,' Ramsey admitted. 'He may have pulled his weight. But it was a team effort.'

'Of course, it was,' Ellie nodded soothingly. Ramsey went to reply, but then paused as a thought struck him.

'Tinker's *not* late, is she?' he asked. 'The boy would be here too. He's never late. Bloody eager beaver. This is about us, isn't it?'

'Maybe Millie wanted her Uncle Ramsey time?'

'Please don't call me that. This is about bloody Simpson, isn't it?'

Ellie nodded, all attempts at pretext gone.

'He's been sniffing around again,' she said. 'He's left us alone for a few weeks, but he's coming out of the woodwork again, now the Danny Flynn case is done and dusted. I wondered if he'd been talking to you at all?'

Ramsey shook his head.

'Wish I could say otherwise, but he's been pretty quiet with me of late, too,' he replied. He felt comfortable talking about this, as Ellie already knew he was currently being blackmailed by Nicky Simpson, who was paying his mother's nursing home bills in return for information on Ellie and her investigations. Ellie, when learning she had a mole in her team, had understood Ramsey's predicament, especially when he chose her over Simpson at his own risk, and since then had quietly allowed Ramsey to provide Nicky Simpson with news on her cases; doctored, of course, to send him in the wrong direction when possible.

However, from the sounds of things, Simpson might not have been so easy to fool after all.

'Let me know if that changes,' she replied, nodding thanks as Sandra brought her tea over. 'I think he might be checking in soon.'

'Oh?' Ramsey sipped at his own mug, his eyebrows rising. 'Do we have something big and juicy coming in?'

'Possibly,' Ellie was looking towards the door as she spoke. 'Robert wanted us here as he had something for my, well, more *unauthorised* side of the business.'

'The pro bono work,' Ramsey sniffed. Since Ellie had brought him into her confidence, he'd been a lot happier taking the occasional unpaid gig, now understanding the end result was better for all of them. 'And Tinker and Casey?'

'Can come in later on this,' Ellie replied. 'I got the impression a large team would overwhelm the client.'

'And the client doesn't want to visit your swanky boardroom?' Ramsey whistled. 'This must be someone very dodgy.'

Ellie chuckled.

'They can't be that bad,' she said, rubbing Millie's head. 'We allow you into the offices after all.'

Ellie's phone beeped. Picking it up, she stared down at the message on it for a long moment, before puffing out her cheeks and whistling to herself in the same way Ramsey had a moment earlier; although while he had been more mocking, this was deadly serious.

'It's a big fish,' she said, looking up at the door. 'Robert's meeting her now and bringing her directly here.'

'Her?' Ramsey raised an eyebrow at this. 'Come on, give me a little more.'

'You used to work for her,' Ellie placed the phone back down. 'And a favour from her will go a long way to proving my innocence.'

Ramsey frowned at this, as he mentally worked through a list of the people he'd worked for over the years. And then, as if a lightbulb switched on inside his head, his eyes widened.

'Mama Lumetta?' he whispered. 'Mary, Mother of God, it's her, isn't it?'

'Is there a problem if it is?' Ellie asked, her tone clipped as she watched the door. 'Because if you have issues, now's the time to make a discreet withdrawal.'

'No, no, I have no issues with Mama Lumetta,' Ramsey smiled. 'That is, I don't think so. Although her sons might not be the biggest fans.'

He looked over to the window now, an almost wistful expression on his face.

'We were an item once,' he said. 'For about a week. It was a couple of years after her husband passed on.'

'Why only a week?'

'She realised I'd stolen from her,' Ramsey continued to smile as he remembered the moment. 'It was the whole reason I got together with her, there was something I wanted, and she had it. Man, she was pissed. And then she hired me instead.'

'You're lucky,' Ellie nodded as Robert Lewis, with a young man in a suit and an older woman beside him, entered through the main doors to the diner. 'Most people lose their hands.'

'I'm too cute for amputation,' Ramsey rubbed his nails against his shirt as he slid out of the booth to meet the three arrivals.

Robert was in his early forties, his dirty-blond hair cut short to mid-length, and parted to the right. It wasn't doctored, either, as the temples were peppered with a slight dusting of grey. He wore a charcoal-grey suit over a pale-blue shirt, but, unlike Ramsey, wore no tie, instead sporting an expensive looking gold Rolex on his wrist as the only sugges-tion he was doing well in business. The man beside him was obviously with Mama Lumetta, wearing the navy-blue suit and black tie of a chauffeur, or a bodyguard, his head closely shaved, giving him an ageless look of either in his twenties or in his thirties. He was taller than Robert, and had the build of a boxer, and if it wasn't for the leather driving gloves he still wore on his hands, Ellie would have pegged him for security.

Of course, there was every chance he was both.

The woman, obviously Mama Lumetta, was a woman in her late sixties or early seventies, with permed, white hair. She was hard-faced, likely through the years of organised crime weighing on her shoulders, and was slim, almost skinny in looks, but hid this under a long, grey and black fur coat. As she held her hand out to Ramsey, Ellie saw it was dripping in gold chains and rings.

'Ramsey Allen,' she smiled warmly, her face softening as she saw the old rogue. 'So good to see you.'

'And you, Maureen,' Ramsey kissed the offered hand, and didn't take offence as Mama Lumetta examined her rings the moment he stepped back, jokingly checking whether he'd stolen any of them. Waving to the booth, Ramsey noticed Mama Lumetta glance at Millie, and then choose to sit on the other side, Robert sitting beside Ramsey as he returned to his seat.

'Not a dog lover?' Ellie asked.

'No,' Mama Lumetta replied. 'Not of little dogs.'

'You'd consider this a little dog?' the answer surprised Ellie.

'My dogs would snap yours up in a mouthful,' Mama Lumetta shrugged. 'But enough of animals and their eating habits. We're here for one reason, and one reason only.'

She turned, nodding to the driver.

'Wait in the car, Lorenzo,' she said.

The driver, now known as Lorenzo, frowned, looking around.

'But you'll be alone,' he muttered.

'I'm never alone when I'm with friends,' Mama Lumetta smiled. And, as Lorenzo walked huffily out of the diner, she sighed.

'Good man, loyal as anything, but is a little overprotective.'

'That's not a bad thing,' Ramsey replied.

As a response to this, Mama Lumetta made a half-shrug of agreement, before turning to Ellie and leaning closer as she continued. 'Give me your terms,' she said. 'For I have need of your services, Ellie Reckless, copper for criminals.'

3

NEW CLIENTS

ELLIE LEANT BACK AS SHE REPLIED, NOT ALLOWING MAMA Lumetta to intimidate her.

Of course, by moving backwards, she'd probably done the exact thing Lumetta had wanted, which slightly annoyed her.

'Well,' she started. 'If you want something done legally, we charge a percentage of the item's worth—'

'Let us not talk of scripts and boilerplate replies,' Mama Lumetta held a hand up to silence Ellie. 'I am here, not in your offices. This is not legal. I cannot do "legal" in this situation, as I am already doing that.'

Ellie paused, frowning.

'What do you mean?'

'What Mrs Lumetta means, is she's employing you on two fronts,' Robert explained. 'We've already sorted out the details of that. As you know, Mrs Lumetta is a rather influential and well-known businesswoman.'

Ellie had to physically force herself not to smile at this; Mama Lumetta was indeed a businesswoman, but that wasn't why she was influential or well known. The Lumetta family were the main criminal organisation of the west coast of Ireland, and over decades had established a solid grip on the restaurants of London, Liverpool, Birmingham and Manchester, with warehouses across the country, and with ambitions heading towards the east coast of America, in particular Boston. Even after the patriarch, Alvaro Lumetta had passed, Mama had managed to keep control of the empire from all attackers.

She was also a still-standing ranking member of the criminal underworld, following the attempted coup by the Lucas family a few months earlier, and possibly even bigger in size and scale than Nicky Simpson.

'Last night, or rather early this morning, Mrs Lumetta had one of her supply vans hijacked,' Robert continued, passing over a sheet of A4 paper for Ellie to look at. 'In it were almost three thousand litres of their finest extra-virgin olive oil, in glass one-litre bottles. All of this was taken, and the driver of the van was shot and killed before they torched the van and left.'

'So, it's a murder enquiry,' Ellie said softly, reading the sheet. 'The police are involved. They have to be.'

'Of course, they are,' Mama Lumetta replied. 'An employee of mine was murdered. Set fire to. Stock stolen. This is a major crime.'

'Then I don't understand where I come in?' Ellie glanced at Ramsey, to see if she was the only one who didn't get this, and was grateful to see he too had a confused expression on his face. 'Apart from the official recovery of your stock, which can't be more than a few grand?'

She counted on her fingers, glancing at some numbers on the sheet Robert had given her.

'Your extra-virgin olive oil is sold for what, a tenner? Sold for half that, so about fifteen grand in stock. I get you're pissed that your driver was killed, and you lost a van and stock, but two of these three things are insurable, so why bring us in?'

'I was told you were thorough, and I'm impressed,' Mama Lumetta replied, carelessly avoiding the question. 'I have three customers all angry their stock is not arriving. I need to show them I care. I'd rather find the bottles and retrieve them, than spend months in legal litigation trying to gain back money lost.'

'And of course, if you can get the bottles back under the counter, you double your money,' Ramsey replied without thinking. 'Not that a successful businesswoman like you would ever think of something like that.'

'Mrs Lumetta has hired us to find the bottles,' Robert continued. 'And, if we find all of them, she'll waive the percentage and give us the worth amount.'

'Fifteen grand just to find some bottles?' Ellie looked down at Millie for a moment before replying. 'So, what was really stolen?'

Mama Lumetta didn't answer this for a long moment, simply watching Ellie carefully, as if judging how much to tell her.

'All you need to know is I had almost three thousand bottles of my family's extra-virgin olive oil taken from me, and a loyal employee killed,' she eventually spoke. 'And I will not only pay your company the full cost of the lost property but also give you whatever your personal payment is.'

'Be careful what you wish for,' Ellie steeped her fingers together. 'My payment is one favour, given without question or argument at a time or place of my choosing – if I find the bottles you lost, that is. If I solve your case, you owe me whatever I ask for, but it'll always be something you can give and afford. I'm not demanding stupidly expensive things, and most of the time these favours are burned to further other cases.'

Mama Lumetta nodded at this.

'I heard about Callahan, and Danny Flynn,' she said. 'I'm good with those terms. Especially as I heard Callahan decided *not* to honour this, and the same night his private files were leaked to the press. And Danny Flynn honoured the deal, even after you used his favour to stop him committing murder.'

'Danny was in a tough spot,' Ellie replied. 'I gave him an out, it was his decision to keep the debt.'

'That you did showed me you won't take the piss,' Mama Lumetta said, the last word sounding strange in her slightly sing-song, Italian accent. 'So don't take it now.'

Ellie nodded in response. She understood very well what Mama Lumetta meant by that.

Find my bottles, and don't ask what's in them.

'Were the bottles the only thing in the van?' she asked.

'What else do you think could be there?'

Ellie considered this.

'Some vans have grooves,' she said, 'in the flooring. You could place things into it.'

Mama Lumetta smiled.

'There may have been things under the pallets,' she said. 'Packing out the space. Trinkets and suchlike.'

'Gold? Diamonds?'

'All I will say, is there was some gold there,' Mama Lumetta admitted. 'Gold I'd like to know the location of.'

'So why hire us to find the bottles?' Ellie asked, but then stopped, holding up her hand. 'Actually, don't answer that.'

Mama Lumetta was hiring Finders, because the bottles were the legal stock. And when they found who stole the bottles, they'd also know who stole the gold.

'Mrs Lumetta has agreed to employ Finders on a consultancy basis, which means you'll be able to examine everything connected to the theft and murder on her behalf, and enter all crime scenes as her designated investigator,' Robert explained. 'She'll also provide your team with a per diem of a hundred pounds, each, per day.'

At this, Ramsey straightened.

'Now that's more like it!' he exclaimed happily.

'So, we are agreed?' Mama Lumetta spat in her hand and held it out to Ellie, who, after a moment, reluctantly spat into her own palm, took the hand and shook it.

'If you can send me the details, sure,' she replied. 'But if I find you killed your driver, I'll be sending the details to the police.'

'I'd expect nothing less,' Mama Lumetta rose, nodded to Robert, and then walked over to the door of the diner. As she did so, three men and one woman, all sitting in different seats, and who had been there since before Ellie had even arrived, all rose and followed her out.

'Now that's impressive,' Ramsey muttered. 'She scoped out the place and had her people in here before she'd even signed the contract to use us.'

Ellie leant back on the booth seat, wiping her hand with a napkin and looking over at Robert, who was already rising from his own place.

'You want to join us for brunch?' she asked. 'You could tell us what we just agreed to.'

'I will, but I need to go get the paperwork first,' Robert was already tapping on his phone. 'I have a feeling we need to be one step ahead of the police on this one, and we're already a day behind.'

'The hijack,' Ramsey said, looking up at Robert. 'Can you do me a favour? Find out if forensics is done with it, as we might need to go visit. That is, if they haven't taken the bloody van away by now.'

'You should go with Tinker for that,' Ellie stopped, checking her phone. 'I told her to wait outside in her car until the meeting was over. Casey too.'

'If anyone's heard anything, I'll let you know,' Robert stepped back as Sandra, now with a plate of sausage, egg and chips for Ramsey arrived, eyeing Millie warily. Nodding to Ellie, Robert left the diner as Ramsey tucked into his early lunch.

'What?' he asked, his mouth half-full of sausage.

Ellie sighed, covering Millie's eyes with her hand.

'You could at least have left her a bit of sausage,' she said as, laughing while eating, Ramsey turned his back on the poor, tired, hadn't-been-fed-in-utterly-ages Cocker Spaniel.

'You heard Mama Lumetta,' he continued. 'Buy your dog something from your own per diem.'

Ellie waved a hand, calling Sandra over. While they waited for the others, she would do just that.

'Can I get a plate with just a sausage on?' she asked.

'We don't do just a sausage,' Sandra sniffed.

'But you offer additional sausages for a quid, right?' Ellie forced a smile. 'So, I'd like an extra sausage.'

'Extra on top of what?'

'Sandra, stop being a jobsworth and give the bloody dog a treat,' Ramsey paused from eating. 'Add it to my bill.'

And, as Sandra, sighing very loudly, left the two alone in the booth, Ramsey turned to face Ellie.

'You tell anyone I bought Millie a sausage and I'll deny everything,' he hissed. "One has a reputation to uphold, you know.'

'Sandra, can you also give me an extra couple of pieces of bacon and two slices of toast added onto Ramsey's meal?' Ellie called out, grinning at the horrified thief as she leant back. 'Might as well get a bacon toastie out of you while I wait for the others.'

Ramsey muttered something incomprehensible and likely obscene as he continued with his food, and Ellie checked her phone again, texting Tinker, telling her the meeting was over, and it was time to go to work. She was about to press "send" when the door to the diner opened, and Tinker Jones, in her usual olive-coloured German Army coat worn over a pale T-shirt and blue jeans, and her curly blonde hair pulled back into a ponytail, but without her usual baseball cap on, entered, followed by Casey. He was as bookish as he ever was, in a black hoodie and jeans, a backpack over his shoulder, and a skateboard in his hand. It was half-term holidays, and he'd been allowed by his mum to rejoin Finders; partly because he made a little holiday money, but mainly because it kept him out from under her feet.

If she knew what he was really doing, she'd ban him from visiting us forever, Ellie thought to herself. The son of Bryan Noyce, Casey knew of the affair his father had with Ellie, and had a far more personal reason than the others to help her find his father's actual killer. And, in his spare time, he'd been data stripping forums on the dark web, looking for anything that could give him that smoking gun, to no avail.

Yet.

'Sorry, had to pick up the child,' Tinker explained as she slid into the booth.

Casey, however, stopped, staring at her.

'First off, I'm not the youngest here, and I'm definitely not answering to "the child"—' he started, but Ramsey held up his fork, pausing him.

'If you're not the youngest, then who is?'

Casey pointed at the Cocker Spaniel on the booth seat.

'She's five.'

'Which is thirty-five in dog years,' Ramsey returned to his food. 'Nice try, though.'

Casey didn't reply, silently accepting the answer.

'And second?' Ellie prompted.

'And second, Tinker was late arriving at mine,' Casey slid into the booth now, his point made. 'I was waiting outside.'

'I didn't say I only just arrived because of the child, but that I had to pick him up,' Tinker looked uncomfortable as she changed her story.

Ellie caught on this, turning to face her old friend.

'You okay?' she asked, concerned.

At this, Casey glared at Tinker.

'Tell her,' he said.

'Tell her what?'

Tinker squirmed in her seat.

'I need to borrow Casey,' she said, looking down at the table. 'Just for a couple of hours.'

Ramsey placed his cutlery down now, sensing sport.

'Tinkerbelle Jones, share with the class,' he joshed. 'What's so important?'

Tinker didn't even snap back about his use of her full name, and Ellie frowned at this. For her to forget to even play that game with Ramsey meant something odd was going on. Especially as she was apologising for being late to a meeting she hadn't been invited to, and had obviously not read the messages about it, or had been so distracted it wasn't taken in.

'Tink, seriously,' she whispered. 'What's going on?'

'I'm being blackmailed,' Tinker replied slowly, looking up at Ramsey, daring him to make a joke at her expense.

Ramsey, seeing the glare, decided better of mockery right now.

'Okay, who by, and how can we help?' he asked instead.

Tinker puffed out her cheeks and shrugged noncommittally as she looked back to the table.

'I don't know,' she said. 'I don't know who's doing it, or why.'

'What are they asking for?' Ellie glanced at Casey. 'And why does she need you? I'm guessing something computer related?'

'She was hacked,' Casey explained. 'As of right now, I don't know how bad. But someone got into her files, removed photos, old emails, stuff like that.'

'Ouch,' Ellie leant back. 'Any idea how they got in?'

'Probably my old army password,' Tinker replied sullenly. 'Which means it's likely someone from back in the day.'

Ellie nodded at this, as Ramsey pushed his now empty plate away.

'You were a squaddie, right?' he asked. 'Not mocking, you've never really talked about it.'

'I was a Corporal in the Rifles, yeah,' Tinker replied. 'Left after my twelve years. No drama, no issues. Still see a lot of my crew, never thought I had a problem with any of them.'

'Until now?'

'Someone knows about my past,' Tinker growled, and Ellie could see it was a sore subject. 'And they think they can cause someone I cared about pain at my expense.'

She looked back at Ellie.

'No ransom yet, no blackmail letter, just a note telling me retribution is coming,' she said.

'Well, that's not ominous at all,' Ramsey shook his head, glancing across the table at Casey. 'You're fixing this, right?'

Casey nodded. 'I need to check her system, but I'll work out what's going on,' he promised. 'As long as we're not needed here?'

'We're waiting for the details right now from Robert, but it looks like we're hunting stolen olive oil bottles,' Ellie smiled. 'And yes, as it's Mama Lumetta we're working for, we can pretty much guarantee the bottles are more than just oil.'

As if hearing his name, Robert walked back into the diner, a sheath of papers in his hand. As he walked up to the booth, Sandra appeared out of nowhere, passing him a mug of coffee before disappearing.

'Hey!' Tinker exclaimed at this. 'She hasn't bloody taken my order yet! How do you get service?'

Robert smiled as he sipped at his coffee.

'I'm just more likeable than all of you,' he replied, spreading out the sheets on the booth table. 'So, who wants to learn about olive oil hijacking and murder?'

4

EXTRA VIRGINS

'Meet Maureen Lumetta,' Robert showed an image of the elderly matriarch. 'Current CEO and owner of *Lumetta Oils*, who stock warehouses and restaurants around the world. She's also, unconfirmed, the head of the Lumetta crime family, who have criminal empires around the world, coincidentally in every city she has a warehouse or restaurant.'

'Handy,' Tinker said, tapping on the menu so Sandra could finally take her order, Casey having already sent his in by email earlier, and now tucking in to a sausage sandwich. 'Who are the two men?'

Robert moved the image aside to give a clearer view of the next two photos, that of men in their forties, stocky and balding, and obviously closely related.

'Tommaso and Matteo Lumetta,' Robert continued. 'Older and younger sons, respectively. Tommaso is the heir apparent to the family, but Matteo is a more respected and liked boss. If they came to a vote, he'd likely win. But that's not how things work in crime families.'

'Are they both loyal to Mama?' Ellie asked. 'Maybe we have a couple of suspects here?'

'Oh, we definitely have that,' Ramsey replied. 'They hate each other, and when they're not doing that to their fullest extent, they're hating their mother.'

'You know them?' Ellie added.

Ramsey shrugged.

'I've not spoken to them for a few years now, but I know them both,' he replied. 'Last I recall, we weren't on bad terms, either. Want me to speak to them?'

'Yeah, that might be an idea,' Ellie looked down at Millie, as if expecting the Cocker Spaniel to have an opinion on this. 'But that said, go lightly. They might not know Mummy's been robbed, and as you said, they don't get on with her. Last thing I want to do is start some kind of land war purely because I gave away some information that wasn't mine.'

'I can do that,' Ramsey nodded. 'Tommaso usually plays cards at one of the Mayfair casinos. I don't know if Matteo's in town, he usually stayed close to the home base in Dublin, but I can ask about.'

'Do either of them fit the bill?' Tinker asked.

At this, Ramsey actually chuckled.

'You've seen *The Godfather*, right?' he asked. 'Where you have the three sons, Sonny, Fredo, and Michael? Sonny's the gung-ho one, not really built for thinking, while Michael's the intelligent one who ends up taking on the role and Fredo is ambitious but a little dumb and useless, and easily led?'

'Which one of them's Fredo?' Tinker smiled.

'Both of them,' Ramsey replied. 'But they both think they're Michael, and act like they're Sonny. They're both dangerous and usually very, very stupid.'

'Maybe not anymore.' Casey was still reading through the papers. 'Especially if one of these did this.'

'Okay, so we have two possibles who have reason to take out the van,' Ellie nodded. 'Do we know what was in it?'

'Exactly what was said,' Robert showed a Customs form. 'Just under three thousand glass litre bottles of extra-virgin olive oil, stacked and wrapped in pallets of fifteen by fifteen.'

'Long wheelbase Sprinter,' Tinker read from a sheet beside it. 'They pretty much packed it out to its top weight. The suspension would have taken a battering there. And you're talking at least a thousand miles of driving until all deliveries were made. Harsh on the van.'

'Apparently they sent deliveries every week, but with differing levels,' Robert read from some handwritten notes, most likely taken when he spoke to Mama Lumetta before she came to the diner. 'Sometimes it's London, sometimes they go to Liverpool, Manchester, all over the place.'

'Say fifteen grand a pop, four times a month, that's only sixty grand a month, not including the petrol, wear and tear on the vehicles, all that,' Ramsey frowned. 'That feels a little small.'

'That's the legal stock,' Ellie nodded at the sheets. 'The fact we've been called in means that they use this to mask the actual stuff.'

'She did mention they have a raised floor in the van, for suspension,' Robert replied. 'Only about an inch, but it's enough to slide various contraband in. Never drugs, though, according to her.'

'Bonds, cash, jewels, the list is endless,' Tinker nodded. 'Put them under the pallets and unless you really know for sure there's something there, you're not opening it up, because you'd have to take everything out first.'

'She admitted there was gold under the pallets, and this was stolen,' Ellie pursed her lips. 'If it was stolen gold, in easy to carry chains or necklaces, there could have been maybe another ten grands worth stolen here.'

'Tell us about the hijack,' Casey said, finishing his sandwich. 'And not because it sounds more exciting than bottles of oil. I'm curious how they managed it.'

'It was well set up,' Robert admitted. 'Paulo Moretti was the driver, and had been working for the family for decades now. He'd drive to the UK every couple of weeks, and had become a well-known face at the Dover Customs. So much so that he regularly passed through faster than anyone else in the queues.'

'So, what was different this time?' Ellie asked.

'Probably the contraband,' Ramsey replied. 'They most likely only send something like this once a month, maybe every couple of them. Which means—'

'Which means it was an inside job, and something of great worth,' Ellie added. 'You're not committing murder and starting off a war unless the money's worth it. So, where did they stop him?'

'He was diverted off the M20, and onto the A20 while en route into London because of roadworks,' Robert explained. 'I checked, there were definitely closures. But then, for some inexplicable reason, he turned off the A20 before Maidstone and headed down Hospital Road, following the country lanes around Hollingbourne.'

'Did anyone else do this?' Ellie asked. 'Maybe it was a shortcut or something?'

'Not that we can work out,' Robert looked at Casey. 'Although now your team is involved, they might find something?'

Ellie nodded, waving Robert to continue.

'Anyway, he pulls up in the middle of nowhere, through a gate that says no entry, and that's where he's shot, the cargo is taken, and the van burned.'

'Are we sure of this?' Tinker asked. 'Perhaps he was taken earlier, maybe at a service station, and someone else drove the body and the van to this location?'

'Apparently, he usually stayed in a truck stop a few miles from Customs after a late-night arrival, but this time he didn't,' Robert admitted, checking the sheet of paper for any other facts that could be seen as relevant. 'There's every chance he could have planned to, and then was driven by gunpoint to this location.'

'Or maybe he was led there,' Casey suggested. 'If he was using sat nav, he might have been looking for the fastest route, especially if he was already off the motorway and stuck in single-lane traffic. Someone could have hacked it.'

'Hack the sat nav?' Ellie shuddered. 'That sounds familiar.'

Casey nodded. A couple of months earlier Ellie and Tinker had almost *died* when someone had hacked into their own car, turning the brakes off in the process.

'In a way, yes,' he said. 'But to do it, you'd need to be able to get into the van, attach the right equipment. Which means probably at the depot where he started.'

'Or at Dover,' Robert checked the notes. 'He left the van when he spoke to Customs.'

'Were either of the sons at the depot?'

'No,' Robert checked the notes. 'Matteo lives in Dublin, and Tommaso lives in London. Mostly. He travels around a lot.'

'We're looking at the sons, but is there anyone else who'd

benefit from this?' Ramsey asked, leaning back so he could see everyone at the booth. 'It's not our first rodeo where someone with a vested interest in the outcome has caused a major financial issue for a rival. We might not know what Mama Lumetta was couriering, but we know it was likely to be over fifteen grand's worth of stock. If she's bringing a chunk of finances into the UK, illegally, that means she's looking to pay someone under the table. Buy something off books, perhaps.'

'And if she can't pay it, she can't move on,' Ellie nodded. Danny Flynn had a similar issue when he called Ellie and her team in; a debt needed to be paid, and the means to pay it stolen. 'So, what is she likely to be spending her money on? And what sort of money can she get her hands on usually?'

'If it's illegal purchases, she wouldn't be able to use anything in her accounts, or anything she has on books,' Robert considered this. 'There'd be a paper trail, and I get the impression she'd rather there wasn't one.'

'So, she has an opportunity to buy something, pay something, perhaps, or maybe she has a debt she needs to pay, quietly,' Ellie mused. 'She uses her regular delivery driver to bring the cash, or something of equal value across, but someone knows it's in there.'

'If she has a secret bottom in the van, they'd have to remove the bottles to get to it,' Tinker suggested. 'The bottles might not be the issue here.'

'No, she wants the bottles,' Ellie shook her head. 'She said to us in the meeting that she'd rather find the bottles and retrieve them than spend months in legal litigation trying to gain back money lost in the theft. Sure, she could look at double the money, but I got a real impression she wanted us to find the stock, and not look that hard into what the stock actually was.'

'The labels are counterfeit notes,' Casey slammed his hand on the table. 'The bottles are made of diamonds.'

'What are you talking about?' Ramsey sighed.

'If we're looking at bottles of olive oil as the items she wants back, then these need to be doctored in some way to give her the profit she needs,' Casey said. 'The gold she said was in the van can't have been that much, or it would have been too obvious, and Customs would have found it. And the Customs note says there's three deliveries, two of nine hundred bottles, and one of eleven hundred and twenty-four. That's about two hundred and twenty-four more than the other two, and until we find another waybill that can confirm this or not, they're rogue bottles.'

He paused, looking at the ceiling, his mouth moving as he thought through a problem.

'You said it was fifteen by fifteen on each pallet, right?' he asked.

'That's right,' Robert checked the numbers. 'Why?'

'That's two hundred and twenty-five bottles a row,' Casey thought aloud. 'Four rows high is nine hundred. Five rows high is one thousand, one hundred and twenty-five.'

'If there's only two hundred and twenty-four extra, then there's a bottle missing,' Ellie leant forward. 'Why send an almost filled pallet? You'd have the full amount.'

'Unless one of the bottles was needed, maybe as a bribe?' Ramsey nodded. 'Which then makes us ask, what's in the bottles that makes them worth a bribe? Expensive whisky, perhaps?'

'That's a thought,' Robert nodded. 'Although it'd look darker in the bottle.'

'Not by that much. If the glass is green-tinted, you might not notice,' Ellie was tapping on her phone's calculator. 'Contraband whisky for, say, something worth fifty quid a bottle, seventy-five centilitres in size, so seven hundred and fifty millilitres ...'

'That's about three hundred whisky bottles' worth, if we only look at the extra two hundred and twenty-four bottles in the shipment,' Casey replied before Ellie could get an answer. 'At fifty quid a bottle, that's fifteen grand.'

'And if we looked at the whole third pallet?' Tinker asked. 'Fifteen still sounds low, and I'm aware we're using an average figure here.'

'We're looking at about fifteen hundred bottles worth once they're split into the new bottle sizes,' Casey continued. 'If it's fifty a bottle, then they've had just under seventy-five grand worth of stock stolen.'

'I know we're reaching, but that's a definite possibility,' Ellie took a piece of sausage Casey hadn't eaten from his sandwich and passed it to Millie, who snapped it up eagerly. 'We have to go with whatever's in the bottles as the contraband until we know any better. But we also need to know where that extra bottle went, because there's definitely a discrepancy there.'

She looked across at Tinker.

'Do you need Casey right now for your thing?' she asked, but Tinker shook her head in reply.

'Nah, I can look into that later today,' she replied. 'Let's get on with this first.'

'Good, then we need to check the van.' Ellie motioned to Millie to drop from the booth as she rose. 'I'll go with Casey and have a look at whatever's left, see if we can get any other clues as to what happened. Tinker, go down to Dover and see if you can get some time with the Customs guys who let Paulo Moretti through. Maybe they know more than they're letting on.'

'I'm guessing you want me to delve into the belly of the underworld, speaking to my loyal underlings and gaining what I can on the criminal empire of the Lumetta family?' Ramsey replied a little over-dramatically.

'Well, I was going to ask you to find one of the sons and have a chat with them, but if you'd rather do all that, have at it and let slip the dogs of war,' Ellie smiled, ruffling Millie's head as she spoke the last line. 'Just don't get killed. It's a real pain when we have to sort the paperwork out.'

'And me?' Robert smiled. 'I mean, if I'm part of your diner meetings now and all that?'

'Speak to Mama Lumetta again, and see if you can find out anything on any rivals we need to worry about, and what was in those bloody bottles,' Ellie smiled. 'And if you do well, we might let you share lunch with us again. Oh, and check into her driver. Might be nothing, but there was something there between them, more than an employer vs employee thing.'

'Maybe they're lovers?' Ramsey suggested. 'She might be old, Elisa, but she's not dead.'

'Great, can't wait to get involved in that hot mess.' Robert gathered up the papers as Ellie waved for the bill. Sandra, having been waiting sullenly by the counter with it in her hand, walked over, slapping it onto the table.

'I bet you're a cat person, aren't you?' Ellie replied, passing a debit card over for payment, while the others all left the diner, each off on their respective assignments.

'You'll never know,' Sandra smiled, a dark, concerning one as she stared at Millie, expecting the dog to attack.

With that, Ellie took Millie's lead and, with the dog now off the seat, she walked out of the diner, unable to resist the urge to look back, seeing Sandra now attacking the booth's leather with a sponge and some antiseptic wipes.

'Some people have way too much time on their hands,' she muttered to the Cocker Spaniel, stopping on the street. There was a nagging thread tugging at her; something warning her about this case. Too many things weren't being said to her, and there were too many unknown elements here. Ellie knew Mama Lumetta was keeping things close to her chest, but at the same time Ellie worried about what would happen the moment she, or her team, worked it out.

A problem for later, she decided, nodding to Casey, waiting outside the diner for her to emerge.

'Are we taking her?' he said, pointing at Millie.

'You have a problem with that?' Ellie bristled, expecting a fight.

'No, it's just ... it's a murder scene, right?' Casey replied. 'You rarely allow *me* to go to those, let alone five-year-old dogs.'

Ellie laughed as she walked with Casey to the car park. 'She's seen a lot in her life,' she said. 'I think she'll be okay.'

5

SIDE LANES

IT TOOK CLOSE TO TWO HOURS FOR ELLIE AND CASEY TO ARRIVE at the hijack site. The route had taken them out of London, down the M25 and eastwards on the M20, and during it Casey had spent some of that time questioning Ellie on whether she'd found out anything more on the murder of his father.

Unfortunately for both of them, she hadn't.

But, surprisingly, Casey was actually understanding on this; after all, he'd been working with her close to two months now, and he'd seen how fast things went when you were hunting for answers, while not giving away to the masses that you were *hunting for answers.*

He'd also been investigating the death of his father in his own time, in particular through the numbers and spread-sheets that he'd gained access to, after hacking into Bryan Noyce's work accounts.

Again, though, he hadn't found anything.

If she was brutally honest, Ellie hadn't expected him to. She knew Nicky Simpson, the man who Bryan had cooked the crooked accounts for, wasn't stupid. He'd have covered his tracks well, especially after the murder. And Ellie's current choice for "police mole who killed her boyfriend", DS Kate Delgado of Vauxhall's Metropolitan Police, hadn't shown up in any paperwork connected to him, for obvious reasons.

They'd keep checking though, and during the drive, they'd come up with several ways to progress the enquiry. Casey's suggestions had been cyber-based, using algorithms and the "dark net", which Ellie still didn't completely understand, while hers had involved thumb screws and pulling out fingernails, but the two sets of potential results were similar.

When they arrived at the single-lane turn off where the van was, though, all conversation ceased. It was now mid-afternoon, and the police would have been on site for close to ten hours by then, as the burning van had been called in early that morning. Ellie had assumed this would have been ample time for forensics to do their thing and get out, but as she pulled up, she saw police squad cars were still blocking the road in.

'You going to do what you did last time?' Casey asked with a smile, and Ellie winced a little as the memory returned. The last time Ellie and Casey attended a crime scene, she'd deliberately rear-ended Delgado's car to cause a distraction, resulting in a punch in the face from the irate and possibly corrupt detective.

'I was thinking of being more professional this time,' Ellie suggested. 'This is Maidstone nick, and they don't know me.'

'What you're actually saying is they don't know how unprofessional you are,' Casey smiled, pulling a box out of his rucksack.

'What's that?' Ellie asked, curious what the item Casey was now slotting together could be.

'A drone,' he replied, attaching some propellers. 'I'm

expecting them to tell you to get lost, so I'll fly this over the top, see if I can see anything.'

'There's a big blue tent over it,' Ellie pointed past the cars, at the blue gazebo that covered the charred remains of the van. 'I don't think you'll see much.'

Climbing out of the car, she motioned for Casey to join her.

'We'll try my way first,' she said, leaning back in and lowering the back windows by an inch. 'We'll leave Millie in here for the moment. It's not hot, so she'll be fine.'

As Millie watched Ellie with what felt like a modicum of betrayal at being left behind, she closed the door and straightened her jacket, walking with Casey over to the police constable guarding the police cordon.

'Sorry, nobody past this,' he said, almost apologetically. He was young, slim and nervous, blue latex "crime scene" gloves on his hands, even though he was nowhere near the scene itself. Ellie reckoned he couldn't be more than six months out of Hendon Police College and remembered very well how she'd felt back then. They'd probably told him to wear the gloves as a precaution for clumsiness. That, or he was super eager and hoping that, by wearing the crime scene apparel, they'd allow him to have a peek. One of the PCs at the City of London's Temple Inn Unit had been just the same, and, according to DCI Alex Monroe the last time they'd met up, he was now assisting the divisional surgeon, so it wasn't unknown.

'Who's in charge?' she asked, relaxing her tone so it didn't sound aggressive.

'DCI Richmond,' the constable replied, relaxing a little in response, the confrontation he'd been expecting now disappearing. 'She's with the van at the moment. You are ...?'

'Ellie Reckless, Finders Corporation,' Ellie flashed a card, held in her old police warrant wallet. She'd hoped it'd give an element of professionalism, but now worried, as she did this, that it might look as if she was trying to impersonate an officer. 'We're the investigators hired by the owner of the van to learn what happened.'

'I thought that was our job?' the constable frowned.

'You're solving a murder,' Ellie smiled. 'I'm locating stolen goods. We'll keep out of your way, but I do need to examine the vehicle.'

She held up her hands, currently in similar blue latex gloves.

'Look, I brought my own PPE and everything,' she winked. 'Just like you. Probably from the same supplier. We can be Smurfs together.'

The constable looked around the crime scene, as if trying to work out what to do in this obviously unfamiliar situation, eventually pausing as a woman, well-built and muscular with short black hair, emerged from the forensics team.

'Guv!' he cried out gratefully. 'Visitors.'

The woman, likely the DCI Richmond the constable had mentioned, tightened her eyes.

'Let them pass, Robinson,' she said, waving for the PC to let them through, in case he didn't understand the order. Motioning to Casey to follow her, Ellie nodded thanks to the now named PC Robinson and did just that, slipping under the cordon as she walked over to the new arrival.

The van was in the middle of the road, with undergrowth leading to a fence on the left, the other side of it a grass verge, maybe ten feet or a little less, to the railway tracks beside. Near the van was more scrubland, where some bushes and trees had grown beside the fence, hiding it from view, and this was mirrored on the other side of the pathway, by what looked like the edge of a small wood. As she observed this, her attention was diverted back to the woman as she walked to intercept them.

'I'm DCI Lucy Richmond,' the woman said, her gaze feeling more like a visual examination than a welcoming expression. 'And you are?'

'Ellie Reckless, Finders Corporation,' Ellie replied, starting her spiel once more. 'This is Casey Noyce, our computer expert.'

'He looks twelve.'

'That's the future, old woman,' Casey forced a smile. 'And I'm fifteen.'

'Oh, well, that makes everything alright then,' Richmond replied, looking back at Ellie. 'I've heard of you, DI Reckless.'

'If you have, then you'll know I'm no longer that,' Ellie replied, inwardly groaning. If Richmond knew her history, there was a strong chance this could become awkward.

'I do, and it's a bloody shame,' Richmond held out a hand to shake. 'You were screwed over. Anyone with half a brain can see that. I hope you find the bastard who set you up and get them kicked out of the force. No place for them.'

'I didn't think I'd reached Maidstone's ears,' Ellie frowned.

'I wasn't here at the time of the ... well, the whole cluster bomb it became,' Richmond explained. 'I'm an East London copper, originally. Mainly Stratford and West Ham, so we had our crossover here and there with you Mile End buggers, before you moved to South London, anyway. Even arrested Danny Martin a couple of times, but the Twins always managed to get him off. Well, until they couldn't, that is.'

'Yeah, the Lucas Twins had a way of doing that with their own,' Ellie smiled. 'Why the move into Kent?'

'Promotion, as London weren't really pushing me,' the DCI explained as she looked back at the van. 'Nasty bit of business there. What's your connection with it?'

'My company – that is the company I work for – has been hired by Lumetta Oils to recover the stolen items.'

'Olive oil.'

'Extra-virgin olive oil,' Ellie corrected. 'Apparently there's a difference.'

'About a fiver a bottle,' Richmond smiled. 'So, you're not here about the murder?'

'Only in as much as the victim was the driver,' Ellie replied. 'We're just here to get an idea of what happened. We'll more than likely be moving onto suppliers after that.'

DCI Richmond considered this for a moment.

'The van's still being looked over, but you're more than welcome to observe from the side,' she said. 'Does the boy understand about crime scene etiquette?'

'The *boy* is going to stand way back and let his drone do the investigating,' Casey muttered, nodding to Ellie and walking sullenly off to the edge of the road.

'Casey Noyce,' Richmond said softly as he left. 'I recognise that name from the court case. The informant's son?'

'You did pay attention in class,' Ellie was surprised at the comment. 'Yeah. I promised his father I'd look after him if anything happened. I only started to take that promise seriously a couple of months back.'

'Well, better late than never,' Richmond clicked her tongue against the top of her mouth. 'You spoke to Customs yet?'

'No, my team will do it later, though,' Ellie said. 'Should I be expecting problems?'

'We didn't get any, so I don't think you will,' Richmond led Ellie to the burnt-out Sprinter van. 'So, this is it. We think they took out the stock, left the body and sprayed some sort of accelerant all over the inside of the van before lighting it. They weren't that bothered though, as it only burned the body, the wooden pallets in the back of the van, and the upholstery of the cabin. The dashboard is a little melted and the radio's buggered, but it didn't catch the petrol tank, which means no boom.'

'You think they wanted the boom?'

Richmond pondered the question.

'Honestly? I think they were quick, professional, and the fire was just a precaution,' she said. 'I'd be stunned if a single fingerprint was left, even before they covered their tracks.'

Ellie nodded, looking over at the van. The outside wasn't burned, but the open doors showed a different scene. The sliding door was on the right, as the van was a left-hand drive and the open back doors were still being checked by people in disposable PPE suits.

'Pallets were left?'

'We think they took the stock from the pallets by hand and left all the packaging behind,' Richmond waved around the open space. 'It's a bit out of the way for a forklift to turn up. Didn't need them anymore, probably thought they'd help with the fire.'

Ellie crouched, looking through the door.

'The body? Paulo Moretti?'

'Shot in the neck, the bullet going through the right-hand side of the throat, exiting out the back and shattering the driver's side window as it left the van,' Richmond pointed at the left-hand side of the van, where the window was closed, but broken into pieces, a visible gunshot hole in the middle. 'It's continental, so the driver's side is opposite. I think the angle of the bullet meant the killer would have been standing here—'

At this point, she stopped to the left of the side door, aiming an imaginary gun at the corner of the cargo space behind the driver's seat.

'—and bang, kills the driver, standing to the back of the pallets, while the bullet carries on. No idea where it landed, the bloody thing could be anywhere. I'll still look for it, though.'

Ellie walked up to the side entrance to the van, making sure she didn't interrupt a forensic technician, wiping down the door for prints.

'How did they get the bottles out?' she asked. 'I was told we had three columns of pallets, each four rows high, with one more at the front.'

'Yeah, we think they just cut the pallet wrappings and removed them in packs of eight,' Richmond shrugged. 'As I said, the pallets were left in here to burn. Probably what they poured the accelerant on to get the fire burning.'

'And you're sure it's an accelerant?' Ellie noticed Casey walking over to the open driver's door, looking up at the shattered window, before peering into the space under the dashboard. Not seeing this, Richmond shrugged.

'My people tell me ignitable liquids can leave behind irregular patterns on the surface of a floor, and this has that,' she explained. 'However, they then talk about high vapour pressures, low flash points and upper and lower explosive limits, and it's around then my eyes glaze over.'

Ellie smiled as she nodded, looking back into the van.

'Did they find anything else?'

Richmond paused, as if deciding whether to say anything, and then nodded.

'Tiny trace amounts of gold on the floor or the van,' she admitted. 'From where the pallets were. We think they packed out the base with contraband and this was taken with the bottles.'

Ellie didn't say anything, but this matched Mama Lumetta's statement about gold being in the van.

'The body—'

'Coroner has it,' Richmond replied. 'Left a few hours back. Hoping for cause of death soon.'

'I thought he was shot in the throat?'

'He was also set fire to. I don't know which of these ended him.'

'Oh, yeah, fair point.' Ellie was going to continue, but was distracted by a whirring noise. Looking to the side, she saw Casey was starting up his drone.

'Do you mind?' she asked Richmond, nodding over at him. 'Gives us an excellent overview.'

'As long as you share anything you find,' Richmond replied as Casey sent his drone into the air, checking on the screen of his controller as he did so.

'Any idea of the vehicles that stopped the van?'

Richmond strolled back to the gate now, pointing at the ground.

'Two or three SUVs, or Land Rovers,' she said. 'Definitely enough to take the stock away. The problem is there's a lot of movement, so it's hard to see if it's three cars, or one that left and came back twice. After all, they could have had all night to sort this. The fire makes a real pain of working out the time of death. And even then, Paulo could have been shot hours before they set him alight.'

Ellie stopped, watching DCI Richmond.

'So, what do you think was taken?' she asked.

'Expensive olive oil?'

'Fifteen grand of olive oil enough to kill a man for?' Reckless tried again.

'Look, that's your job,' Richmond sighed. 'I'm looking for a motive for Moretti's death, sure, but there could be a dozen reasons. I'm looking into him right now, and it looks like he was seeing someone on the side in London every time he came over. Maybe this was a jealous lover? It doesn't have to be the sons.'

Ellie smiled.

'I didn't mention the sons,' she said.

'Yeah, but you're thinking it,' Richmond shrugged. 'We all know it's serious levels of *Game of Thrones* in that family. If they haven't attacked each other by lunchtime, it's classed as a national holiday.'

Ellie looked back to the van, trying to envision Paulo Moretti's last moments. Shot in the throat, the window smashing as the bullet went through it ... was he trying to hide, or was he looking for a way to save his life?

'You brought a dog.'

It was a statement more than a question, and Ellie was brought back to the moment as Richmond pointed back across the cordon, to where Casey had let Millie out of the car.

'What the hell are you doing?' Ellie asked, getting irritated now. Casey had been so useful in the previous cases they'd worked on, but right now he was playing the part of a petulant, bored child—

Playing the part.

Casey had changed the moment Richmond had commented on his age, as if working to her expectations. He'd walked off to play with a drone rather than examine the van, but she had seen him move towards the dashboard when nobody was looking. If he was releasing Millie, there had to be a reason.

'She's cooped up,' he whined. 'It's not fair. I'm going to play over there with her.'

He pointed to a patch of grass about twenty yards from the van, and over towards some dense bushes.

'Sorry,' Ellie turned back to Richmond. 'I didn't have anyone to look after her. She was supposed to stay in the car.'

'As long as he remembers it's an active crime scene,' DCI Richmond sighed, looking back at Casey and Millie. He had a rucksack on his shoulder, and had pulled a ball out of it, throwing it for the Cocker Spaniel to chase. 'I'm sure it's fine. So, what do you intend to do next?'

Ellie was about to answer this when there was another interruption, a commotion at the cordon once more. This time it was a Mercedes, black and very expensive, which had pulled up, and a large, balding man had exited. His clothes were tailored and expensive and he had the build of a rugby player, stocky but muscled.

Ellie recognised him immediately.

'What the hell is this?' Tommaso Lumetta hissed, ignoring the protesting PC Robinson as he broke the tape, striding through it. 'What are you doing with my property?'

'Your property?' Ellie asked, confused. 'I was under the assumption this was owned by Lumetta Oils.'

'Yeah, and I own Lumetta Oils,' Tommaso hissed. 'I'm the—'

'Son of Mama Lumetta,' DCI Richmond interrupted. 'Who, the last we heard, *was* the owner.'

'She retired,' Tommaso replied, his eyes flitting from woman to woman.

'Really?' Ellie pursed her lips, pondering this. 'Because she wasn't retired when she hired me to find her missing stock this morning.'

Tommaso paused his attention on Ellie now, smiling, his teeth stained yellow from years of smoking.

'Maybe she hasn't realised it yet,' he said darkly. 'She hired you? Well, I'm *firing* you.'

'That's not how it works,' Ellie squared up to Tommaso now, confident this bluster and attitude was hiding something. 'So why don't you tell me what's really going on here?'

'Why don't you tell me why that kid's climbing a tree?' Tommaso asked, and Richmond and Ellie looked around to see Casey, already halfway up the side of a dense bush, waving to a police officer, currently calling him back down.

'Millie's ball went into the tree,' he said, reaching the top. 'I'm just getting it back.'

As if emphasising the point, Millie barked agreement at this.

'This van is my property, and I didn't give you permission to poke around it,' Losing interest in the tree-climbing antics across the track, Tommaso returned his attention to DCI Richmond.

'There was a body found—' she started.

'Yeah, and the body's gone, isn't it?' Tommaso Lumetta made a pantomime of looking around as he interrupted her. 'Just like I want you gone. And this bitch my mum hired.'

Ellie chose better than to rise to this; Tommaso was angry and wanted a fight. Instead, she looked back to Casey, climbing back down with the ball. What she also saw, and the police hadn't, was that he'd also placed on blue latex gloves in the process, ones he wasn't wearing when he climbed up, which he now took off.

'Got the ball,' he exclaimed triumphantly, holding the ball up, before dropping it carefully into the bag. Then, walking with Millie, he returned to Ellie's car, helping the Cocker Spaniel back into the back of it before getting in himself, all while Tommaso's assistants and likely body-guards glared at him from the nearby Mercedes.

Richmond, however, was still staring at Tommaso.

'This is an active crime scene, an active *murder* scene, in fact, and we'll finish when we're damn well done,' she hissed. 'So piss off back to your pretty little car and wait for me to allow you in. Or, piss off to wherever you crawled out of. and wait for my officers to call you.'

Tommaso glared at Richmond.

'You can stay, but she goes,' he conceded. 'She ain't police.'

Richmond went to snap back again, but Ellie held up a hand to halt her.

'Fine, you win,' Ellie sighed at Tommaso. 'I'll leave. But I won't be stopping the case until I hear from your mum, so you'd better get on the phone with her, yeah?'

Tommaso grunted a noncommittal reply and, with a nod to DCI Richmond, Ellie pulled off her blue latex gloves, tossing them into a forensics waste bag before returning to the car.

'You'd better have a reason for all that,' she said to Casey as she got in.

'Maidstone Services isn't far away,' he replied as he

nestled the bag in his hands. 'Can we stop there? But like, leave right now?'

Nodding, Ellie started the car, reversing out of the small side road, and returning to the A20.

IT WAS ANOTHER FIVE MINUTES BEFORE THEY REACHED THE services, and only then did Casey seem to relax.

'Okay, so what the hell?' Ellie asked. 'What scheme did you enrol Millie into?'

Casey opened the rucksack, and in it, Ellie could see a broken shard of bottle, held upright in the bag by Casey's legs.

'So, I used the drone, yeah?' he said. 'And you were right. I couldn't see anything under the tent. So, I started looking around the van. I thought maybe someone threw something away, maybe tried to hide evidence. And we're right by train tracks, so I wondered if they tried to throw it over the fence. Especially as the police were only focusing on the van.'

'Okay,' Ellie pulled a pair of new latex gloves out of a box in the glove compartment, slipping them on as she motioned for the rucksack to be passed over. 'What did you find?'

'This was caught in the top branches of the bushes beside the road,' Casey continued, gently passing the bag over. 'You couldn't see it from the ground, but it glinted in the sun when you looked down on it from a drone.'

'So, you pretended you'd trapped a ball up there and went and got it,' Ellie smiled. 'Good call.'

Pulling the chunk of broken bottle out, Ellie saw it was a Lumetta Oils bottle, the label on the front torn and half missing, but showing it was a 2021 vintage. There was no liquid in it, but there was blood on the broken tips of the neck and shoulder remains, and also spattered onto the back of the label.

'Why throw an empty bottle of oil into the bushes?' Ellie examined the bottle. 'It's an impact shatter. Like a nail ...'

She shuddered.

'Or a bullet struck it,' she said, looking back at Casey. 'Well done. I wouldn't have seen the glass in the light.'

'I didn't see the glass, I saw the glint,' Casey tapped the bottle, 'of what was in it.'

Ellie turned the bottle, looking down the neck. It was empty, and the sides should have, at best, been slick with oil, but there was definitely some kind of shimmering substance there, coating the sides.

'That's not oil, and it's sure as hell not whisky,' Casey leant back in his seat. 'I don't know what it is, but someone killed for it.'

'I'll get this looked at,' Ellie nodded, placing the bottle into an evidence baggie she had in the back of the car, one big enough to hold it, being careful not to slice the sides of the bag with the shattered neck. 'Although technically we should be giving this back to the police.'

'They said share, not pass over,' Casey replied smugly. 'And besides, there's something off with that copper.'

'Oh aye?' Ellie smiled. 'And what's that?'

'She didn't like Millie,' Casey grinned. 'Oh, I have something else, too.'

He reached into his jacket pocket, pulling out what looked to be a small circuit board. It was singed around the edges, likely from the flames, but had been spared the brunt of the fire.

'What is it?' Ellie took the small piece of circuitry, turning it in her hand.

'I'm not sure, but it definitely isn't part of the van,' Casey replied, tapping his chin as he spoke. 'I found it under the dashboard. I think it's how they overwrote the sat nav.'

Ellie passed it back.

'Find out,' she ordered. 'Do whatever you need to do.'

Casey nodded, already examining the circuit board as Ellie sat back in the driver's seat. So far she had a piece of rogue circuitry, and a smashed bottle of olive oil that didn't seem to be olive oil, broken most likely by the impact of a bullet. Was this against Paulo's upper chest when he was killed? The angle could just about match although it'd be a hell of a deviation, and if so, was he trying to steal it, or using it to plead for his life?

And then there was Tommaso Lumetta. A man who not only believed he was in control, but that he wanted everything closed down around the van. Ellie wondered how his brother and mother would react to this rather arrogant assumption.

Leaning back and ruffling Millie's head, Ellie went to start the car, but stopped, staring over at the service station.

'You want a drink?' she asked. 'I'm going to buy Millie a treat for helping us there.'

'But I did the work!' Brought back to the moment, Casey looked at her, irritated.

'And that's why I'm buying you a drink as well,' Ellie smiled. 'Come on, let's get something to take the taste of burned rubber out of our throats. And I might have an idea about that circuit board.'

6

CUSTOMS AND EXERCISE

TINKER HAD BEEN FOLLOWING ELLIE FOR MOST OF THE JOURNEY up to the M20, but once they turned off to go look at the van, she carried on in her battered Land Rover Defender, heading east to Dover, and the Customs Officers that had waved Paulo through.

It had taken another half an hour to arrive at the port, and after a couple of wrong turnings, Tinker was eventually shown the correct building to ask her questions in. Parking up and pulling on her army coat, Tinker opened the door to the building, a stark, sixties block of windowed concrete, and walked up the stairs.

Robert had called the office in advance, asking about the van, and during the discussion had mentioned there would be someone else coming to follow up on this, so this should have been a cakewalk for Tinker, entering an office that not only expected her but also had the correct information for her.

Of course, it wasn't that easy.

'Lumetta Oils,' the woman on the reception desk,

possibly named Olivia – although Tinker hadn't heard it clearly and had now passed the window of opportunity to ask for clarification – wore wide-rimmed pearl glasses framing her thin face, a blouse that looked like it had been sewn in the eighteen hundreds, and had a harshly pulled back almost-white bun of hair. She muttered to herself as she clicked through the files for the previous day. 'Ah yes. Here you go. Came in before midnight, last ferry. Not many people on it, that time of night. Mercedes Sprinter Van.'

'That's the one,' Tinker replied. 'I was hoping I could—'

'Oh, we can't tell you anything about it, and we can't print you any of the records,' possibly-Olivia replied. 'I told the man on the phone that. He should have told you.'

Tinker forced a smile. Robert had indeed told her this, but he'd also said the woman on the phone, most likely possibly-Olivia, sounded like she was a bit of a jobsworth, and probably needed a face to face, anyway.

'That's completely fine,' Tinker replied, keeping her face emotionless. 'I don't need your reports and forms, as we have those from the owner.'

'Oh,' possibly-Olivia looked up, pushing her glasses up her nose, a little thrown by this. 'So, what is it—'

'I was hoping to speak to the Customs Officers that passed the van through,' Tinker interrupted. 'They were the last people to see Paulo Moretti alive, and I was hoping they might have seen or heard something which could help our case.'

'They won't be able to speak about their work.'

'Again, I don't want that,' Tinker was finding it harder and harder to keep a snarl from appearing on her face. 'All I want is an opportunity, hopefully to see if they can give any insight as to why a respectable and regular driver, one of many years' service, would take a diversion out of his way in the middle of the night, ending with his death in a lay-by in the middle of nowhere.'

Possibly-Olivia thought about this for a moment. Tinker could see her working out whether or not this was an argument she wanted.

Apparently, it wasn't.

'Brian Watson and Jimmy Mantel were on the docks last night, and I believe they both spoke to Mister Moretti. Brian's not in today, but Jimmy starts his shift in—' she looked at the clock on the wall, showing the time to be three-fifty pm '— about ten minutes, so he'll likely be in the break room downstairs.'

'Thank you so much,' Tinker's smile was genuine as she gathered her items. 'I'll just—'

'You can't enter the break room without a pass.'

Tinker froze in place, forcing the urge to scream deep into her soul.

'And how would I get that?' she kept a tone of politeness in her voice as she asked.

Possibly-Olivia actually smiled now, a winner's half smile, like she'd beaten Tinker in this conversational joust, holding up a lanyard and plastic card.

'I give it to you once you sign the visitor's book,' she said, tapping on a lined notebook beside her. It had space for a name, company, car registration, time of entry, time of exit and a signature. Sighing, Tinker took a pen, wrote in all the requisite boxes and, placing the pen calmly beside the book, received the pass graciously, placing it around her neck as she left the reception area, hurrying before her dreams of taking the lanyard and strangling possibly-Olivia with it became reality.

The break room was a quick stroll back through the building; in fact, Tinker had even passed it on the way up to the main reception, making her wonder why she'd even had to sign for a pass. However, she hadn't looked in when she did so earlier, and at least now she couldn't be questioned as to her movements by even more jobsworths.

Now, with the aforementioned pass in her possession, ready to show to anyone who wished to see it, she walked into the room, noting a young man with short blond hair in the corner, standing by the sink and the high cabinets above the countertop, reaching into one of them as she cleared her throat.

'Mister Mantel?' she asked, and the man turned around with a start, obviously not expecting anyone else to enter the room. He wore a white shirt with black lapels, a black tie and trousers, all under a navy jacket with a fluorescent vest over the top. On the back in black letters were the words H.M. CUSTOMS & EXCISE.

'Who wants to know?' he replied cautiously. 'I'm about to go on shift.'

Tinker almost smiled at this. The caution was fine, but then to reply with a second statement, effectively confirming the statement. *This was a man who didn't do lying well.*

'Tinker Jones, Finders Corporation,' she replied, flashing her card, making sure it looked as close to the way a police officer showed their warrant card as she could. Ellie had them made a month or two back; they were official cards that stated they were accredited insurance investigators working for the Finders Corporation, but they'd been designed to look like police warrants, even down to the leather wallets that held them. And, as Ellie had once said to her, most likely in a pub and over a drink or three, *the more officious the ID, the more a normal person wants to assist.*

Jimmy Mantel didn't want to assist. Tinker could see that from his expression.

'This about the man?' he asked.

'Which man would that be?' Tinker shot back.

'The Italian guy. Olive oil dude who got burned alive last night.'

Tinker waved Jimmy towards a chair, moving to sit opposite him.

'Olivia said you were the last person to see him alive.'

Jimmy frowned.

'Who's Olivia?'

'The woman upstairs, hair in a bun, wide glasses?' Tinker was now even less sure of possibly-Olivia's name.

'Oh, her,' Jimmy nodded. 'Didn't know her name. But yeah, we might have been.'

'Did anything look off when you spoke to him?'

Jimmy shrugged, not looking Tinker in the eye.

'Not really,' he replied. 'I mean, you see so many of these, yeah? Men with vans, earning a crust. Brian usually deals with him, as he's a daytime driver. I do nights.'

'But he was nights yesterday?'

Jimmy shrugged again, giving the impression of a man who really didn't know or care about this. Tinker mentally noted, however, that Brian Watson wasn't on his usual shift.

'Poor bastard probably got through Calais late,' he suggested. 'They've been dicks recently. Loads of lorries have been delayed. Although we're just as bad, I suppose. Anyway, I'd never met the guy before.'

'Did you see his stock?'

'Yeah, that's our job,' there was a hint of sarcasm, maybe a small piece of smugness in the reply. Jimmy was perhaps even mocking the woman in front of him for not knowing what his role there was. 'We checked the back. Three pallets, four high—no, wait, the back one had five, because it was taller than the others. Just about fit in the van, definitely buggered the suspension. That's a shitload of weight. Those glass bottles aren't light.'

'How would you know that?' Tinker frowned. 'Do you weigh the vehicles?'

At this Jimmy rose, walking to the cabinet.

'Because he gave me a bottle,' he said, pulling out a glass bottle with a LUMETTA OILS label on it. 'Said he always had three spares in case one or two of them broke. Gave me one, gave Brian one.'

'Do you always take bribes?' Tinker asked icily.

At this, Jimmy paled a little at the accusation.

'Weren't no bribe,' Jimmy shook his head, as if convincing himself rather than the woman in front of him. 'And as you can see, I brought it in here for everyone. I don't need to have issues hanging over my head on declaring things, thank you very much.'

Tinker nodded, watching Jimmy. *She could understand that.*

'And Brian? Did he do the same?'

'Why should he?' Jimmy was surly as he replied. 'What he does with his bottle is his choice.'

'Was he nervous?' Tinker asked, changing the subject. 'The driver?'

'No more than they usually are when they have to speak to us,' Jimmy chuckled. 'He was heading off to bed down.'

He paused, remembering something.

'There was one thing,' he said. 'Rubbed me wrong a little.

When he was stamped through, Brian – that's Brian Watson, who you already mentioned – he stopped him, talking about where he intended to sleep.'

'How do you mean?'

'Well, Brian asked if he meant to stop at the truck stop at the start of the M20, and then told the guy to carry on to Maidstone Services instead. Said there'd been some break-ins on trucks, a couple of EU Nationals attacked, that sort of thing. I looked into that later, just curious, like, and I couldn't find anything on it.'

'Brian said this?'

'Yeah.'

'You know Brian long?'

At this, Jimmy laughed.

'Bloody should do,' he said, his nerves now gone. 'He's my cousin. Older by a few years, but he's been around forever. Got me this job when I left school, too.'

Tinker picked up the bottle, turning it in her hand as she considered this.

'The seal's broken,' she said as she twisted the bottle cap.

'Well yeah,' Jimmy admitted. 'I tried a little. And Louise put some on her roll this morning with some balsamic vinegar. I prefer Shreddies though, so I didn't join her.'

'Louise?'

'Morning shift.'

'And?' Tinker waggled the bottle. 'Any good?'

'It's alright,' he sniffed. 'I mean, it's nothing to write home about, and I don't reckon it's worth the money, but it was free, wasn't it?'

'And Brian got the same bottle, but kept it to himself?'

Jimmy nodded, but then stopped, pausing mid-nod.

'No, actually,' he replied. 'The driver, Paulo? He gave him

one from the back of the van. These are 2022 bottles, and Brian had a 2021 bottle. But there was nothing on the waybill about years on the bottles, so I don't know how many were which. Brian knew the driver better, so I just assumed he'd been given a better quality one from the top of the pallet.'

Tinker leant back in the chair as Jimmy rose, checking the clock.

'Are we done? My shift starts in a minute.'

'One quick question,' Tinker rose to meet him. 'You said Paulo Moretti usually travelled by day. How did Brian Watson know him?'

'Oh, he usually does days too,' Jimmy replied, doing up his jacket as he spoke. 'One in four of his shifts crosses over into the night shift, so it was just coincidence they were meeting.'

Tinker didn't think this was coincidence, as much as she didn't think the bottle of olive oil Brian had been given was the same as the one Jimmy had received.

'Is Brian on shift today?' she asked, following Jimmy to the break-room door.

'Nah, he rotates back on days tomorrow,' Jimmy shrugged. 'Prick isn't answering his phone, though, so I'm guessing he's having a duvet day. You know, staying in bed and watching shit TV.'

He looked uncomfortable as he continued, as if he was expressing emotions he didn't like to show.

'I'm really sorry. I met the guy for about a minute, he seemed nice, and I'm sorry he's dead,' he finished. 'But I really can't help you.'

'Believe me,' Tinker smiled, nodding farewell. 'You've helped more than you could possibly imagine.'

TINKER HAD BEEN PLEASANTLY SURPRISED WHEN POSSIBLY-Olivia gave her the address details of Brian Watson with no fuss; apparently her concerns about GDPR extended to the paperwork the Customs and Excise Department dealt with, but not the addresses of its employees.

Watson lived in a small semi-detached house on a side street off the Folkestone Road, a hill climb if ever there was one, and Tinker decided, with no car parking on the street immediately outside, that she'd rather park down the hill and walk up, than park the other side and have to trudge up the hill to her jeep once the conversation was over. And so, she parked the Defender around fifty metres down the street, walking the steep incline to the house before knocking on the door.

However, the term "knocking" may have been a bit polite, as, after the long drive, the conversations at the docks, the second drive and the steep hill walk, Tinker was getting tired, and it was a more full-fist banging on the door than polite rap.

'Mister Watson!' she shouted. 'Can you open up, please?'

In retrospect, Tinker could have realised she sounded more like a bailiff than an insurance investigator, but the moment had passed, and now she waited expectantly as, on the other side of the door she heard a bolt scrape back, and then the door itself was opened a little, enough for an inch of light to break through as part of Brian Watson's face peered nervously at her.

'Yes?' he asked. Tinker held up her ID for him to see before speaking.

'I'd like to talk to you about Paulo Moretti—' she started,

but, at the name, Brian tried to slam the door in her face, the wood bouncing from her steel-toe-capped army boot, wedged into the doorframe the moment it had opened. As the door ricocheted back, swinging in, Tinker could see Brian Watson, in his dressing gown, sprinting up the stairs.

'Mister Watson!' she shouted, entering the hallway and chasing after him. She knew she shouldn't, but as the door was technically now open, she wasn't breaking in. By the time she reached the top of the stairs, however, she saw him run back out of a bedroom, a bottle of Lumetta Oil in his hand, barging past her and running into the bathroom, slamming the bathroom door closed behind him. Shaken for a second, Tinker followed at speed, smashing the closed bathroom door aside to see Brian Watson frantically pouring the olive oil from the bottle into a sink.

'What the hell are you doing?' she hissed, snatching the bottle from him and turning it back up. The liquid looked more like weak orange squash than olive oil, and was watery, although with the slightest metallic sheen upon it. There was only about ten percent of the liquid left in the bottle as Brian Watson fell against the bath, sobbing.

'It's not mine!' he wailed. 'I was holding it for a friend!'

'You took it from Paulo Moretti,' Tinker replied icily. 'How can you be—'

'He was picking it back up!' Brian sobbed. 'I mean, he said it'd be picked back up later today!'

Tinker stared down at the man in the dressing gown.

'Why were you pouring it away?'

'Because you were coming to arrest me!'

'I'm not a police officer!' Tinker exclaimed, pulling at her army jacket. 'Do I *look* like a bloody police officer?'

Brian wiped his eyes.

'I've known Paulo for years,' he whispered. 'Every week he'd come through, usually with olive oil bottles. And, over the years, we got talking. He had a side hustle. I don't know what it was. But for the last three years, every couple of months, he'd give me a couple of bottles as a gift. I'd hold them for him, he'd take it back a day or so later, and in return they'd give me a monkey.'

'They?'

'The person who picked it up,' he explained. 'Never Paulo; by then he was on his way home.'

'Do you mean five hundred quid, or an actual monkey?' Tinker took the bottle into her hands, turning it around as she stared down at it. 'What's in it?'

'I don't know, I never looked,' Brian muttered to himself. 'And now I've spilt most of it in the sink.'

'How much did Paulo give you?' Tinker asked. 'I mean, in total over the years?'

'Five hundred each trip, and about fourteen times in total – so seven grand, and he would have owed me another monkey for this one.'

'So, thirty of these bottles over three years?'

Brian shook his head.

'Twenty-nine,' he corrected. 'He only gave me one last night.'

'Any reason why?'

'Didn't ask. He said I'd be getting the same benefits, so I guessed he meant the same money.'

Curious, Tinker examined the bottle again. There was something in the bloody thing that not only had people kill for it, but Paulo had to definitely be making at least a couple of grand for each bribe, or the five hundred was overkill for a holding fee – and this definitely put aside the fifty-pound bottles of whisky idea, and now pushed the value of the stolen items up tenfold, if not even more.

'Were the orders the same size each time?'

'Yeah, but I got the feeling the special bottles weren't,' Brian replied. 'I think usually it was half a pallet's worth. Maybe a hundred bottles? This time it was half the truck. Like something big was going on. Always a different year to the normal bottles. You know, the ones the actual wholesalers are getting.'

Tinker considered the statement for a few seconds before nodding. It made sense that they'd have smaller, regular trips with whatever this was. But, that meant not only was this most recent trip out of the ordinary, the fact it had been hijacked so easily meant it was definitely an inside job.

'I'm taking this bottle before you pour the rest out,' she said, rising from the ground where she'd been crouching beside Brian. 'Oh, one last thing. I spoke to Jimmy? James? Your cousin, who you were with last night? He told me you spoke to Paulo, telling him to not sleep at his usual spot.'

Brian thought about this for a moment and then nodded.

'There were reports of people being robbed at the truck stop,' he said. 'I knew this was one of his ... well, his special deliveries, and I didn't want to see him taken down.'

'You mean you didn't want the money to stop.'

'I liked him,' Brian shook his head. 'He was a good man.'

'And you don't find it strange the one night he doesn't do his usual routine, is the night he's murdered and robbed thirty minutes down the M20?' Tinker asked, almost mockingly. 'Who told you, Brian? Who gave you this heads up?'

Brian placed his head in his hands as the realisation of what he'd done finally hit home.

'I did this to him,' he groaned. 'I told him to move on and they took him.'

'Who's the *they* you're talking about here, Brian?' Tinker watched from the door dispassionately. 'Who told you?'

Brian looked up; his eyes red with tears.

'It was another driver for Lumetta Oils,' he said. 'Antonio something. They left the UK on the ferry before Paulo arrived. Said he'd stayed at the truck stop the night before, that people had been robbed, and told me I had to tell Paulo, make sure he didn't risk it. I knew what he'd be bringing, so assumed Antonio also knew, and I thought this was the smart move.'

'How many times do Lumetta Oils come through Dover?' Tinker placed the remnants of the olive oil inside her jacket.

'Twice a week,' Brian replied, clambering to his feet. 'They usually loop. One leaves as the other arrives.'

'And you didn't find it strange that nobody else mentioned this, apart from someone working for the same company as Paulo?' Tinker shook her head. 'And I thought you guys were supposed to be smart.'

And, with Brian Watson complaining loudly that he was smart, although easily led, Tinker realised he knew little more than he had already said and, now with a splitting headache starting, she took the remains of the olive oil bottle and left his house, returning down the hill to her Defender, and a long drive home.

7

FAMILY TRIES

RAMSEY HADN'T SPOKEN TO ANY OF THE LUMETTA FAMILY IN A long time, and the thought of sitting down with either Tommaso or Matteo was a little daunting, to say the least. It was true that he used to work for Mama Lumetta back in the day. It was also true the two of them had been more than close frequently, having an actual relationship for around a week, total, but Ramsey also knew this was a secret never to mention, primarily because either brother would have him killed for defiling their mother, especially so soon after his father's passing.

Which, in a weird way, Ramsey completely understood.

He'd called a few favours in and learnt his target was in East London that day, in a back office of one of his many small enterprises; in this case, a hand carwash in Shoreditch. A place where most of the clients turned up in their vehicles to what was once a petrol station – the pumps now removed and replaced with high pressure washers – as cars drove in and looped around the conveyor-belt-style cleaning service, eventually leaving the other end with a washed and dried car. It was a quick and easy valeting business, mainly paid for in cash, and usually the queue for cars to be cleaned went down the side road the entrance was on.

Ramsey arrived by cab. He had his own car, and could have brought that, but he didn't want to hunt for street parking, and he wasn't looking for a full-service car wash on it either. His car was a classic, an old Rover, and the dirt, grime and rust they'd wash off while cleaning was pretty much what kept it together.

As he arrived at the car wash, however, another man was walking out. A tall, spindly thin, black man in a pale suit-jacket not unlike the one *Doctor No* wore in the Bond movie of the same name; the collar non-existent and done up at the neck. The man was now smiling as he saw Ramsey walk up.

'Bloody hell, Allen,' he exclaimed in actual delight. 'I heard you were in jail.'

'I was: got out,' Ramsey smiled in return, but he was way more guarded. 'Strange to see you here, Darius.'

'Getting my car cleaned,' Darius replied.

'People usually stay in the car when they do that.'

'I'm a special case.'

'You've always been that,' Ramsey now grinned, warming. 'Life treating you well?'

'Can't complain,' Darius held his hands out, as if allowing Ramsey to see him in all his glory. 'I have three betting shops in the City now. I'm the *Ladbrokes* of London.'

'I might be wrong, but I think *Ladbrokes* also has shops in London,' Ramsey corrected.

'Yeah, but mine are better,' Darius shrugged, uncaring. 'Always go independent. Help your local businesses.'

He looked back at the building.

'You seeing Matteo?' he asked conversationally, but Ramsey could see the cogs turning.

'Catching up,' Ramsey replied noncommittally. 'In the area, all that.'

'Yeah, me too.' Darius's smile was now looking plastered on, his eyes cold while the smile gave the impression of joy. 'Don't be a stranger now, yeah?'

'I'll make the effort to see you soon.' Ramsey shook hands with Darius, knowing that both men knew this was a lie. And, with that small moment of greeting passed, Darius turned and, almost as if instantly forgetting Ramsey was even watching him as he left, Darius was gone as quickly as he appeared, and Ramsey, straightening his tie, carried on with his journey.

The sight of a well-dressed man, complete with "old school tie" walking past them to the back offices didn't even distract the washers as they worked on the cars, and Ramsey couldn't help but feel a little wounded at this, like his clothing hadn't been exciting enough for them.

But, this didn't matter, as he wasn't here for them, he reminded himself as he walked up the stairs, aiming for the upper-level back office. As he'd said to Darius, he was here for Matteo Lumetta.

Matteo was the younger of the two Lumetta brothers, although there wasn't much between them. He was, like his older brother, stocky with a body made for fighting, built from muscle and scar tissue, his hair thinning and combed over, and dyed black as well. He'd been a bare-knuckle fighter when his family lived in Ireland in the eighties, and now ran Dublin with an iron fist: one used for punching out his rivals with outstanding success, as his strategising skills were sadly lacking. He preferred the immediacy of a shooting game to one of thought and planning.

A Fredo who thought he was Michael, but acted like a Sonny.

'Mister Lumetta,' Ramsey said as he was allowed into the office by one of Matteo's guards, after spending a good few minutes standing outside while he was patted down. 'I was surprised to hear you were in London. I thought you concentrated on Ireland these days?'

'I've got things in London that keep me active.' Matteo looked up from the desk he was working at. 'Mister ...?'

'Allen.' For the second time that day Ramsey felt slighted. 'I used to work with your mother. I knew you when you were a teenager.'

Matteo squinted at Ramsey for a long, awkward pause before grinning.

'Ramsey Allen,' he said, finally recognising the man in front of him. 'Cutthroat shite and backstabbing petty thief. You got old. And what, you tried to cover that with this upper-class bollocks?' he waved at Ramsey's herringbone jacket. 'You can cover shite in gold, but it's just gold-covered shite,' he finished with a flair, the Dublin accent peeking through as he spoke.

Ramsey bristled but allowed Matteo to finish. He remembered the Matteo of old, a young man who never expected to be the least most important person in the room, even if he had to bring the others in it down to his level.

'Good to be remembered,' he replied through clenched teeth.

'So, what do you want?' Matteo returned to his papers as he spoke. 'A job? A loan?' He looked back at Ramsey with a smile. 'Address of a good tailor?'

'I'm working for your mother,' Ramsey kept to the facts. 'That is, the company I work for is.'

'The company you work for,' Matteo stopped looking at the papers now, leaning back in his chair as he finally took in the man standing in front of him. 'That's something I'd never expected to come out of your mouth. Unless it's a lie. I'd understand if it was a lie, as that's what you used to do all the time.'

'No lie,' Ramsey replied, watching the men who'd escorted him in as they walked up behind him, sensing danger. This felt a little concerning, a little too real, but he pushed on. 'I work for an insurance investigator. *Use a thief to catch a thief* and all that.'

'And what about honour amongst thieves?'

'That never existed, Mister Lumetta. And you would know that.'

'Would I?' Matteo smiled coldly, and Ramsey could still feel the men behind him, close enough to breathe down his neck.

'Look, Matteo,' Ramsey forced a smile. 'I knew you when you played gangster in the streets with your friends. So, if you want me to play gangster with you now, I'm more than happy to. But I'm here as a favour.'

Matteo waved his hand, and, as if by magic, the two men behind Ramsey stepped back, returning to their original positions.

'Tell me then, *old family friend*,' Matteo said, emphasising the last three words mockingly. 'Why did Mama hire you?'

'I think we both know why,' Ramsey was tiring of the game now. 'Paulo Moretti.'

'That's a matter for the police,' Matteo's smile finally dropped. 'I believe a DCI Richmond is running that case, as she's already spoken to me. Maybe you should speak to her.'

'We're not investigating that,' Ramsey replied. 'We're looking for the three thousand stolen bottles.'

'The bottles?' Matteo bellowed with laughter at this. 'Christ, you've gone down in the world!'

'Have I?' Ramsey waited for Matteo to stop. 'Because let's face it, we both know one of those pallets wasn't filled with olive oil.'

Ramsey held his ground but couldn't help but flinch a little as Matteo burst upwards out of his chair, his face reddening as he stared down at the man in front of him.

'And what exactly *were they?*' he hissed.

'Something worth killing for,' Ramsey decided to play it smart; not mentioning what the bottles could have been, but seeing whether Matteo would give something up. 'Something I think you know about.'

'And why would you think that?'

'Because you work from Dublin, and yet yesterday you flew back to London for no reason,' Ramsey replied defiantly.

At this, Matteo waved around the office, calming down.

'I have books to check.'

'Books any of your employees could have sorted,' Ramsey was warming up now, walking over and tapping one sheet. 'You came to London because you knew there was a shipment arriving. What I can't work out is whether you were here to pick it up, or intercept it.'

'You should speak to Tommaso about that,' Matteo shrugged. 'He runs Lumetta Oils now.'

'I thought Maureen Lumetta did?'

'So does she,' another smile flitted briefly across Matteo's face. 'It changes depending on who you speak to.'

'And if I was to ask you?'

Matteo walked around the desk now, walking up to Ramsey.

'I am my mother's son,' he said. 'And I do what she says.'

'And if Tommaso went against her?'

'He is the elder,' Matteo puffed out his cheeks. 'I may not agree with him all the time. Look, Ramsey. I don't come here because of shipments. I come here because I was asked.'

'Who asked you?'

Matteo looked away, and Ramsey realised there was something more going on here than the man was letting on.

'A family friend,' he said. 'I will not explain their identity more than that.'

'I see, but I need one thing clarified,' Ramsey spoke carefully. 'Is it family or a friend? The two are very different.'

'A friend who was once almost family,' Matteo admitted, and Ramsey couldn't help but pick up on the past tense on speaking about this friend. 'Someone who was concerned I might be overcome during a power struggle.'

'Someone was muscling in on Mama Lumetta?' Ramsey was surprised at this. 'Or do you mean your brother?'

'Tommaso and Mama are complicated,' Matteo replied. 'Have been ever since my father passed.'

The finality of the statement concerned Ramsey, and he chose to keep away from it for the moment.

'Look,' he said. 'Mama Lumetta hired us to locate and retrieve the stolen stock, but couldn't confirm who she believed stole it. The obvious suspects are you and your brother, who both happen to be in London at the same time they hijacked the van. Which does kind of give the suspicion you either knew it was being hijacked or you suspected it could be – which gives knowledge of the contents – or you did it yourself.'

'If I'd stolen the contents, do you think I'd be sitting in the back of a car wash?' Matteo asked, and although his tone was now light, mocking almost, Ramsey knew this was put on, and that Matteo was currently boiling hot with anger right now.

'Then who did it?' Ramsey asked. 'Tell me who it was, let us get your stock back, and then you can do whatever you want to them. Who's arrogant enough to go against you, and at the same time, who has the information required to do this?'

'Nobody does, that's the point,' Matteo finally snapped, looking back at Ramsey, and for the first time he could actually see concern on the man's face. 'I knew. Tommaso knew. Mama knew. Paulo knew. Bar maybe a couple of people outside the family, that was it. Mama hired you to find it, and that says she wasn't involved. But what if she *did* do this, and you're there to make her look good? Ineffective as ever and there to make a noise while she does what she needs to do?'

'I'd hardly say we were that,' Ramsey replied. 'You could always ask Nicky Simpson how ineffective we are.'

'I will do,' Matteo smiled, looking over at a screen, where on it a familiar car was arriving. 'He's here now.'

Ramsey fought the urge to run, his curiosity overcoming his fear.

'I didn't know you worked together,' he said, keeping his voice calm.

'We don't,' Matteo replied, walking over to the screen, looking at it. 'Mister Simpson is looking to open a few of his poncy health clubs in Dublin, and that's my manor.'

'How did you make contact?' Ramsey couldn't help himself.

'Mama's driver,' Matteo was distracted. 'He's a member of one of his clubs. Suggested I speak to him.'

Ramsey couldn't help acknowledge the timing, but held his ground. He was beside the desk now, his hand resting on the papers.

'Well, before he arrives, let's conclude this chat,' he said calmly. 'You think your mum could have done this?'

'It's her, or Tommaso,' Matteo scrunched his nose, walking over to his guards. 'I could imagine Tommaso doing this to her, but he wouldn't shoot Paulo. Go welcome our guests, will you?'

'Why not?' Ramsey frowned, ignoring the second part and now moving away from the desk, his hands behind his back, remembering the earlier comment. 'Because he's a family friend?'

'Because Paulo was our half-brother,' Matteo sighed, finally turning back to Ramsey, pausing for a moment and frowning as he realised the man had moved. 'Never formerly acknowledged, but my father, he, shall we say, played around? And Paulo resulted from one of those affairs. We always knew, and his mother was looked after. As was he.'

Ramsey didn't want to look into extra-marital affairs, considering he'd had a dalliance with Mama Lumetta herself, but he couldn't help himself.

'How was your mama with Paulo?' Ramsey asked, his hand now sliding into his pocket as he tried to look casual. 'I understand how you and Tommaso could see Paulo as family, but she could look at Paulo and see a painful reminder of her husband's indiscretions.'

Matteo breathed out a long and frustrated sigh at this.

'We all have bastards in our families,' he said eventually. 'Sometimes they're given the keys to the kingdom, and sometimes they're just the driver.'

Ramsey was about to continue, noting the backhanded comment about Paulo not becoming more powerful, when the door opened and Nicky Simpson entered the office. Muscled and lean, wearing expensive jeans, a Ralph Lauren shirt with half the buttons undone under a navy-blue blazer, his wild, sun-lightened hair roughly pulled back into a small ponytail, revealing his tanned, well-moisturised face, his eyes lit up as he saw Ramsey standing in the room.

'It must be Christmas,' he smiled. 'Ramsey Allen. Your mum doing okay?'

'She is, Mister Simpson,' Ramsey nodded, wanting more than anything to not be there right now. 'Thank you.'

'And why are you here with my new friend Matteo?' Simpson asked, looking at his new friend Matteo, as if expecting an answer. 'Is his ex-DI friend, Ellie Reckless, here?'

'He never mentioned he worked with the police,' Matteo's eyes narrowed. 'But Mister Allen here is an old family friend. He came to say hello, offer his condolences to the death of one of our organisation.'

Interesting, Ramsey thought to himself. *He doesn't want Simpson to know about the stolen bottles.*

'I was passing,' Ramsey added, relaxing a little as he spoke to lessen his nervous body language. 'I heard Matteo was here, over from Dublin, and I came to pay my respects. I knew him and his brother when they were children.'

'You're old enough,' Simpson smiled, but it didn't reach his eyes. 'Who would have thought it, that you had influence in other areas?'

'I wouldn't say that,' Ramsey said, perhaps a little too quickly. 'I'm just a facilitator.'

'That you are,' Simpson replied and Ramsey could see he was irritated at Ramsey being there. 'But if you've finished facilitating, perhaps you could piss off like a good little flunky?'

Ramsey bit back a reply; Simpson's money was paying for his mother's rest home, and as far as Nicky Simpson was concerned, this meant Ramsey worked for him. Nodding at Matteo, Ramsey started to back out of the room.

'Say hello to your brother for me,' he said. 'And I'll hopefully speak to you soon.'

Matteo waved a hand, almost dismissively, and Ramsey turned to leave, but a hand on his shoulder stopped him.

Nicky Simpson was frowning.

'Who died?' he asked. 'This member of the organisation you came to offer condolences for?'

'Renata,' Matteo replied before Ramsey could speak. 'Used to babysit me when I was a kid. Knew Mister Allen a hundred years ago or something.'

'And you came to offer your respects over that?' Simpson tutted as he shook his head. 'This was the best you could do to get an appointment?'

'What can I say?' Ramsey shrugged. 'Any opportunity is an open door to make new friends, right?'

'You're a vulture, Ramsey Allen,' Simpson smiled. 'That's why I like you. Don't be a stranger.'

And, this said, Nicky Simpson turned back to Matteo, the well-dressed thief beside him now forgotten.

'I was hoping your older brother would be here for this?' he asked. 'He gave me the impression he was brokering the deal.'

Ramsey didn't hear the answer, as the doors were closed in his face as he backed out, and the conversation was replaced by the sounds of pressure washers and hoses.

Walking back out into the street, Ramsey considered what he'd learnt. For a start, his gut didn't think Matteo was involved, but his alliance with Nicky Simpson was concerning. That said, if he heard right, it was Tommaso who brokered that deal. Maybe he stole the stolen items to fund something to do with it?

The one thing that had surprised Ramsey, though, was the news of Paulo Moretti's parentage. If he was a Lumetta, a recognised in any respect one, then he could have made a play for the crown at any time, perhaps get offered the "keys to the kingdom", to paraphrase Matteo. From the looks of things, he hadn't, staying a simple driver, but at the same time …

Shrugging off the feeling of dread that travelled across him, Ramsey looked around for a taxi back to Finders. With luck, he'd arrive back before the others, and snaffle all the biscuits the company brought in for team meetings in the afternoon.

After all, once a thief and all that.

Talking of which, as he walked out of sight of the building, he pulled a folded sheet of A4 paper out of his pocket. It was one of the papers on the desk in the back office, something he'd grabbed while Matteo had walked to the screen and folded up behind his back, sliding it into his pocket before Nicky Simpson had entered. It had been an impulse, a split-second act he'd stopped giving in to a long time ago, but he'd seen it and felt it could be important. And so, when he had the opportunity, he'd taken it.

Borrowed it.

Opening it up, he examined it carefully, realising it was indeed what he'd suspected when he'd seen the LUMETTA OILS logo on the top of the sheet.

It was a shipping order.

It wasn't dated last night, but two months earlier. There were three deliveries on it, all to differing locations. The driver's name, though, was Paulo Moretti.

Matteo Lumetta was checking Paulo's previous deliveries, in particular this one.

Ramsey looked up, waving a passing cab down, folding the paper once more and this time slipping it into his jacket. There was a strong chance the three delivery locations on this sheet were the same ones Moretti was supposed to deliver to today, but just from the stock numbers on this, he knew at least one amount was massively different.

All Ramsey had to do was work out how this could help them with who stole the stock, and why they had to kill Moretti to do so.

8

CIRCUIT BREAKERS

AFTER THE BREAK AT THE SERVICE STATION, ELLIE HAD TAKEN A diversion before heading back to the office; she knew she needed to know more about the piece of circuit that Casey had found attached to the Sprinter's burnt out sat nav and, while they took a break at the service station, she put a call in. Pulling into a car park in North Greenwich, she made her way along the lanes, aiming for the back end of the car park, where, secluded and almost out of sight, a hideously painted Lamborghini was parked in the far corner waiting for her. Standing beside it was a tall man; almost seven feet tall and stick thin, he looked like someone who'd had his aspect ratio stretched too far vertically. Well dressed, wearing a collection of *Prada, Tom Ford* and *Gucci*, he smiled as Ellie arrived; his hair short and brown, matching the groomed stubble on his face.

'Big Slim,' Ellie grinned as she exited the car. 'Good to see you haven't lost it again.'

Big Slim patted the top of his car. A few weeks earlier, Ellie had repossessed the car from a wannabe crime lord who'd stolen it from him, while also, and rather stupidly, telling everyone about what he'd done. The favour owed for this had been paid back a day or two later though, when one of Big Slim's experts, Jeet, had checked a recently crashed car for ways it could have been tampered with, after it caused a short circuit while driving that almost killed Ellie and Tinker.

'I paid off my favour, Reckless,' Big Slim said gently, as if reminding a friend who might have forgotten.

At this, Ellie nodded.

'I know,' she said. 'I'm here to owe you one.'

Big Slim's eyebrows raised at the statement.

'Oh,' he smiled with realisation at the turning of the tables. 'I think I can come up with something.'

He rapped on the top of the car, and from the passenger side the door opened and another man emerged. This was a small Indian named Jeet, a man who Ellie also knew, and who'd found the cause of the accident the last time they'd been together. He had some kind of nervous tic in his neck that meant he was constantly twitching, and he flinched slightly as he walked around the car, a laptop in his hand.

'I understand you've got something for me?' he asked, already looking for whatever the item was, as if expecting Ellie to already have it in her hand, just waiting to pass over.

'My computer guy does,' Ellie nodded to Casey who, eyeing Jeet up cautiously looked back at her.

'You sure about this?' he asked with the reluctance of someone who really didn't rate the person he was looking at.

'I am,' Ellie said, motioning again. 'He's good. Believe me.'

Reluctantly, Casey pulled the singed circuit board out of his pocket, passing it over.

'Found it attached to the wires of a Mercedes Sprinter

van,' he explained. 'The charred edges were because they set the van alight. I think it was used to overwrite the sat nav.'

Jeet pursed his lips, already walking to the back of the car park, using a bench as a makeshift table after throwing a small towel across it.

'There's gaps,' he explained. 'In the wood. Don't want anything falling through.'

Ellie didn't reply to this, as she felt this was more a statement than a conversational comment, and so instead looked back at Big Slim as Casey and Jeet huddled together over the bench.

'So, what's the favour you want from me?' she asked.

Big Slim looked awkward as he considered the question.

'Look, I get it if you don't want to do this, but it'd mean a lot,' he said. 'I'm connected to a biker group. A motorcycle club.'

Ellie tried not to smile at this, but failed.

'What, you're one of the "Sons of Anarchy"?' she sniggered. 'Never really saw you as that sort of type.'

'Motorcycle clubs aren't filled with criminals,' Big Slim snapped. 'And between us, I don't think you can play from the high ground here. You were never cleared of murder, remember? Just allowed to walk out of the court.'

Ellie bristled at the comment, but had to reluctantly accept it.

'You're not exactly whiter than white yourself,' she replied, keeping her temper. 'Or had you forgotten our last job? The Lamborghini you had stolen, which you yourself—'

'Bought unknowingly,' Big Slim held his hands up, warding off her next attack before she started. 'Look, all I'm saying is we all have secrets, and I'm sure that's the same with the *Screaming Angels* – that's the name of the club – but they're mainly middle-class men or ex-army officers, riding expensive Harleys every weekend and raising money for charity in the process.'

Ellie conceded the point, holding her own hands up in surrender, deliberately mirroring Big Slim's earlier motions.

'Okay,' she said. 'Nice guys, ride bikes, allowed you to join so they obviously have some issues to work through ...'

'So, last night I get a call from one of them; Minty,' Big Slim replied. 'Don't ask about how he got the name; long story and a not surprising punchline. Anyway, he called and told me that yesterday evening, someone turned up and trashed the clubhouse. There's a couple of members there and they tried to stop this, and one's now in hospital, and the other might not ride again.'

'They were injured so badly?'

'No, just really scared off by the attack,' Big Slim replied. 'The one scared off. He's a bank manager from Lewes. Doesn't usually find himself in confrontations.'

'So why are you coming to me with this?' Ellie asked, frowning. 'It sounds like something any number of people could fix.'

Big Slim looked over at Jeet and Casey, the latter now pointing excitedly at Jeet's laptop screen.

'The attacker was one of yours,' he said. 'Tinker Jones.'

Ellie actually stepped back in surprise at this.

'You're sure?'

'There ain't that many people who could kick the shit out of bikers named Tinkerbelle, are there?' Big Slim's eyes narrowed. 'And the Disney fairy didn't have army combat training, to my knowledge. It was her, alright. Came in like a banshee possessed, demanding to see one of the club members, and then, when nobody could help, she took the place apart.'

Ellie bit her bottom lip as she considered this. Tinker had arrived at the diner with a story of blackmail, someone having hacked into her files and removed sensitive material. Could this have been connected?

'What was the name of the person she was looking for?' Ellie eventually asked.

'Suggs,' Big Slim replied. 'Old member, ex-army. Rifles, I think. Why?'

'Tinker was a Corporal in the Rifles, and she said she believed an ex-army contact was blackmailing her,' Ellie was running a hand along her hair, smoothing it down as she considered this. 'I'm not saying what she did was right, but I think there could be more to this than a random beating.'

'I'm sure there is, but there needs to be recompense made,' Big Slim shook his head, and Ellie could see he was squaring up for an argument. 'I'll check into Suggs, get info for her—'

'For *me*,' Ellie interrupted. 'I want to know what I'm getting into before I speak to anyone. But I'll get Tinker to fix what she did, I promise.'

'I know you will,' Big Slim smiled now. 'That's why I was going to contact you, regardless.'

Ellie sighed at this. If she hadn't needed Big Slim's help right now, the chances were she'd have gained another favour from him. But the fact of the matter was she needed his help right now, and this at least balanced the books. Taking a deep breath, she looked back at Casey and Jeet.

'Anything?' she asked.

'It's crispy fried, but yeah, there's something,' Jeet replied with his customary neck twitch. 'This didn't hack the van; it hacked his phone.'

'Did we see a phone?' Ellie asked Casey who shook his head.

'It would have been connected through a USB port at the front of the van, just under the media screen,' he explained. 'Probably through CarPlay or an Android equivalent. Chances are if it wasn't too badly burnt, the police would have taken the phone to examine. Maybe even the USB wire, too.'

'So, what does the thingie do?' Ellie nodded at the circuit. 'And how does it help us?'

'Someone placed it in the van, and used the van's own Wi-Fi to connect it,' Jeet explained. 'There's a cellular SIM in the dashboard, so you can call emergency support if the van breaks down, usually by pressing a button that connects you straight through. This also gives the van a kind of basic Wi-Fi on the road, while also connecting to the sat nav's servers, checking for road issues. Closures, roadworks, all that sort of thing.'

'So, Paulo was led somewhere, rather than following the correct path?'

'It looks like he was using a navigation app on his phone,' Jeet was peering closely at the screen now. 'Probably Waze, or Google Maps, one of those.'

'Why would he use that over the van's own sat nav?' Ellie pulled her phone out, checking it, worried it was currently being hacked. 'It can't get into phones remotely, right?'

'For the second question, don't be an idiot, it's not connected to any power source, and for the first question, they're used because they give up-to-the-moment traffic data,' Jeet replied knowledgeably. 'Take Waze, for example. It's great for drivers because all drivers who use the app place notes on it. You're driving down a road, for example, and there's a car accident in front of you? Well *beep boop beep*, you tap on Waze, press the "major accident" icon and boom, there's an accident marked on the map. And then it sends this out to anyone nearby. So, someone's in a car half a mile behind you when you do this? Their Waze is told "hey, there's an accident ahead" and instantly works out the best route that avoids it in real time.'

'Clever,' Ellie admitted.

'Yes and no,' Casey replied. 'The reason people are turning off apps like Waze and Google is because they're constantly looking for the quickest or shortest routes for you, depending on your preferences. Which means you could be driving down a dual carriageway with no issues, and then you're suddenly sent down five country lanes, all because Waze, or Google Maps, or whatever app you're using checked a ton of road journeys in a millisecond and decided this new route was thirty seconds faster, and therefore better for you. Problem is, now you're behind a tractor, or you're having to be more careful because of the twists and turns, and you'd probably have a far better experience just driving down the A-road and eating that half a minute. You might even get there faster because you're not behind a tractor, or being more careful.'

'How do you know all this?' Ellie frowned. 'You can't even drive yet.'

'Waze is free on phones,' Casey shrugged. 'I use it when I'm on my electric skateboard.'

'Of course, you do,' Ellie shook her head. 'I don't know what came over me. So, Paulo was using this?'

'It looks that way,' Jeet nodded – although it could have

been a rather extreme twitch – as he placed his laptop away. 'This would be connected to the van's media display unit, but also to the wires that lead to the Wi-Fi. Which means anyone using CarPlay, or whatever, is effectively turning the circuit on, as the connection powers it.'

'And what exactly does the circuit do once it's on?' Ellie was tiring of the conversation.

'It allows someone to remote-change the route you're going,' Jeet explained. 'Basically, someone can see the route you're taking on their own device, maybe a phone, more likely a laptop, and then add a diverted stop. This then changes the sat nav, as it's now looking to take you to the diversion first. However, this circuit hides all that in the background, so the driver wouldn't have known he was being directed. He doesn't realise there's a second location, he only sees the final destination.'

'So, he goes down the motorway, and there's a diversion,' Ellie thought aloud. 'This was real?'

'Unless crime lords can close off motorways,' Jeet smiled. 'They probably arranged for him to drive down it last night, knowing the roadworks were up. The roadworks probably started at ten in the evening, that's the usual time for things like this, so all the hijackers had to do was make sure he got onto the motorway after that. And then, the moment he came off, the sat nav would have been constantly trying to find the best option for him, and he would likely have been going down whatever route it was taking.'

'Here,' Casey eagerly pointed at a line of code. 'When the van reached the A20 at Leeds Castle, a message was sent to the screen, saying there was a three-car smash ahead, and the road was currently closed.'

'While it did this, the line of code here also added the

village of Hollingbourne as an extra, diverted location, which meant that instead of carrying on down the road, whoever was driving the van now turned right up Hospital Road,' Jeet puffed out his cheeks. 'It's good coding. Top level stuff.'

'And then, about a hundred metres down the road, he found himself captured,' Casey added. 'Anyone with a phone could have done this, as it would have linked to the van's Wi-Fi, and you could follow the IP on a tracker. Like when you "find my phone" on something moving.'

'And, when the van was in the right location, they pressed send and waited,' Ellie nodded. 'So, they knew Paulo was going to be travelling through roadworks.'

'If he'd crashed for the night in a car park, the motorway would have been opened by the time he woke,' Casey said, realising what he was saying. 'Whoever told him to carry on signed his death warrant.'

'Also, this was a UK circuit,' Jeet looked at Big Slim as he spoke. 'It was a short-term device, completely disposable and would have burned out after an hour.'

'Which means it was put into the van in Dover?' Ellie wasn't expecting this. 'How long would it take to install?'

'With access to the van, a matter of seconds,' Casey replied. 'I found it quickly, so it wasn't hidden or anything. They relied on Paulo not looking under the dash at midnight. But if they had to break into the van, it could have taken longer.'

'Could it have been done on the ferry?'

Jeet clicked his tongue against his teeth.

'Could be, but it's risky,' he said. 'Delay at Customs and you're screwed. Likely this was done as the van landed.'

'So, when Paulo was talking to the Customs Officers,' Ellie

nodded. 'Tinker's having a chat with them, so we'll see what they say.'

Looking back at Big Slim, Ellie held out her hand.

'I'll fix what we discussed,' she said. 'And I'll find out what's going on.'

'If you find any of the *Screaming Angels* actually had a part in whatever this is,' Big Slim replied, 'and Tinker had a valid reason for what she did? I'll fix it myself, and I'll make sure she has a front-row seat for the show.'

Ellie nodded her appreciation, and with his help no longer required, Big Slim nodded to Jeet, and the two of them climbed into the Lamborghini, screeching off out of the supermarket car park and towards the A2.

'I heard a bit of what your favour is,' Casey said, walking back to Ellie. 'I'm guessing it's Tinker's blackmail problem?'

'When you met her, did she tell you anything more about this?' Ellie asked, opening the driver's door of her own car and getting in. 'Because this isn't like her.'

'What, taking out biker gangs?'

'Taking out potentially innocent biker gangs.'

Casey climbed into the passenger seat, putting away the circuit and leaning back over the chair to ruffle Millie's head as she panted happily.

'I'm seeing her tonight,' he said. 'Hopefully, she'll tell me more about what's going on.'

'Oh, she will,' Ellie replied as she started the car, her voice emotionless and cold. 'Because I'm coming with you.'

9

RIFLES

Tinker hadn't expected Ellie to be waiting outside her apartment with Millie and Casey when she arrived back, but at the same time she hadn't discounted the possibility. Casey would have told Ellie what he knew during the day, and as he didn't know much, that wasn't a lot, but Ellie's face was a lot icier than Tinker had expected.

Something had happened.

'You okay?' she asked as she climbed out of her battered Defender.

'That depends,' Ellie replied, straightening as she spoke. 'I'm just a little curious about something. Beat the living hell out of any biker gangs recently?'

'How—' realising she'd been rumbled, Tinker looked over at Casey, but knew it couldn't have been him. She hadn't said anything about the attack earlier on.

'Big Slim's a member of the club,' Ellie replied. 'I had to ask him for a favour, offering one back. Can you guess what the favour he asked of me was?'

Tinker nodded, wincing a little internally.

'Sorry,' she said, leaning against the Defender. 'Look, can we talk in the pub on the corner? The building committee doesn't allow dogs inside my apartment.'

Ellie went to argue, most likely say something like "the building needs a new committee then" or similar, but instead sighed, letting out a long breath, nodding.

'One drink, you tell us what's going on, and I decide if or how you're going to apologise to the *Screaming Angels*.'

Tinker went to reply she was a grown woman and could make her own decisions on whether she should apologise to anyone or not, but there was a part of her that knew Ellie was right, and so she nodded acceptance at this, already walking towards the pub, the *Royal Oak*, on the corner of her street. It was dog friendly. Tinker and Ellie had met there for Sunday lunch a week earlier, but now it was late on a weekday, and the end-of-day workers had turned up, almost filling the place with conversation and work-based testosterone. In the end, Tinker, Ellie and Casey requisitioned a pub table outside and beside one of the front windows; an all-in-one bench and table system that Millie could sit under, with a plastic pop-out bowl of tap water to sip on beside her while Ellie passed her treats.

'So, do you want to start at the beginning?' Ellie asked as she placed a pint in front of Tinker, and the two Cokes she'd also been carefully carrying in front of both her and Casey. Tinker took a long draught of the lager before replying.

'I left the army,' she said.

'Well, we got that,' Casey said sarcastically, but stopped when both women turned to look at him. He quickly back-tracked, finding something incredibly interesting in his glass of Coke.

'I know this story,' Ellie said, looking back at Tinker. 'I've never pushed you on it.'

'I left because I had an inappropriate relationship with a superior officer,' Tinker admitted. 'I was a non-com, as in *non-commissioned officer*. They were higher. And they were married.'

Casey's eyes widened.

'You didn't!' he hissed in the way someone being told salacious gossip spoke.

'I did, and it cost her a marriage,' Tinker replied, and Ellie watched Casey, trying to work out whether he picked up on what Tinker was actually saying. 'It got out, I started getting shit for it. Not for being gay, or whatever you wanted to call it, but for being a marriage breaker. That was the last thing I ever wanted to do.'

'You never do. Trust me, I know that one well,' Ellie said sadly, and Casey looked at her, went to speak and then stopped himself, turning instead back to Tinker.

'So, what, they kicked you out for being gay? That's a bit shit,' he said.

'I voluntarily resigned,' Tinker shook her head. 'I couldn't be there anymore. It used to be my everything, and now all it was ... well, it was just memories.'

'And someone's blackmailing you on this?' Ellie asked.

'In a way, yes, and in a way, no,' Tinker replied. 'I left a few years back, and Jemima – that was her name – she stayed in the Rifles. Changed battalions too, went from First to Fourth Battalion, moving from Chepstow to Aldershot.'

'How many are there?' Casey asked, genuinely curious. 'Battalions, that is?'

'Eight, although technically seven now,' Tinker replied. 'Fourth Battalion was seconded to the Rangers about a year back, and is now the Fourth Battalion of Ranger Regiment. Basically, they were created to become the UK equivalent of the American Green Berets.'

She looked across the road, almost wistfully.

'If I'd stayed, I could have been in it too,' she said. 'Working with the Army Special Operations Brigade, doing all that unconventional warfare shit you see in movies …'

She looked back at Ellie, smiling.

'Instead, I'm stuck with you,' she continued. 'I'd have a better survival rating over there.'

'So, someone's blackmailing Jemima?' Ellie asked, ignoring the attempt at diverting the subject. 'Because I've never seen you shy away from a fight before.'

'She's going for a promotion,' Tinker explained. 'We keep in touch here and there. Couple of reunions, a wedding or two, maybe a funeral. Usually, I hear from old mates in the infantry about what's going on. And a few weeks back I heard she was going for a big role.'

'And coincidentally, this is the same time you get hacked?'

Tinker shrugged.

'It's shitty they're going for her sexuality over this,' Casey muttered, but at this Tinker shook her head.

'It's not that,' she replied, lowering her voice. 'That's not enough these days to cause a problem.'

'Then what was it?' Ellie asked, leaning closer and lowering her voice to match.

Tinker looked around the front of the pub, at the other people, caught up in their own conversations and, finally nodding to herself quietly agreeing to give up this secret, she spoke.

'It was five years ago,' she started, taking a sip of her pint to either take a moment to consider her next words, or lubricate her throat for a long speech. 'We were on patrol in – well, let's just say it was somewhere hot. We'd had information that some insurgents were in the area, but we weren't to confront unless confronted. There was an incident, and by the end of it we had someone in custody. But this was all off the books. Our commander decided to be a hero, and started interrogating him, even though we weren't supposed to be involved. And we weren't at base, we were on the ground floor of this guy's home, with him zip-tied to a chair.'

'Sounds like it was your commander's fault, not yours,' Ellie continued.

'Yeah, but at this point the commander, all gung-ho and filled with this belief he's doing the good fight, has a heart attack right there in the room, collapsing while he's leaning over the prisoner,' Tinker replied. 'We don't see this, and we sure as hell don't realise what's going on, as all we see is our commanding officer going in at the insurgent. We think he's about to give him a slap or something, but then he staggers back, collapsing, clutching his chest, and the prisoner's right hand is free. We jump to conclusions.'

'You think your commander was attacked by him?'

Tinker nodded.

Jemima goes off on one, beats the shit out of him. Guy's a mess, and at this point we learn from the medic what really happened to Peterson, our commander.'

'So now you've got a prisoner, unarmed and secured who's been beaten for something he never did.'

'Jemima was a mess, couldn't believe what she'd done,' Tinker explained. 'And I got that because we're breaking a ton of laws here.'

'What laws are we talking about?'

'Laws which could have you doing military time

because we could be court-martialled,' Tinker replied. 'Our careers were over the moment she attacked an unarmed and tied prisoner, no matter what the belief had been. We were lucky, the room only had a couple of people in, and we'd turned off any body cameras the moment Peterson went off on this bloody stupid idea, but although we knew people could see how this looked, and why we did what we did, it was still bad. So, while she sits with Peterson, I sort things out. I untie the prisoner, toss the cable ties and the chair out of the room. At least this way I can claim it was self-defence, and we didn't realise when Peterson fell, it wasn't the insurgent attacking. But we knew it was coming out.'

'So, what happened?' Casey asked.

'I was a non-com officer, so I took the flack,' Tinker explained. 'I said it was me who attacked, stating Jemima wasn't even in the building at the time, it was just me and Peterson, and I was following his orders, leaping to a knee-jerk reaction when he fell. And he backed me up, because he knew this was all because of his bloody stupid hero complex in the first point. He'd been shipped out, I think, even given a desk job because of his heart, and only when we returned to Chepstow did any of this shit hit the fan. But during this time, Jemima and me, we'd become close because of this. You find that when people share a moment together. And we started an affair, but it got out.'

Tinker stopped at this, and Ellie couldn't work out whether she was taking time, remembering the moment, or trying to find a way to mentally forget it.

'At the same time Peterson was having some kind of guilt trip, and people were talking about the incident again,' she continued. 'I knew I'd screwed things up for Jemima with the affair, and I was getting some personal flack—not for my sexuality, but for being a marriage-breaker.'

Again, Ellie decided not to comment on this.

'I spoke to my superiors and explained I intended to leave,' she said. 'I also pointed out if I went, this whole thing could be put at my feet and, with me gone, it was decided to be swept under the rug. Everyone else went on with their lives.'

'But someone found out the truth.'

Tinker smiled sullenly.

'Not of the incident,' she replied. 'But the medic, when he came in to check Peterson he hadn't been in the original meeting, where Peterson decided to interrogate the poor bastard, and because of this, his body cam was still on. He didn't see the other room or the prisoner, but on camera, you could clearly see Jemima as she spoke to Peterson, kneeling beside him and comforting him as he lay on the floor.'

'Jemima, who wasn't supposed to be in the building at the time,' Casey added, now understanding.

'And they showed these to the court-martial?' Ellie asked.

'No, the medic understood the situation, and realised what was seen in the footage. It wasn't classed as relevant to the case because the medic wasn't in the room earlier, but all it took was for someone clever to put two and two together and realise although I'm claiming responsibility, Jemima, who's claimed as being absent from the scene, is there beside me. And it's a few months later by now, I'm on my notice and she was transferring at this point.'

Tinker sipped her drink again.

'The medic, I can't remember his name. Mason, perhaps? I want to say Gavin something? Anyway, he sent some footage images, five or six photos in total to me in that friendly "you should know about this" way, mainly for my defence if some-thing came up, but it was never needed. The army had already accepted my resignation, everything got swept away, and I left.'

'Have you spoken to Jemima since?'

'A couple of times,' Tinker nodded. 'She mended her marriage, classed me as a bi-curious blip and moved on. Which I get, I really do. The situation gave us an artificial closeness. And, as far as I know, she doesn't think about me at all.'

She sighed, placing her hands behind her head as she stretched her arms.

'But now, someone's gone into my account and found those photos.'

'So, they're looking for a way to stop her promotion?' Casey's face darkened. 'Or are they looking to do something worse?'

'I genuinely think it's the latter,' Tinker nodded. 'I think whoever this is, they're looking for a way to make her do what *they* want her to do, in particular once she has that promo-tion. Remember, she's working in the Army Special Opera-tions now, and that means secrets. Things they can use to possibly destabilise the country if they can turn her.'

She took another long draught of the pint, slamming the now almost-empty glass onto the table in anger, surprising a couple of the surrounding drinkers who, not expecting the noise, startled at this.

'And that's my problem,' Tinker, ignoring the glares aimed at her, continued. 'I don't know who actually wants to do this. I spoke to a few of my mates and there's one or two people who have dropped off the radar, people who had reasons why they might want something like this.'

'Let me guess, one of them was a *Screaming Angel*?'

Tinker gave a soft, embarrassed grin.

'Yeah, which is why I went there,' she said.

'Do you know how they got in?' Casey, already working on his tablet, pulling up data from some dark-web page forum he'd logged into, asked.

'They got into the system through my old army password,' Tinker replied. 'Which means if they came in that way, they had to have connections into the Rifles, or even my personal details, to get hold of it.'

'Who had knowledge of the photos?' Ellie asked.

'Me, Jemima, Peterson, my army lawyer, the medic who contacted me ... that was it,' Tinker replied, her eyes scrunching as she tried to remember anyone else who might have known. 'There were two people in the battalion, in my unit, who had issues with both of us. And I decided to start there. But one of those couldn't have done it.'

'Why?'

'Because they're dead and have been for two years,' Tinker shrugged. 'And no, it wasn't me that did them in; before you ask.'

Casey grinned, returning to his tablet.

'And the other one?' Ellie prodded.

'Seems to havè an alibi, so they're out of the picture,' Tinker sighed, looking up at the sky. 'But they were a lead. I had to look into it, and my patience was worn down a little.'

'Okay, so the one who's dead,' Casey took a sip of his Coke as he stared at his tablet screen. 'Are there people who could've worked with them? Like, is it somebody using their ID to take *your* ID? Can it be a hacker?'

Casey turned the screen around to show a chain of emails. All of them were through Tinker's account.

'Don't worry,' he said, seeing Ellie's surprised expression. 'I didn't hack it; Tinker gave me the details when we drove to you this morning. However, as you can see here, I'm in her account, I have a chain email thread in front of me with three, maybe four people on it, and just through looking at the emails, I can see personal information from several of the others. All I need to do is spoof a couple of IPs and I can start to really dig in. So, if I can do this in five minutes, there's a very strong chance someone else hacked into an account that's inert, say, from someone who died, and then got into your emails through a back door. And they don't even need to control your emails, just be able to open them up and screen-shot anything in them. Like photos from a medic that warn you of a possible issue. Then they delete the emails to hide the fact they opened them.'

'So, what we have here is someone who knew about the pictures, but didn't have copies of them, or a way to get the originals,' Ellie mused. 'The only option they have is to hack you personally, and get them that way. Once they have these images, proof Jemima was at an incident she swore on oath she wasn't at, they can leverage her into God knows what.'

Tinker nodded.

'That's about the skinny of it,' she replied. 'And right now, what I *do* know is I need to find the hacker and the black-mailer fast, because I have an ex-friend one step away from losing everything.'

'We'll add it to the list,' Ellie raised a glass. 'And if it is connected to the *Screaming Angels*, and you *were* in the right, I know Big Slim would love to get involved.'

10

LATE NIGHTERS

AFTER FINISHING UP WITH TINKER, ELLIE HAD DROPPED CASEY back at his house before returning to her apartment, situated slightly west of Shoreditch. She'd intended to walk Millie before she fed the Cocker Spaniel, but after entering her apartment and changing into some more comfortable clothes, she stopped as the door buzzed.

Walking to the buzzer, effectively a plastic phone on the wall with a screen beside it, Ellie looked through the CCTV camera at the two police detectives standing at the door, waiting patiently for an answer. The man, tall, slim and in his thirties was looking around the street while the woman, wearing a shapeless grey overcoat, and with her blonde hair pulled back, glared directly at the camera and, by default, directly at Ellie.

'What can I do for you tonight?' Ellie pressed the intercom button and asked through the speaker. Hearing this, the man looked up at the camera, joining his partner.

'Evening, Ellie,' he said. 'Sorry for calling so late. We

thought we'd check in, find out how things are going with you?'

Ellie chuckled at this.

'Checking in like we're old friends, eh, Mark?' she replied. 'I think we stopped being that a while back. And I was never friends with Kate.'

'Can we come in?' DI Mark Whitehouse sighed, obviously tiring of this as he glanced at DS Kate Delgado, standing beside him.

'No,' Ellie replied. She didn't want them there, but she also didn't want them standing outside her door when she wanted to walk Millie, so reluctantly added, 'What kind of conversation is it gonna be Mark?'

'Nothing official, I swear,' Whitehouse replied. 'Just a talk.'

Sighing audibly and knowing this was against her better judgement, Ellie buzzed them in. After a few seconds, there was a knock at her door. Opening it up, Ellie saw Whitehouse and Delgado standing in the corridor outside.

'Not letting you in until I see your IDs,' she said. 'You could be anyone.'

Whitehouse looked pained, and Delgado looked furious, but they both did this, playing whatever game Ellie wanted to play here. And, as they pulled out their warrant cards, Ellie took a moment to recall her onetime relationship with the two Vauxhall detectives. Once upon a time, Ellie had been a DI, a Detective Inspector, under Detective Chief Inspector Alex Monroe and on her way up the promotion ladder, labelled "one to watch", after Monroe and Reckless had transferred to Vauxhall from Mile End. The then-Detective Sergeant Mark Whitehouse had been her partner at the time, and they'd worked well together for years. Even the then-Detective Constable Kate Delgado had been a team player.

But, after the death of Bryan Noyce, everything had changed.

The punch, no more than a slap she'd given him, the one that drew blood from his nose, had only been spoken of with two people, the two who had now entered her apartment. Whitehouse had argued this with her many times, pointing out forensics had spotted the blood when they took her clothes for DNA testing, but she knew without a doubt Kate Delgado had grassed her up.

Because Kate Delgado was a traitor.

She couldn't prove it yet, but it was only a matter of time. And, when she had enough favours lined up, she intended to flick them like dominos, each one getting closer to proving Nicky Simpson and Kate Delgado not only worked together, but that both set her up, and murdered the love of her life.

She was brought back to the moment by barking; Millie was losing her mind as she faced Delgado, currently glaring down at the dog.

'Your dog needs to be put in a muzzle,' she muttered.

'My dog doesn't like you because my dog is an excellent judge of character,' Ellie smiled in response.

'So, when are we going to get a tour of your flat?' Delgado looked around, changing the subject and now ignoring the still-barking Millie. Ellie knew this was more a professional curiosity than a friendly request.

Delgado wanted a chance to look for incriminating things.

'Do you have a warrant?' Ellie carried on smiling, walking with them into the main living area.

'Of course not,' Delgado replied, as if this was the most stupid question ever.

'Then never,' Ellie replied, folding her arms as she faced the detectives. 'So, which one of you is going to tell me what's really going on here? It's been a long day and I really don't need any more shit to deal with.'

'We had a call from a detective in Maidstone today, asking about you,' Delgado replied. 'Seemed to think you were trying to interfere with an investigation.'

'DCI Richmond, by chance?'

'That's the one,' Delgado replied icily, a cold, thin-lipped half-smile now on her face. 'She wanted to know a bit more about DI Ellie Reckless, and as you used to work in Vauxhall, they put it through to us.'

'She wanted to know why you were turning up at a murder inquiry,' Whitehouse added, obviously uncomfortable with the whole situation.

'I wasn't there for that, I was looking at a separate but unrelated case, involving a stolen shipment.'

Delgado sneered at this.

'Careful, Reckless,' she said. 'You're starting to sound like a copper, and we both know you're not one of those.'

'I've been asked by the owners of the product to find the stolen items,' Ellie ignored the jibe. 'The murder can be investigated by the police; I'm not even trying to solve that.'

Whitehouse still looked uncomfortable as she spoke, and Ellie suddenly realised what the issue was here.

'Why don't you ask me the question, Mark?' she said.

'Ellie, I think we should—'

'Ask me the bloody question.'

Mark shuffled, puffed out his cheeks and then straightened.

'Ellie, are you working for the Lumetta family?'

'And what about it if I am?' Now understanding where

this was going, Ellie squared her feet. 'They're an olive oil distributor.'

'You know damn well who and what they are,' Delgado snapped.

'You're right, I know the accusations levelled against them, but my company has been hired by Lumetta Oils to find stock that's been stolen from them,' Ellie raised a finger, pointing at Delgado before she could speak. 'And don't for one moment give me one of your "holier than thou" lectures. I saw first-hand how policing works, remember? We worked with corrupt people all the time if it meant the bigger bastard was arrested.'

'And now you just cut out the middleman, and work for them directly,' Delgado sneered.

'I don't know what your problem is with me, Kate, and to be brutally honest I'm over it.' Ellie turned and walked away from the two detectives. 'You seem to think that I'm corrupt, and that's your choice, your opinion, no matter how wrong it is. But it doesn't mean that you get to come here regularly and make my life hell.'

'Ellie—' Whitehouse started, but stopped as Ellie spun back to face him.

'I don't work in your remit, and I don't *live* in your remit, so go back to Vauxhall and solve some actual crimes with your *new* allies.'

Whitehouse looked as if he wanted to argue this, but eventually shook his head.

'Don't act as if you're the victim here, Mark,' Ellie continued, interrupting whatever martyr-ridden response he was about to give. 'You showed your loyalty the day you turned against me and forced me to leave my job. Others didn't.'

'You mean DCI Monroe?' Delgado laughed. 'He's not

exactly a blinding character witness. He's been suspended more times than—'

'Are we done?' Ellie interrupted, and Delgado opened and shut her mouth a few times.

'Ellie, we're just worried—' Whitehouse started.

'I said *are we done?*' Ellie repeated, her tone darker, her voice colder. 'You don't have anything I need to know about, and I sure as hell don't have anything *you* get to know about. Return to your patch, detectives, and leave me the hell alone.'

Whitehouse and Delgado stared at Ellie for what felt like minutes, but was actually only a few seconds, before Whitehouse reluctantly nodded, waving Delgado out of the apartment, followed by Millie, barking all the way until the door was closed behind them, when she sneezed, wagged her tail and sauntered back to Ellie.

Now alone in the apartment, Ellie crouched down, hugging the Cocker Spaniel.

Sometimes it was really hard fighting for what was right.

———

RAMSEY ALLEN HAD FELT TOO WIRED TO GO HOME AFTER speaking with Matteo, and, after returning to Finders, he'd eventually gone for dinner in London with some friends – well, more a group of onetime cutthroat bastards, now too old to do anything more than reminisce about the old days – before deciding to end the night in a small Mayfair casino he knew, off-the-books, that still for some reason allowed him credit.

It was in the basement of a restaurant, just off Berkeley Square and smack bang in the midst of the Embassy district.

As people played poker and blackjack around him, the shouts of the kitchen next door could be heard, the chefs calling out orders for the affluent diners upstairs. The diners included a selection of diplomats and ambassadors from around the globe, most of whom had no idea of the gambling occurring beneath their tables – which, in Ramsey's opinion made it that little bit more authentic.

What he hadn't expected, however, was to see Tommaso Lumetta in the casino, playing blackjack with two other gamblers when he arrived. He almost turned around and left the building there and then, but there was a little piece of pride, a smidgin of territorial arrogance that stayed with him.

This was his casino, after all. Why should he leave because someone else was there?

Walking up to the table, he took a deep breath and, forcing a casual smile, sat two seats down from Tommaso, placing his chips down onto the baize in front of him as he waved for some cards. He started slow, making small bets to start with, working out the heat of the table as he watched his rivals, but as he did so, across the baize and never taking his eyes from his cards, Tommaso spoke.

'I saw your boss today, Ramsey,' he said by greeting. 'I don't rate her highly.'

'You're not the first to tell me that. Still, needs must and all that,' Ramsey replied noncommittally, wondering if this was Tommaso trying to scope out what Ellie knew.

'She had a kid and a dog with her,' Tommaso smiled, still looking at his cards, playing a chip on the table ahead of them. 'Stick.'

'Oh yes?' Ramsey waved his hand to the dealer, cancelling his dealt hand of cards. He could have stuck, like Tommaso, but he could guess the man had a better number than he did. He had a crap hand, and he didn't want to risk it.

'She struck me as very unprofessional,' Tommaso continued. 'When I heard you were working for her, well, I felt sorry for you. You know, sorry to see how far you fell.'

There was a quiet moment as the dealer placed two more cards in front of each of the players; Ramsey took a peek at the two he had now in front of him, and forced every poker-playing nerve in his body not to wince at his unlucky cards. An eight and a five: thirteen. A royal card would kill his hand, in fact anything over eight would do that. And he knew every low card that followed would make it more likely he'd go bust. Tommaso on the other hand peeked at his two cards and relaxed as he leant back on his chair, obviously happy with what he had.

'She gave me loyalty,' Ramsey replied. 'She might have arrested me back in the day, but I was a mess. And, when I came out she helped me start a new life.'

He turned now to face Tommaso, and the stocky, balding man finally met his eyes.

'And I don't recall getting any Lumetta Christmas cards while I was in prison,' Ramsey continued.

'We only give the people who add value those,' Tommaso gave a tight, momentary smile as he looked back at the table, and the dealer's cards. 'Not the *whores*.'

'The what?' Ramsey was stunned at the insult. 'Nobody—'

'You screwed my mother, and in return she gave you trinkets, gifts,' Tommaso tossed his hand away, leaning back in his chair. 'You think I never knew of the affair? Matteo was too young to understand, but I wasn't. I saw everything, old man. You screwed for finance. *Whore*. Only lasted a week, too, before she felt sorry for you and gave you a salary after kicking you out of her bed.'

Ramsey looked around the casino as Tommaso spoke; there was no way he'd speak such words without knowing he was in the stronger position, as there was no way of working out how many people in the room had connections, or even loyalties to Ramsey Allen. As he did this, he could make out three suited men in the corners, all strangers, and all likely there because of Tommaso.

'If you were a less guarded man, I'd ask you to step outside,' he snapped, anger overcoming his common sense. 'I loved your mother. I thought she loved me. And I would have done anything for her, even if we didn't last longer, as you say, than a week.'

'And now you hunt stolen olive oil,' Tommaso slow clapped his hands. 'Oh, how you've risen. Although you were always only one step higher than the toilet cleaner while you worked for us.'

Ramsey decided he'd had enough. The casino wasn't where he wanted to be right now. Rising from the chair, he tossed the dealer a chip.

'The bad luck that brought us together can go to hell,' he said. 'I'll leave now and—'

'You think it's due to *luck* I'm here?' Tommaso seemed surprised at the comment. 'I'm here because I was *told* this was where you ended up most nights. I was *looking* for you.'

Ramsey felt his stomach fall at this, and noticed, out of the corner of his eyes the bodyguards begin to drift closer.

Tommaso, seemingly also tiring of the game, rose, also cashing in his chips.

'You stole from me,' he said. 'And I'd like to discuss that. But not here. Not in front of *respectable* people.'

Ramsey had no choice; he was surrounded. And, more importantly, he knew the phone signal down here was terrible.

Who was he kidding, he thought to himself. *Even if he could call Ellie, one of her magical favours couldn't arrive in time to save him.*

'You seem to hold all the cards, so lead the way,' he said, forcing his voice not to waver as he followed Tommaso into the kitchen, the men boxing him in, one on either side, and one behind him.

In the kitchen, the chefs, seeing the new arrivals and wanting nothing to do with it, moved to the other end, giving Tommaso and Ramsey privacy.

'So, what did I steal from you?' Ramsey sighed theatrically. 'Your childhood? Your innocence? Did you walk in on me and your mother—'

'Earlier today you took a sheet of paper from my brother,' Tommaso spoke softly, calmly, interrupting Ramsey, but giving the impression he hadn't even realised the older man was talking. 'Did you think he wouldn't miss it?'

Ramsey went to argue this, to say he took nothing, but he stopped himself. If there hadn't been CCTV in the room, one glance over the desk once Matteo sat back down would have given away Ramsey's theft. It was impulsive, and it was now regretted.

'I saw a clue,' he said. 'To the case your mother hired us to solve.'

'My mother, my mother ...' Tommaso ran the word over his tongue. 'You act as if she has some kind of control in *my* company.'

'Last I heard, it was still hers,' Ramsey felt a little defiant as he spoke. *If he was going to be killed in a Mayfair kitchen, he sure as hell wasn't going to do it as a bitch.*

'My mother has sadly come to a place in her life where she can no longer manage Lumetta Oils, and has allowed her first-born child, me, to replace her,' Tommaso replied, holding up a finger to silence Ramsey's inevitable reply. 'Unfortunately, nobody has told her this yet. But they will.'

'What was it?' Ramsey asked, almost mockingly. 'How much did you lose?'

'Not your concern.' Tommaso picked up a discarded meat cleaver; a sharp-edged chunk of metal with a heavy, flat reverse side. He held it in his hand, as if checking it for weight. 'You're off the case.'

'I'm off the case when I'm told that by my superiors,' Ramsey challenged.

'You have been,' Tommaso smiled. 'This is an order from my brother's new partner.'

For the second time, Ramsey felt his stomach flip-flop. *Nicky Simpson had said this?* Then that meant Nicky Simpson had been the one who told Tommaso where to find Ramsey.

'Nicky Simpson doesn't control me.'

'He seems to think he does, old man. Why would that be?'

Ramsey had no answer to that.

'Where is it?' Tommaso changed tack now, looking back from the cleaver to Ramsey's sweating face. 'The sheet of paper you stole from my brother, from me?'

'Here,' Ramsey said, pulling it out, unfolding it and placing it down. 'I thought it might help us understand how the delivery—'

'Ch-ch-ch—' Tommaso made a silencing sound, waggling his finger with one hand while waving the cleaver with the other. 'Did you show anyone?'

'No,' Ramsey said. It was true, he hadn't *shown* anyone. But he decided the question hadn't included "have you scanned it, and intended to show people the following morning", so kept quiet.

Tommaso took the sheet, read it, and then passed it to one of his bodyguards who, after lighting one of the gas hobs, set fire to it.

'You had adulterous acts with my mother, shaming her, and shaming my family. You took our money for lacklustre work, and as well as that, you stole from me,' Tommaso said, and his voice was now cold and emotionless. 'Do you know what would have happened to you in the old days for theft?'

Before Ramsey could reply, the bodyguards on either side grabbed him, the one to the left grabbing his left wrist and slamming it, palm down, onto a wooden chopping block.

'They would have their hand chopped off,' Tommaso was feeling along the edge of the cleaver now, smiling to himself as he saw a thin line of blood appear on his index finger. 'People who shamed a family? They'd lose fingers. Which do I do with you?'

'You could let me go with a sternly worded written warning?' Ramsey struggled to pull back the hand, but it was being held down by his wrist, the guard's hand pressed down on his own, leaving his four fingers exposed.

Tommaso stared down at them.

'Your boss needs to be sent a message,' he said. 'You need to be sent a message. *They* need to be sent a message.'

'They?' Ramsey tried to pull away again, desperation obvious in his voice. 'Who are the "they" you're talking of?'

'Nobody steals from the Lumetta family,' Tommaso snarled, ignoring the question. 'You have any last words?'

'Yes,' Ramsey threw every ounce of insolence and arrogance he had into his reply.

'My work was never lacklustre, you sanctimonious prick.' This said, Ramsey braced himself. And, with a scream of rage and almost psychotic anger, Tommaso Lumetta decided not to reply to this, and instead swung the cleaver in a vicious arc, slamming it down onto Ramsey's fingers.

11

HANGOVER CURES

ELLIE HAD A TERRIBLE NIGHT'S SLEEP; SHE DREAMED OF BRYAN again. They'd been together on a London bus, one of the old ones where you could jump on and off, but he'd slipped and lost his handhold, falling onto the street as Ellie cried out, shouting herself awake. And, when she woke up, she found her phone had been ringing for most of the night, but, having placed it on silent, she hadn't noticed.

There had been some texts too. Nobody could get hold of Ramsey; he wasn't at home, and Tinker had heard from one of her mutual friends he'd been taken from a Mayfair casino by Tommaso Lumetta, stopping a game of blackjack in the process as they all walked out via the kitchen.

However, there was another text, sent an hour ago, from Ramsey that simply said

Am fine

Ellie frowned. There was something going on here, but she didn't know what it was.

There were also messages from Rajesh Khanna; he was the main SOCO, or Scene of Crime Officer for Mile End police, and had worked with Ellie professionally for many years, but because of his position in the force, had also found himself on the team investigating the allegations against her. In fact, he was the one who noted the bloodstains that damned her entire case. Even though he saw she was being framed, though, it was eventually his own evidence that forced her to leave. It hadn't sat well with him, however, and after a few months, when she started at Finders and Rajesh learnt what her plans for retribution were, he offered his services, on an off-the-books basis, whenever she needed them. And this went out to the team too, although many of them had their own side deals, usually involving favours or cash, with him.

Apparently, from the texts, he'd been examining the broken bottle Casey had found the previous day, as well as a second, more intact bottle Tinker had given him late that evening, probably before she met up with Ellie and Casey. He'd also snagged a look at the Maidstone coroner's report on Paulo Moretti, and had some thoughts, ones he said he'd give at the diner around ten in the morning, as he started his shift at Mile End at twelve.

Checking the time and seeing it was almost eight-thirty, Ellie forwarded the message around, telling everyone to meet at Caesars for ten. She walked Millie around the block for her morning ablutions and then fed her, before grabbing a quick shower herself.

She felt like shit. After Delgado and Whitehouse had left, she'd fallen deep into a bottle of whisky, and now the whole damn thing was gone. Which, although she couldn't remember drinking all of it, explained why she felt so terrible. So, with an Alka Seltzer knocked down followed by a strong black coffee, she sat back on her sofa and nuzzled Millie weakly while she waited for her metabolism to fix this God-awful state she was in. After half an hour, she felt well enough to grab some clothes and put them on, and with sunglasses firmly placed over her bloodshot eyes, she emerged into the outside world.

'MAN, YOU LOOK LIKE CRAP,' SANDRA THE WAITRESS HALF-gloated as Ellie slid into her usual space in the booth. 'I feel so sorry for you, I won't even give you shit about the mutt.'

Ellie nodded gratefully as she clambered onto the seat, patting to her side so Millie could jump up and be with her. As the spaniel did this, Ellie leant back against the booth, fighting the urge not to throw up. She only looked frontwards again when Sandra placed a glass of some weird brown liquid in front of her.

'Flat Coke mixed with orange juice,' she said. 'Called Mud, because, well, it looks like it. The Coke soothes the stomach, and the vitamin C helps fix you up.'

Ellie tried the drink as Sandra walked away; it wasn't half bad. And she was even beginning to feel ready to face the day when Tinker walked into the diner. *No, hold that.* Tinker stormed into the diner and looked ready to kick off a fight.

'So, you're alive then,' she snapped, standing at the end of the table, not moving to sit down. 'I called you a dozen times last night. Did you hear about Ramsey?'

Ellie shook her head.

'Just the texts,' she said, 'and then Ramsey sent one saying he was fine, so I assumed it was something to be discussed today.'

'You're damned right it'll be discussed,' Tinker looked back at the door, as if waiting for someone to enter. 'You were all over my problem last night, but you didn't give a shit about Ramsey's.'

'Now wait a second, Tink, that's harsh—' Ellie started, but then paused as she had to force the weird Coke and orange drink back down her throat before she threw it up. '—but true. I had a relapse last night. Whitehouse and Delgado turned up at my door. Ended up crawling into a bottle of Jameson. My phone was on silent, or do not disturb, or bloody something, and when I woke up, I found I'd missed everything, but I still don't know what I missed.'

As Ellie started talking about Whitehouse and Delgado, Tinker's pose had softened slightly at the realisation of how Ellie's night had gone down, but she still hadn't sat herself at the booth.

'Tommaso Lumetta went looking for Ramsey last night,' she said. 'Found him in his usual haunts, took him into the kitchen.'

'I'm guessing not for a late-night snack?' Ellie weakly joked, but Tinker's stone-cold lack of any humour to this stopped her in her tracks.

'Why?' Ellie frowned. 'Just for asking about?'

'He did more than ask about,' Tinker shook her head. 'He stole a shipping document.'

'Oh, that bloody idiot,' Ellie sighed. 'I've told him a—'

'*Don't.*'

The word was soft, but heavy, echoing in the diner.

'Don't you dare belittle what he did,' Tinker continued. 'He took the sheet because it had addresses on it, and he wanted to do good by you. *Impress* you. And because of this, Tommaso Lumetta took a meat cleaver to his fingers.'

Ellie stared in utter horror at Tinker, unsure if she'd even heard her friend correctly as, through the doors, Ramsey walked into the diner, helped by Casey. He was dressed, as ever, in tie, shirt and blazer, but he looked tired, drawn, and his left hand was heavily bandaged up, currently strapped to his chest.

'I didn't know,' Ellie said as Ramsey walked to the booth, sitting down. 'Ramsey, I swear, I didn't know.'

'I didn't want you to,' Ramsey replied, looking over at Tinker. 'Oh, sit down, for God's sake. You're not doing anything.'

'I'm going to kill him.'

'Kill who exactly?' Ramsey forced a weak smile. 'Tommaso for doing it? Simpson for grassing me up to him?'

'Wait, what's Nicky Simpson got to do with—' Ellie started, but then stopped, placing fingers at the bridge of her nose, pinching hard.

You screwed up, Reckless. You fell into a bottle while your people needed you. And the man you want dead more than anyone in the world was probably behind it. You bloody half-arsed bitch.

'Tell me about the injury,' she said.

'Tommaso held my hand out and slammed a meat cleaver down onto my fingers,' Ramsey looked down at his heavily bandaged hand. 'It was a comment about thieves having their hands cut off. He wasn't psychotic, though, just angry. And, as he brought it down, he'd spun it around so the flat end, not the blade, hit them.'

'Jesus,' Ellie whispered.

'I was lucky—' Ramsey replied, but was interrupted by an almost incomprehensible sound of anger from Casey.

'I was lucky,' Ramsey continued when the teenager had stopped, 'because I was wearing my signet ring and my lucky gambling ring on my left hand. The cleaver struck my fingers, and crushed the gaming ring, and denting the signet ring terribly, but this took a lot of the force out of the blow. And instead of shattering all the bones in my fingers, he simply broke three of them with the attack.'

He looked at his hand again, as if looking through the bandages.

'Even though it wasn't the blade end, there was still a lot of blood, and me screaming, so it was probably quite horrific looking, and his guards let me fall to the ground, probably not wanting to be near me at that point. As he left, he said I was "lucky Nicky Simpson still needed me to use my fingers, eventually", which meant that Nicky had told Tommaso where I was, but had demanded I wasn't to be permanently disfigured in the process.'

'So, I kill Simpson then,' Tinker went to rise from the chair.

'For God's sake, Tinkerbelle, let it rest,' Ramsey shook his head. 'If anyone's going to kill that insufferable, healthy bastard, it's me. My fingers will heal, and currently I'm more annoyed at the loss of my lucky gambling ring.'

'They had to cut it off,' Casey mentioned. 'Not so lucky.'

'It stopped my finger being crushed, so it's a score draw right now,' Ramsey replied as he looked at Ellie, for the first time that morning properly *looking* at her.

'You look like dried excrement,' he said, mockingly. 'Nasty night?'

'Nowhere near as bad as yours,' Ellie replied as Sandra walked over, placing a mug of tea in front of Ramsey.

'Number four?' she asked, nodding at the menu. Ramsey, however, shook his head.

'Not today, my dear, just some toast,' he replied. 'Something I can eat one-handed.'

Sandra left after taking everyone else's breakfast orders, and for a moment, things felt a little more normal.

But Ellie hadn't missed Ramsey's comment.

And Ramsey, it seemed, hadn't finished.

'When you came to Finders, and you started this team, I was here because you'd been good to me, but also because I liked the money. I didn't understand why you did these favours, and I was stuck in the middle of you and Simpson, with him paying for my mother's care, as long as I spied on you for him.'

He paused at this; everyone at the table knew of this after he'd admitted it during the Danny Flynn case. He'd told Ellie first, and then, when she'd told everyone why she was banking favours, he'd let everyone know the truth as well.

'And then you told us why you hated him so, and I agreed I'd do my part. For the team,' he continued, as he glanced at the bandaged wrist, and then back at Ellie.

'Not anymore,' he said. 'I'm in. All the way. This wasn't a message from Tommaso – well, it was, but you know what I mean – this was a message from Simpson, showing me I still worked for him, and my transgressions would be punished. And I can't live like that. I want him removed.'

'My plan isn't to kill him,' Ellie reminded him. 'I need to prove my innocence.'

'Yeah, but after that, we can kill him, right?' Tinker asked quite seriously, reaching across the table and squeezing Ramsey's hand. 'After all, you've got Tinkerbelle and Captain Hook here working for you, and Peter Pan's your cyber expert, so I think we can make sure he never grows old, if you know what I mean.'

Ellie chuckled, but then groaned as a wave of nausea ripped through her skull.

'Okay, so if we're not killing anyone, can someone tell me whether Ramsey's sacrifice was worth it or not?' she asked. 'Because if it wasn't, then we have to have a serious chat here about boundaries.'

'It was,' Ramsey half-smiled, shrugging his shoulders as he did so. 'That is, it has to be. Otherwise, I did all this for nothing.'

'Before he went to the casino, Ramsey came to the office,' Tinker explained. 'He took the sheet of paper and he scanned it.'

'Tommaso might have it back, but we still have a copy,' Casey continued, pulling out his tablet and already opening it up. On the screen was a document. 'As you can see here, it's a few months old, but it's definitely a consignment from Lumetta Oils, driven by Paulo Moretti, and stops at three locations in London before he returns home.'

'Matteo was poring over this when I arrived to meet with him,' Ramsey explained. 'It was obviously important enough for him to spend time on.'

'Casey sent this to me late last night, and I sent it to Brian Watson, the Customs Officer I spoke to yesterday,' Tinker took over the story. 'He emailed back a couple of hours later and can't be a hundred percent, but he's convinced this is the same set of addresses Paulo had a couple of nights back. And, he was also absolutely sure this isn't the usual list of addresses he goes to. There's one in Mayfair that he thinks is the same, but there's definitely one he didn't recognise from the usuals that were on this list.'

She pointed at one of the addresses, a warehouse in Shoreditch.

'This one,' she said.

'Registered to a company called "Whipcrack Holdings",' Casey read from a website listing. 'No trading records, nothing out there saying who they are, just a list of directors that could be anyone. Although, one of them, Carl Fredricks, happens to be connected through several other smaller businesses, to Matteo Lumetta.'

'So, the delivery of the bottles is to a trusted location,' Ellie considered this. 'That makes sense. Especially if these aren't stock as such.'

'The address is close to where Matteo had his car wash,' Ramsey pursed his lips as he thought. 'But I don't think he had anything to do with it.'

'He was over from Dublin the day it happened,' Ellie replied. 'That's pretty suss to me.'

'True, but he said he was over as a favour to a family friend,' Ramsey gratefully took a plate of toast from Sandra as she started passing out the breakfast orders. 'He said some other interesting stuff, too. Like how Paulo was his half-brother.'

'His what?' Casey, obviously not having heard this before, looked up.

'That's what he said,' Ramsey smiled, happy he'd got one up on the teenager. 'Never formerly acknowledged apparently, but it was well known Daddy Lumetta slept about, and personally, I'd be stunned if this was the only bastard in the basket. Matteo said they always knew, and his mother was looked after, as was Paulo. It all sounded quite civil, although he did make a comment about the bastards in the family. It was quite profound, so I remembered it. He said sometimes the bastards of the family were given the keys to the kingdom, and sometimes they were just the driver.'

Tinker frowned.

'Well, Paulo's the bastard driver, so who's the bastard with the keys?' she asked.

'A question for another time,' Ellie rubbed at her temples. 'I can't imagine Mama Lumetta being too happy about this.'

'She had her own skeletons, believe me,' Ramsey was almost wistful at this. 'I can't understand how Paulo was happy to simply be a driver, though.'

'Maybe he didn't want to go up against the brothers?' Tinker suggested.

'Or Tommaso, singular,' Ramsey nodded. 'Matteo also spoke about him. Said he was his mother's son, and did what she said, but Tommaso was the elder. Which meant he'd always stay loyal, but to whom, I'm not sure.'

'He was making something out of it all,' Tinker replied, eating half a sausage as she spoke, using it on the fork as some kind of pointer. 'He was giving Brian, the Customs guard, two bottles every few deliveries, as he went through and then, a day or two later someone would contact Brian by WhatsApp, and pick it up from him, giving him a monkey, in cash, for his troubles.'

'That's five hundred pounds,' Ramsey said knowingly to Casey. 'Does your generation even know what cash is?'

'Of course,' Casey looked dismissively at the old man. 'How else could we roll around on it in our TikTok videos?'

Ramsey chuckled, wincing halfway through a laugh.

'They punched me in the gut, too,' he said to Ellie as she looked concerned at him. 'Hurts to laugh.'

'Although he won't be getting five hundred for the most recent one now,' Tinker added.

'Because Paulo Moretti's dead?' Casey asked.

'Because Brian thought I was a copper and poured ninety percent of it down the sink,' Tinker smiled. 'I gave the remains to our resident forensics expert.'

'But he'd have another bottle?' Casey added. 'You said two bottles.'

'Not this time, apparently,' Tinker shrugged. 'Paulo didn't say why it'd changed, but the bribe money was going to stay the same.'

'Do we know who picked up the bottles?' Ellie looked up. 'Did he ever meet the family, for example?'

'No, he never saw them,' Tinker replied. 'Was always done as a drop off and pick up. Got the impression he never wanted to see them, either. But over the last couple of years, he's done about fifteen of these drops. That's twenty-nine bottles, with the last delivery only being one.'

Ellie whistled.

'Paulo's making money here if he's paying out five hundred a shot,' she said. 'Looks like they cut him from the same Lumetta cloth.'

She tapped at her teeth with her tongue.

'Tinker, you said there was about a tenth of the bottle left,' Ellie was counting on her fingers. 'Casey found a broken bottle that had been emptied of something that wasn't olive oil ... I'm thinking this isn't whisky. But even so, there's not enough upsell to make this worth five hundred a bottle. This is something bigger. But what's so big that a litre of it is a grand, minimum?'

'Gamma Hydroxybutyric Acid, or GHB?' Casey was reading from a list. 'Says here the street value is just under seven hundred bucks a litre.'

'Which isn't much above the five hundred he gives the

guard,' Ellie shook her head. 'I think we're on the right path, though. The cost of these bottles will give a better idea of who stole them, because someone killing for a fifty-pound bottle is different from someone killing for a five hundred minimum bottle.'

'Chanel Number Five goes for about seven grand a litre,' Casey was still reading. 'Insulin's about five grand. The list is quite long, and it could be anything.'

'Well, let's hope Rajesh has an idea then,' Ellie could feel her headache lessening, but it was being replaced by a tension headache that was just as bad. As she spoke, she nodded at the door to the diner, where a new arrival walked in.

Rajesh Khanna, in his sixties, with pince-nez glasses over his eyes and currently in a dark suit and tie, a blue shirt and his police-appropriate black turban nodded at Ellie's table, shifting his leather messenger bag around as he approached it.

'You need to walk away from this case right now,' he said by way of introduction. 'Before you all end up like him—' this was aimed at Ramsey, '—or worse.'

'I'm guessing you worked out what's in the olive oil bottles,' Ellie smiled weakly, feeling the frigid chill of death slide down her spine.

'I did indeed,' Rajesh nodded. 'And if I'm right with the numbers, this is bigger than all of us, and just as lethal to anyone who goes looking for it.'

12

AQUA REGIA

RAJESH STARTED HIS SHOW AND TELL BY STANDING AT THE END of the table facing the others.

'Aqua Regia,' he said by way of beginning. 'Concentrated hydrochloric acid and concentrated nitric acid.'

'Is there a test?' Ramsey muttered, looking around. 'Nobody told me there was a test.'

'This was a substance found in the liquid Tinker recovered, and there were trace elements of it in the bottle Casey and Ellie discovered at the murder scene,' Rajesh repositioned his glasses on his nose. 'Also, there was chloroauric acid in the bottles, a small amount of sulphuric acid and finally, they had been diluted with pure water until the liquid they had matched the right shade of yellow.'

'This doesn't sound very much like olive oil,' Ramsey muttered.

'Indeed,' Rajesh smiled. 'When I saw the chloroauric acid on the toxicology report, I guessed immediately what this was. You might call it gold solution. But not the cheap stuff you see in gold plating. This is twenty-four karat gold.'

Ellie and the others looked at each other.

'Gold? How much is a bottle worth?' she eventually asked.

'Uh-uh, this is show and *then* tell,' Rajesh smiled. 'First, let me tell you about my technical prowess.'

'Do you have to?' Ramsey asked hopefully. 'Maybe you could leave us a note, like the Jehovah's Witnesses do?'

'First, I took the approximate hundred millilitres Tinker had salvaged, roughly ten percent of the contents and placed it in a beaker,' Rajesh ignored the thief. 'I used potassium metabisulfite—'

'Bless you,' Sandra, walking past, said, frowning as the table broke into laughter at the mistake. Rajesh patiently waited for it to die down before continuing.

'You make a solution by mixing it with distilled water,' he continued, 'I did this, and then dumped it into the liquid, watching the potassium metabisulfite change the gold in the solution back into its uncharged, metallic form.'

'Like an alchemist,' Casey said, mesmerised.

'No, because I'm creating gold from gold,' Rajesh corrected. 'I'm not pretending in any way to make it from something else. Unless you buy into the "it's olive oil" belief.'

He rummaged about in his messenger bag as he continued.

'After a couple of hours, the gold settled at the bottom, so I dumped off the water, added some newer distilled water and boiled it again before dumping *that* off,' he said, half distracted as he rummaged. 'I did this four, no, five times more using boiling distilled water, and then did it three more times with boiling hydrochloric acid, and then two more with distilled water again. It might sound like a lot of pointless steps—'

'You're not wrong there,' Ramsey muttered, mostly to himself.

'*However*,' Rajesh glared at the thief as he repeated himself. '*However*, this was all done to purify the gold.'

'You wanted to be Doctor Frankenstein as a kid, didn't you?' Ellie said, watching Rajesh as he rooted about in the bag.

'He *wishes* I wanted to be him,' Rajesh smiled, pausing his search. 'Anyway, I poured the water off, and dried the spongy sludge that was left on a hot plate until it was a dry powder, about seven and a half grams' worth.'

'Seven and a half grams of pure gold?' Ramsey was suddenly interested as he sat upright. 'What happened then?'

'I got a metalworker neighbour I know to melt it down,' Rajesh said, triumphantly pulling out a small, golden lump, about the size of a slightly rounded, thickened postage stamp. 'Here you go. This was what Tinker retrieved.'

'Good God,' Ramsey was the first to grab the gold, unsurprisingly, holding it up to the light as he stared at it. 'Seven and a half grams of gold is about—'

'Forty-eight pounds a gram,' Casey was reading from a screen. 'Which makes that lump worth just under four hundred pounds.'

Ellie now looked at the gold lump, taking it from Ramsey, who reluctantly passed it over to her, twisting it around in her fingers, watching it catch the diner's lights as she considered it.

'How did they make the liquid?' she asked.

'They would have melted the gold in its original forms, whatever that was.'

'Whatever that was?'

'Yes. Gold, when it starts, is a variance,' Rajesh shrugged.

'I have a ring, you have a necklace I can see, both are gold so both could be melted down. Now you get a lot of these sorts of things, and melt it all down together, you get the pure gold we see here.'

'But jewellery isn't pure,' Ramsey frowned. 'Some of the "gold" jewellery out there is fluffed out with coppers, nickels, silver even.'

'Exactly,' Rajesh smiled, holding up his gold ring. 'So, once they gather up their jewellery, gold bars, whatever it is they're making the base from, they would then have taken these items, stuck them in a container and covered them with diluted nitric acid to remove the coppers and silvers, nickel, zinc, iron, anything that wasn't what they wanted, just purifying the gold itself. They'd also begin heating it until the impurities dissolved, adding the Aqua Regia I mentioned. It's time consuming, but it does the job, as you can see.'

'So, the Lumettas take the gold they own, either in jewellery, or in gold bars, melt it down, turn it into solution, dilute it to match the other bottles they have, bottle it up with them, ship it to the UK and then, once it's arrived the other end, they return it to the original form,' Tinker rubbed at her chin. 'Is it worth all that?'

'Gold is exempt from VAT, but the Government web page states anyone entering the UK with gold will "pay tax or duty on any goods you're bringing in", which is a bit of a red flag,' Casey read from his screen. 'Anyone buying gold in the UK has to declare to HMRC if it's over ten grand, so I reckon they'd want a substantial chunk of each bottle's worth if it was being brought in legally.'

Tinker started counting on her fingers.

'If I only had a hundred millilitres, and that made seven and a half grams, then a litre bottle would have had—'

'About seventy-five grams of gold,' Rajesh nodded. 'Currently standing, if Casey's right, at just over three and a half grand a bottle. Or just over four grand if you're talking dollars.'

'Paulo was making over three grand a bottle, putting aside the bribe,' Ramsey replied. 'Twenty-nine of these, that's almost a hundred grand he's ripped off his family.'

'I think we also know why they were hijacked,' Ellie sipped at the Coke and orange juice mix. 'Eleven hundred bottles of these—'

'Eleven hundred and twenty-four,' Casey interjected. 'That's four million pounds' worth of gold taken from the Lumetta family.'

'That's why she wanted us to find it,' Ellie nodded. 'And, judging from the anger we saw on Tommaso's face, that's also why he wanted everyone away from the investigation.'

Ellie wanted to swear. Mama Lumetta had pretty much told her this from the start.

'All I will say, is there was gold there. Gold I'd like to know the location of.'

There hadn't been gold hidden. And the traces found on the floor of the van were from the spilt bottle. The bottles *were* the gold.

'Brian said the other times were smaller deliveries, a pallet's worth,' Tinker added, looking at Casey. 'What was the amount of bottles sent to Shoreditch on that shipping thing?'

'A hundred and twelve,' Casey read from the note Ramsey had scanned at great cost. 'That's half a pallet's worth, based on what your Customs mate said, and it comes to about four hundred grand, or just under half a million US dollars.'

'No wonder they were operating this at a loss,' Ellie mused. 'Even with the equipment and chemicals needed to do all this, not to mention the hiring of trustworthy people to turn the gold to liquid and then back, with all that, they're still pulling in three hundred grand a trip.'

'Why the sudden rise, though?' Casey asked. 'It's one thing to send a few hundred grand, but this was millions.'

'Kid's got a point,' Ramsey added. 'We thought the hijack was something to do with the brothers' power struggle, but this is world-changing money for them. If either Matteo, Tommaso or Mama Lumetta gained four million in one go through off-the-books assets, then it's game over for the other two. You could wipe out everyone with that kind of cash.'

'And if you can stop your rival having it, maybe even taking it for yourself, you gain a massive advantage,' Ellie said. 'Ramsey, put it back.'

Ramsey reluctantly removed the small lump of gold from his inside jacket pocket and placed it back on the table.

'So, what's Nicky Simpson's connection to this?' Ellie frowned, asking the table as a whole.

'Possibly nothing,' Ramsey replied, munching sullenly on some toast, eyeing the lump of gold on the table. 'Matteo claimed he was dealing with Nicky Simpson to get some of his health clubs into Dublin, probably as a franchise deal or something, but it felt like a lie, or at least it felt like an excuse for them to meet, if you get my drift. I might be able to find something out if I arrange—'

'No,' Ellie shook her head, cutting him off. 'You're not going anywhere near Simpson. Not now.'

'Elisa, I think you'll find—'

'I think *you'll* find, Ramsey, that I'm your boss, and I don't want you risking yourself anymore until you're fully healed,' Ellie snapped. 'Once you are, you can go back to doing all your bloody silly dodgy shit. But now? No.'

'Yes, mum,' Ramsey smiled. It was mocking, but Ramsey obviously appreciated the sentiment. 'Either way, Matteo coming over to meet with Nicky Simpson, the day his half-brother is killed and four million's worth of smuggled gold is stolen? Definitely looks dodgy.'

'Agreed,' Ellie nodded, looking back at Rajesh. 'Okay, then. Magical gold from liquid aside, what else do you have?'

'What, finding the gold wasn't enough?' Rajesh gave mock outrage at the question, but was already reaching into his messenger bag, pulling out some more sheets of paper. 'So, I had a look at Paulo Moretti. Not literally, there's no way I could get in there to look at the body, but through the coroner's reports and the pictures. From what I can see, they shot him in the neck from mid-range, so about five metres' distance, but from an angle that was low and to the left.'

'Basically, someone stood outside the van, it's a left-hand drive, so he was in the van behind the driver's seat, and someone tried to shoot him,' Tinker replied, nodding.

'Tried?' Ramsey frowned. 'I'm pretty much sure they succeeded.'

'They did, but not in the way they hoped,' Rajesh replied, straightening his glasses. 'Now it looks like Moretti was holding one of these bottles in front of him, maybe even up like a shield, and when the gun was fired, the bullet smashed through the neck of the bottle in his hand, so under his grip, and in the process this deflected the trajectory ever so slightly upwards, so whereas the killer likely aimed at his chest, they actually caught Paulo in the neck, with the bullet continuing to the right through the driver's window, shattering it.'

Rajesh stopped, considering this.

'If he'd stood an inch to the left, the bullet might even have missed.'

'Wouldn't have changed anything,' Tinker replied. 'They'd have simply fired a second time. There was a moment, when Moretti held up the bottle, that he knew he wasn't getting out of there alive. Why else would he use it as some kind of shield?'

Rajesh nodded, before turning his attention towards Casey.

'The bottle you found in that bush, or tree, or wherever it was, had traces of blood on it,' he said. 'Two distinct types, one spattered on the back of it, and one found around the neck. The former matched Paulo, so it was definitely the bottle he was holding, and the blood was likely from the blood spurting from his throat.'

Casey shuddered.

'I don't know if I really wanted to know that,' he muttered.

'Any idea who the other blood is from?' Ellie asked. 'I'm guessing it's probably from the person who threw it into the bush?'

'I think that too,' Rajesh nodded. 'Hypothetically, the bottle was smashed, but we've seen from the evidence Casey retrieved that there was still three quarters of the actual bottle still existing physically, so I'm making a calculated guess that maybe half of the liquid was still in it.'

'A couple of grand's worth of gold isn't worth throwing away,' Tinker pursed her lips. 'So, Moretti is shot, and then someone is told to change bottles, maybe put the gold from the shattered bottle into one of the legitimate, olive oil containing ones, or maybe even an empty spare bottle, before tossing the broken one away, somewhere the police won't find it.'

'That works,' Casey puffed his cheeks as he thought about this. 'I only saw it because I was using a drone.'

'If that's the case,' Ellie continued the hypothesis, 'maybe as they do this, they slice their finger or their hand when they pick it up, or when they throw it. The bottle could slip when they're decanting, and they might shift grip, cutting themselves in the process.'

Rajesh nodded.

'There's a problem here, though,' he said. 'I'm police. And unfortunately for you, this is a clue in a murder investigation. I need to pass this to DCI Richmond, who's running the case.'

Ellie scrunched her face.

'Yeah, I know,' she replied. 'I'd expect nothing less, as it's what I'd have done if I was still in the force. Do what you need to do.'

She gave an overstated wink.

'But if there's any way of working out who this bottle thrower could have been, maybe monitoring the DNA you've found, and checking if it comes up with a match, I'd appreciate the heads up.'

'Always,' Rajesh placed the papers away.

'Do we know if the bullet killed him, or whether the fire did?' Ramsey asked now. 'I'm guessing, as the body was in the van ...'

'He would have bled out well before the van was torched,' Rajesh shook his head, gathering his things. 'They had to remove the pallets, and that would have taken time. Poor bastard probably bled out slowly in a corner. Or, he was lucky, and they caught an artery.'

'How's that lucky?' Casey looked around at this.

'It would have been a far quicker death,' Tinker said, and her voice was emotionless as she spoke, as if she was forcing herself not to consider it.

'Did any of Tommaso's men have bandaged hands?' Ellie

asked Casey. 'I don't remember seeing any of them sporting plasters.'

'I wasn't really checking,' Casey frowned. 'That said, I can easily check. The drone caught them when they arrived. I can zoom in.'

'You think Tommaso did this?' Ramsey whistled, raising his own bandaged hand. 'I don't know, Elisa. He's a psychopath, but he's not an organised one. I can't see him planning this. It's too detailed for him.'

'So, what now?' Tinker asked.

'Now, Rajesh goes to work,' Ellie leaned across, clasping the Indian's outstretched hand. 'I owe you again.'

'You'll only owe me once you're reinstated,' Rajesh smiled before nodding to the others, grabbing his messenger bag and turning to leave.

'Your gold!' Casey blurted.

'It's not mine,' Rajesh grinned. 'I think Ellie knows what to do with it.'

And with that, Rajesh Khanna left the diner.

'Is the answer "give the gold to Ramsey, I think he really deserves it"?' Ramsey asked.

'I would have agreed until you started talking about yourself in the third person,' Tinker grinned. 'Now you just sound like a crazy poor person. Poor because you don't get the gold.'

Ellie picked up the chunk of gold, placing it in her own jacket.

'I think I'll be taking this back to its rightful owner,' she said icily. 'And in the process, she can tell me what the merry hell is really going on.'

'And what do—' Tinker started, but stopped as her phone rang. Rising from the table, she walked away for a moment, listening. Eventually, she walked back to the table, placing the phone onto it as she looked around at the others.

'I'll need to borrow these two,' she said, nodding at Casey and Ramsey. 'If that's okay?'

'Who was that?' Ellie asked.

'That was Dover Customs,' Tinker explained. 'I'd asked possibly-Olivia to call me if anything odd happened.'

'Odder than being called possibly-Olivia?' Casey asked.

'That's my pet name for her,' Tinker shrugged. 'Because of her name being possibly—well, you get the idea.'

'I'm guessing something odd happened?' Ellie asked, trying to steer the conversation back in the right direction.

'Oh, yeah, sorry,' Tinker flushed. 'Brian Watson's dead.'

13

MOTHERS AND SONS

As Tinker, Ramsey and Casey travelled east to Dover and yet another murder enquiry, Ellie contacted Robert, asking if he had details for where Mama Lumetta would be at that exact moment. He'd asked about, checking with her assistant and claiming updates in the case as a reason for the contact, and within fifteen minutes of calling him, enough time for the hangover to finally subside and for Ellie to finally feel human again, she had an address in her phone's memory. And, with Millie now left in "legal doggie day-care" with Sara, the receptionist at Finders, Ellie made her way across London to Wigmore Street, and a third-floor office in a rented building; one with no names or numbers on the buzzer.

This area was an enigma in London; to the side was Harley Street, to the east was Regent Street, to the west was Marylebone and to the south was Mayfair. But here, some areas had been passed by progress, and ancient-looking, onetime council flats, in brutalist fifties and sixties design had been left alone as the surrounding areas became more affluent. However, these were now being bought from the long-term owners, refurbished and reopened as offices, most of which now held plastic surgeons and medical experts. That said, several of the floors had other companies on them, smaller ones that wanted the postcode to "up" their branding, and Ellie assumed, as she buzzed on a door panel at the entrance to one of these blocks, that Mama Lumetta had wanted the same for her own company.

The "company office", as much as you could call it such was on the third floor, and was accessed by a small, and rather unsafe-looking elevator/lift system that seemed large enough to hold two people at best, or maybe someone in a very small wheelchair. Ellie had almost changed her mind when she saw it and taken the stairs, but reluctantly she risked the metal cocoon, and within moments stood outside a door, a simple, grey-painted entrance that could have been either business or residential. It opened, and a young man, Italian and in his twenties opened it to face her. He wore dark blue chinos, a white shirt and a black tie, loose, and he nodded to Ellie, motioning for her to enter.

'Mrs Lumetta is waiting for you in the main office,' he said, with the slightest trace of a northern accent, as they walked into a reception area. It was small, enough for a desk, one which the man now walked behind once more, sitting down under a television that silently played a BBC News channel above him as Ellie waited on a sofa, a selection of restaurant, style and food magazines laid out on the coffee table in front of her. Which made sense, with Lumetta Oils being used mostly by the hospitality industry.

After a moment, the door opened and the driver, Lorenzo, who'd been with Mama Lumetta the previous day, and still wearing his driver's gloves, waved her through into a back room.

If the office *had* once been an apartment, when the new owners took control they'd definitely refurbished, as there were no signs of it left, with the back room now an office, a long, thin window to the left looking out onto Wigmore Street, and a desk at the rear end, facing the door. On the walls were old, framed olive oil adverts from the fifties, including ones from the Lumetta family themselves. And, on the desk were small bottles of oil, the size of mini-bar spirit bottles, obviously marketing giveaways, or something.

'I understand you have news,' Mama Lumetta said, looking up from a trade magazine she'd been reading intently. 'You found my oils?'

'Not quite,' Ellie said, and before she sat, she pulled the lump of gold out and tossed it onto the desk. 'We found that though, so it's a start.'

There was a long silence as Mama Lumetta stared down at the small golden disk before picking it up, biting the edge with her teeth before nodding and tossing it to the driver.

'Found like this?'

'No,' Ellie observed the older woman as she spoke. 'I have people who understand certain things. And, when we found a small percentage of a bottle intact, they were able to gain back part of your missing *four million pounds of lost gold.*'

Ellie stated the number deliberately to garner a reaction, and as she leant back into the chair, she forced herself to relax as Mama Lumetta pursed her lips, obviously irritated at being caught on the back foot.

'Now you know, then,' Mama Lumetta eventually replied. 'It changes nothing.'

'It changes everything!' Ellie hissed, straightening. 'You hired us to find a few grand's worth of missing bottles, not millions in smuggled bullion! The suspect list is completely different!'

She took a breath, waiting for a response. When none came, she continued.

'We thought there could be a power struggle here, but didn't see how,' she said. 'We guessed the bottles had contraband, but didn't know what. The main consensus was perhaps illegal whisky, or something that could up the bottle's worth by a factor of five. That'd be enough to cause a problem, maybe screw with a supply. We didn't expect it to be a factor of a thousand.'

'Where did you find it?'

'A Customs Officer was given a bottle as a bribe,' Ellie replied. 'By Paulo Moretti.'

'This is all you gained?'

'This was all we could get from the remains after he tried to pour it down a sink,' Ellie shrugged. 'Brian thought my woman was police. He'd poured over three quarters of it out before she could get to him.'

'A Customs Officer named Brian,' Mama Lumetta raised her eyebrows. 'Should you be so candid with the names of people who have my stock?'

'Oh, it's *had* more than have, and it doesn't matter,' Ellie smiled. 'He's dead now. Although I have to admit, I'd assumed you'd know.'

'You killed him?' Lorenzo, across the office, was surprised.

'You know I didn't,' Ellie continued to smile, looking over at him. 'I'm guessing the same man that killed Paulo did that.'

'Any news on who that was?' Mama Lumetta asked.

'Well, here's the problem,' Ellie leant forward now, steepling her fingers in front of her chin as she did so, resting her elbows on her knees. 'You see, Mrs Lumetta, by not being told the entire story, we went in half-cocked. We didn't know the stolen olive oil was twenty-four karat gold, for example.'

'Need to know basis, I'm afraid.'

'We also didn't know Paulo Moretti was Matteo and Tommaso's illegitimate half-brother,' Ellie continued. 'One you were quite vocal about, apparently all for keeping bastards out of the family. I'm guessing "delivery driver" was as close as he could get?'

At this, Ellie thought she saw Lorenzo flinch, but by the time she glanced over at him, he'd regained his composure.

'What you speak of is personal,' Mama Lumetta's voice was dangerously low now.

'And that's the problem,' Ellie replied. 'All of this is personal. If we'd known Paulo was a Lumetta—'

'He was *never* a Lumetta!' Mama Lumetta rose from her chair in anger. 'He was a *bastardo!* A parasite! His mother lived in luxury because of one stupid mistake! He wasn't anywhere near as intelligent as his half-brothers! He was lucky we allowed him to drive for us!'

Again, Ellie could see Lorenzo's expression darken at this, but she didn't have time to look into this, preferring to continue verbally jousting with Mama Lumetta.

'Who's the "we" there?' Ellie answered calmly. 'Because here's the next part of the problem. According to your eldest *real* son, you don't seem to be in power.'

Mama Lumetta went to reply again, to shout, but then slumped back into her chair, her face crumpling in real-isation.

'Tommaso,' she said.

'Yes, Tommaso,' Ellie didn't move, but in small, subtle ways her body language changed, becoming more menacing.

'A man who turned up to a murder enquiry and demanded the police leave. Who then told me to stop investigating and then tried to sever one of my team's fingers off with a meat cleaver. *That* Tommaso.'

Mama Lumetta stared at Ellie for what felt like minutes, but was only a few seconds.

'What do you want of me?' she asked. 'To change your deal?'

'Oh, we're definitely changing the deal,' Ellie replied. 'Call it danger money. Or, call it "being lied to and played the whole time" danger money. You double the fee once we find your gold.'

'Fine,' Mama Lumetta nodded. 'Double fifteen is thirty thousand.'

'No,' Ellie shook her head. 'I said double the fee, not just the money. The fee also included per diems and my favour.'

'You want *two* favours?' Mama Lumetta looked up at Lorenzo as she spoke, almost looking for confirmation she wasn't losing her mind. In return, Ellie simply nodded.

'If we find the gold,' she said. 'But I also want full transparency. No more lies. This is the kind of money that, if used wisely, could propel anyone to the top of the chain, not just your sons. Or, it's enough to destroy you. Why in God's name would you try to smuggle four million into London, anyway? Surely there's better places to hide it?'

'She brought it into London because she needed to shore up her interests,' a new, male voice spoke, and Ellie spun in her seat to find a new arrival in the office. Cursing her hangover for slowing her down, she rose, holding out a hand.

'Matteo Lumetta,' she said.

Matteo smiled, shaking it briefly before letting go and

walking over to a sofa at the side of the room, slumping into it.

'DI Reckless,' he said. 'Sorry, *ex*-DI Reckless. I've been hearing all about you.'

'From your new business partner, I'm sure,' Ellie sat back in her chair, watching him as she continued. 'Sorry about the stolen note. My man thought he was helping your mother.'

'He was, but unfortunately my brother has different ambitions,' Matteo made a half-shrug. 'Did he keep his fingers?'

'Yes.'

'Tell him when he's better to come and see me. I'll make amends,' Matteo replied. 'We might not like the man, but he treated Mama there well back in the day, and he didn't deserve to be attacked that way.'

'Can I ask why you're here?' Ellie pressed. 'Ramsey seemed to think you were in London to arrange a health club deal, but that's just the smoke screen, isn't it?'

Matteo looked over to his mother, who gave the slightest of nods.

'I'm working with my mama to take down my dear, darling, older brother,' he said. 'Tommaso's too violent, too much like Papa. He'll destroy us, take us all down with him. He's better off playing with his toys back at home.'

'While you take over control?' Ellie enquired with mock innocence.

'Nobody takes control until Mama passes it on,' Matteo said with what felt to be utter sincerity. 'But when she does, yes, it'll be me.'

'And you'd pass your elder son over for your youngest?'

'Currently, my eldest son's looking to remove me by any

means necessary,' Mama Lumetta replied. 'I'll do whatever it takes to stay in power, and also stay alive.'

Ellie looked over at Matteo now.

'Actually, I'm glad you're here, Mister Lumetta,' she forced a smile again. 'I was hoping you could tell me a little about Whipcrack Holdings.'

As she spoke the name, Ellie saw Lorenzo start a little once more, the slightest of flinches, but enough to know something more was happening here. In fact, Ellie was wondering how involved Lorenzo actually was.

'Carl Fredricks,' Matteo looked up at Lorenzo, and then at his mother as he spoke. 'Nice guy. Old friend of the family. Had legal problems a while back, came to me for help. We sorted it out, he's worked with us since then.'

'He's the one who you've been sending the bottles to, right?' Ellie looked back at Mama Lumetta now. 'The special ones?'

'It's okay, he knows about the gold,' Mama Lumetta sighed. 'You can speak freely.'

'You were checking Paulo Moretti's last shipment,' Ellie said as she looked back at Matteo. 'When Ramsey came to see you.'

'You mean when he stole it from me,' Matteo raised his left eyebrow in mild amusement.

'More borrowed,' Ellie stood her ground here. 'But yes, pretty much. The warehouse isn't far from you, either.'

'Nothing's far from anyone in Shoreditch,' Matteo replied with a smile, but it didn't reach the eyes as he continued. 'You should know that, Miss Reckless. You are, after all, a Shoreditch resident.'

Ellie felt a sliver of ice slide down her spine at this. *How did he know?* Of course, he'd have checked up on her. Maybe

Nicky Simpson mentioned it. Her address wasn't a secret location, either, as shown by Delgado and Whitehouse knocking on her door the previous day.

Did one of them tell him? Did she have to consider moving?

'Is that a threat?' she asked, tired of playing games.

'Not at all,' Matteo gave the impression of utter innocence as he smiled in return. 'Just pointing out that in London we can all be neighbours without realising.'

'Fine,' Ellie rose from the chair now, still faking the smile. 'Maybe I'll go chat with Carl.'

'If you manage it, let me know,' Matteo said, backing to the side a little to give Ellie a clear path to the door. 'He died a week ago.'

Ellie stopped.

'Did you know this?' she asked, looking back at Mama Lumetta, but one look confirmed that the matriarch of the Lumetta family didn't have a clue.

'I hadn't been told,' Mama Lumetta glared at Matteo as she spoke. 'But I'm sure my son was about to tell me this.'

Matteo nodded at this, but again, Ellie felt he was nodding to Lorenzo more than Mama Lumetta.

'How did he die?' Ellie asked.

'Shortness of breath,' Matteo shrugged. 'I don't know. Never asked. Funeral was two days ago.'

Ellie looked back at Mama Lumetta, but before she could speak, Matteo stepped forwards.

'Here,' Matteo passed Ellie a business card. 'Rather than hassling my mother with every question you have, drop me a line.'

Ellie had the feeling this was done as a dismissal, but as she placed the business card into her pocket, she pursed her lips in thought.

'Answer me a couple of last questions before I go, then,' Ellie said, still standing in the middle of the office. 'Carl Fredricks was the man who turned the solution back into gold, wasn't he? Paulo would bring him small amounts regularly.'

Mama Lumetta looked as if she wouldn't reply for a moment, and then nodded.

'His family was known for it up north,' Matteo explained. 'We helped him expand southwards.'

'So, let me see if I got this right,' Ellie looked back at Matteo now. 'A week ago, the guy who takes this contraband and turns it back into gold dies, a few days before a massive delivery, possibly the biggest ever, arrives. Yes?'

'Yeah,' Matteo replied.

'And then, when the delivery is made, your half-brother Paulo is diverted from his route in the middle of the night and murdered while the stock is taken?'

'We don't know why he drove there,' Matteo replied.

At this, Ellie shook her head.

'Oh, I didn't mention, did I?' she said. 'We found the circuit that overran his van's sat nav. Someone put it into the van in Dover. It sent him right to his killer.'

Either Matteo was a great power player, or he truly didn't know this, as his face darkened into one of suppressed fury.

'Someone killed your alchemist, and when that didn't stop the delivery, they took it,' Ellie said. 'This is major. So, my last question to you is this. What's about to happen?'

Mama Lumetta looked across at Matteo at this.

'I don't know what you mean,' she said, but with the sullen tone of someone who knew exactly what was being said.

'You brought amounts of gold in, over the last couple of

years,' Ellie said. 'Fourteen other times. So, maybe three, four million in gold? And then this month you bring four million in one go. You're either hiding it or building a serious war chest, Mrs Lumetta. And if it's the latter, I'd like to know who exactly are you going to war with?'

Mama Lumetta didn't reply.

'You've had your final two questions,' Matteo said, although his voice was more sympathetic now than angry, perhaps worried for his mother. 'I think you should go now.'

'Only once I'm given confirmation,' Ellie said, looking back at Mama Lumetta. 'Do we double the fee?'

There was a long moment of silence.

'I just want my bottles back,' Mama Lumetta replied, and it was the reply of a woman with nothing left to lose. 'I'll agree to the changes.'

'Awesome,' Ellie smiled, walking to the door. 'I'll keep you updated.'

She stopped.

'One more thing,' she said, looking back. 'A request. Lorenzo, isn't it?'

'You said your last questions,' Matteo snapped.

'To *you*, not the hired help,' Ellie smiled winningly, while her eyes glittered menacingly. 'And I'm not asking a question. Lorenzo, you're the driver, and you wear driving gloves, even when you're not driving. I was wondering, could you remove them for a moment?'

'Why?' Lorenzo asked, frowning.

'Because two nights back, someone cut their hand open after killing Paulo Moretti, and so far you're the only one I've seen who's been hiding them.'

Lorenzo looked almost pleadingly at Mama Lumetta.

'She's fishing,' he said. 'I won't do—'

'You'll do what she asks,' Matteo spoke, rather than his mother, and his tone was that of a man who didn't expect to be argued with.

Lorenzo went to reply, then sighed, pulling off his gloves, tossing them onto a chair as he showed his uninjured hands, turning them around.

'There,' he said. 'I didn't cut my hands on a broken bottle. No wounds.'

Ellie frowned. *She'd really thought this would be a breakthrough.* Instead, she nodded, looked at Mama Lumetta and smiled.

'Just being thorough,' she said, finally leaving.

Only once she was out of the office, down the stairs and out into the open air did Ellie Reckless take a breath, calming herself down as she leant against the building for support.

This was bigger than a theft. This was bigger than the current three murders that had happened. Lorenzo and Matteo were definitely involved somehow, but she didn't know how, or what their connections had been in this.

And currently, Ellie still didn't know what *this* was.

14

CUSTOMS DUTIES

Tinker had driven down to Dover in her Defender, which wasn't the most comfortable of cars. Ramsey had sat in the passenger seat, constantly complaining about the vehicle's lack of suspension, while Casey had sat on a bench in the back, reading comics on his tablet and chuckling to himself. The entire journey had been two hours of abject misery, not helped by Ramsey's constant yelps every time a pothole shuddered the Defender, and by default, his bandaged hand.

'You know, I could drop you off,' Tinker had said early on, but Ramsey had stoically refused, probably knee-deep into whatever martyrdom he was intending to use to get out of this.

Tinker had then felt bad about even considering that; Ramsey didn't have to place himself in the position he'd been in, and the fact he was still there spoke volumes.

If he carried on like this, she might even end up liking him.

As they'd driven, Casey had hacked into HOLMES 2, the police network, from his tablet, while sitting on the back seat.

Tinker hadn't wanted to know how he managed it, and instead just left him to his own devices as, his comics now finished, he returned into the system and the information already gathered on Brian Watson's murder.

'Apparently it was late last night,' he said, reading the notes. 'Witnesses said he'd been spooked all day—'

'Probably after meeting Tinkerbelle here,' Ramsey muttered, and then paused, looking wide eyed at her. 'Dear God, it probably was because of that, wasn't it?'

'Carry on,' Tinker said to Casey as she gritted her teeth. 'Find me something that shows this wasn't my fault.'

'He went out to a Dover club, was witnessed around ten pm when he drank a lot of tequila, left about two in the morning and was attacked in an alley nearby,' Casey read. 'Mugging gone wrong, they say. Wallet and phone taken, but not his watch.'

'Is there a reason they'd take it?'

'It's worth more than the phone, by far,' Casey looked up. 'It's a U-Boat Chimera. Italian company, worth about four grand.'

'Well now we know what he was using the bribe money on,' Tinker shook her head. 'Idiot.'

'Actually, it's a good idea,' Ramsey replied, scratching his moustache with his good hand. 'He could buy a couple of watches with the money, claim he's saved up for them, and then let them make him profit. Expensive watches rise in price faster than bank interest rates.'

'Not if you keep wearing them,' Tinker muttered, but she could understand where he was coming from. 'So, they either didn't know it was worth money—'

'Or it was a killing faked to look like a mugging,' Casey had said.

Tinker suddenly screeched the Defender to a halt, swerving onto the side, the force of the braking slamming Ramsey, and his hand onto the dashboard with a sudden explosion of curse words.

'What the utter hell?' he eventually hissed, rubbing his bandage.

'He emailed me about the shipping note around ten pm,' Tinker muttered, not really to anyone in the Defender, but more to herself. 'He checked the addresses, emailed me, left and then died.'

'You can't blame yourself for that,' Ramsey, calming slightly, shook his head. 'You don't know what happened.'

'What if his checking of the note made him a target?' Tinker started the Defender up again, pulling back into the traffic. 'What if—'

'The world is full of what ifs,' Ramsey replied, cutting her off. 'What if your arrival at his house spooked his colleagues, so they'd kill him? What if his pouring of the gold away was enough to get him removed? What if, what if, what if ...'

'You are aware every one of these still ends with me being to blame,' Tinker glared at Ramsey, who simply smiled in return.

'I never said it wasn't your fault,' he replied with mock sincerity, still rubbing his hand. 'Just your reasoning might be flawed.'

'I'm beginning to wish I'd been there when they slammed the meat cleaver on your fingers,' Tinker hissed.

'Why, to save me?' Ramsey innocently enquired.

'No, to help give them a better angle,' Tinker muttered sullenly.

'Hey,' Casey looked up from his tablet. 'Matteo's connected to Whipcrack Holdings.'

'How so?' Tinker was concentrating on the road now, seething with a mixture of anger and guilt.

'He's on the board of directors, but he's not public,' Casey was scrolling down what looked to be a database. 'A holding company doesn't do much, it's just a kind of business entity, usually a corporation or something similar.'

'I've dealt with a few in my time,' Ramsey added from the front. 'Typically, they don't manufacture anything, sell any products or give any services worth a damn. They just hold the controlling stock in other companies.'

'But what companies?' Tinker asked. 'What's Whipcrack hiding?'

'That's gonna be a little harder to find out, as I'll have to request details,' Casey replied. 'At least for one, so I can get that backdoor route.'

'What, and they give these to fifteen-year-old kids?' Tinker raised her eyebrows.

'Don't be silly, I'm not speaking to them as me,' Casey laughed at this. 'I'm Peter Sutcliffe, CEO of some finance company in the city.'

'Wasn't Peter Sutcliffe the Yorkshire Ripper?' Ramsey frowned.

'This is a different Peter,' Casey replied without looking up, already deep into forums once more. 'He does ultra-marathons and likes *Sex and the City*.'

And, as they carried on driving into Dover, he stayed that way.

'I CONTACTED YOU AS SOON AS I HEARD,' POSSIBLY-OLIVIA explained, as she faced Ramsey, Casey and Tinker across the reception desk. Her name was definitely Olivia, confirmed by Ramsey who, knowing Tinker's issue, had asked for it the moment he met her. But it was difficult for Tinker to consider her as anything but "possibly-Olivia", so for the time being, the name was sticking, especially as she hadn't seen Ramsey do this, and there was every chance he'd said this purely to have Tinker call her by the name "Olivia", just for her to say she was wrong, and it was in fact something completely different, purely for his own twisted amusement.

So, for the moment, "possibly-Olivia" it was.

'We appreciate it,' Tinker replied. 'But why call us here rather than to Brian's house?'

'Because the police are there,' possibly-Olivia explained. 'You're not police, so I assumed they wouldn't let you in.'

'She's got a point,' Ramsey winked at possibly-Olivia, and she gave a small coquettish smile back. 'We can always have a root about there once the police have finished. Better to see what else we can learn before that.'

'I can't really help more than I already know,' possibly-Olivia looked saddened at her failure here. 'But after you spoke to Jimmy and Brian, I spoke to Brian late last night, after you did.'

'You did?' this surprised Tinker. 'Why?'

'Because I didn't trust you, that's why,' possibly-Olivia snapped back. 'I've known Brian Watson for years, and I wasn't going to have him strung out to dry by some stranger over a murder he wasn't privy to. But, he said you were alright. That you had his best interests in heart. And that's why I called you.'

If Tinker was in any way insulted by the outburst, she did a good job of hiding it.

'All we know is Brian was mugged and attacked last

night,' she said. 'Was there anything else you can tell us about the events?'

'Only what I was told, and that was said to you on the phone,' possibly-Olivia leant closer as she spoke though, making sure nobody could overhear her as she whispered. 'But there's other stuff.'

Leaning back, possibly-Olivia looked around, nodding at a short, blonde woman at a table behind her.

'Disappearing for a couple of minutes, Brenda,' she said. 'You good to hold the fort?'

As the blonde woman nodded, possibly-Olivia rose from her chair and walked around, exiting the reception area through a door to the side. Motioning for the others to follow her, she walked back down the stairs and out of the building. Now back into the open air, she visibly relaxed, pulling out a pack of cigarettes, placing one in her mouth and then starting with surprise as Ramsey, ever the charmer, leant in with a lighter. Lighting her cigarette, she smiled again at him, and Tinker had to force herself not to laugh.

'So, what's the other stuff?' Ramsey asked, placing the lighter back into his jacket pocket.

'Listen,' possibly-Olivia breathed. 'I wasn't here last night, and therefore I didn't see it, but I heard about it when I got in.'

'Okay,' Tinker kept her tone neutral, allowing possibly-Olivia space to continue. 'And what did you hear?'

'So, Jimmy Mantel worked the night shift last night,' possibly-Olivia explained. 'He always works that shift, while Brian is usually rotating through.'

'Is that usual?' Casey asked, looking up from his tablet for the first time.

'It's not the norm, but you can request it if you want, and

as most people don't like the nights, it's usually given if you ask for it.'

Possibly-Olivia took a long drag on the cigarette before continuing.

'The offices are closed during the night, just a skeleton staff, in case something comes in or out that needs a little more official work done. And so, I heard about this from Stacey, who's one of the overnighters. She said that around two in the morning, there were three visitors.'

'Visitors?' Tinker looked at Ramsey, trying to work out if she'd missed something here. 'What sort of visitors?'

'That's the problem, nobody knows,' possibly-Olivia continued. 'They signed in at the gate, but the book went missing. Nigel whatshisname was on the gate last night and he's a sneaky bastard. Probably paid him cash to lose the details.'

'This happen a lot?'

Possibly-Olivia shook her head vigorously.

'Oh no,' she replied. 'This barely ever happens. And when it does, it's usually mates of the guards popping in, or someone getting their side woman through while it's quiet.'

'Side woman?' Tinker raised an eyebrow at this.

'Or side man, I'm not judging.'

'A side woman or man is someone who's a "bit on the side"—' Casey explained, but stopped when Tinker shot him a glare.

'I know what it means,' she hissed. 'So, going on the fact these three people weren't side people, who were they?'

'Nobody knows,' possibly-Olivia's eyes widened as she nodded conspiratorially. 'But they were seen by Stacey, looking for Jimmy. Two men and a woman. Irish accents. Jimmy goes to meet them, but then disappears. An hour later he's found by the rear staircase, and he's had the living hell beaten out of him. The two men and the woman? Gone.'

'Did Jimmy explain what happened?'

'Nope,' her cigarette ended, possibly-Olivia stubbed it out on a metal ashtray box attached to the wall. 'And when people asked him, he claimed it was nothing, and they should just move on. But Stacey said there was one more strange thing. In the canteen room, there was a bottle of extra-virgin olive oil. Jimmy brought it in the night before, saying Paulo Moretti, the man you were asking about, gave it to him. This morning? It was gone.'

Tinker nodded, already expecting this. Two men and a woman had arrived looking for that bottle, and the chances were these were either connected to the Lumetta family, or whomever Brian had been holding the bottle for.

'I thought you should know,' possibly-Olivia continued. 'What with Brian being mugged and killed last night and his locker being opened.'

'Wait, his locker was opened?' Ramsey picked up on this before Tinker could speak. 'When?'

'Sometime late in the afternoon, maybe early evening?' possibly-Olivia scrunched her nose as she thought about it. 'After you'd been here. Someone came up and told me it'd been opened, but it looked like nothing had been taken. I'd called Brian to tell him, make sure he was aware of the situation, especially as he'd called in sick that day, but he said there was nothing worth stealing in it, and he'd probably mis-locked it or something. Only other people in there who weren't staff were the police, when they came to talk about that driver's death, so we assumed it was just an accident. It was during that conversation we spoke about you.'

This last part was aimed at Tinker, who frowned.

'How so?'

'I told him you'd been asking about him and Mister Moretti, but he replied you'd already visited him,' possibly-Olivia explained. 'I asked if there was any issue here, if there were problems I needed to know about, and he said no, that you had his best interests at heart. And then later on that day, or early this morning even, he—'

At this, possibly-Olivia fluttered slightly, tears welling up.

'—he was killed.'

Tinker placed a hand on possibly-Olivia's arm, trying her best to look and be reassuring.

'We'll find who killed him,' she said, and from the tone of her voice, it was obvious she meant and believed this. 'We'll bring them to justice. Is Stacey still around?'

'No,' possibly-Olivia wiped away a still-forming tear. 'But she gave an excellent description of who they were to the police. The woman was obviously in charge, long red hair, like that girl from the Disney movie *Brave*. Wore the same colours, too.'

'The police were here?' Ramsey was surprised.

'Yes, a detective, woman by the name of Richmond,' possibly-Olivia replied. 'She said she was on the Moretti murder, and had expanded the case to cover Brian, too. She was here yesterday, too, but I hadn't seen her.'

'Did Stacey explain what happened to Jimmy?'

'No, he'd asked everyone to keep quiet,' possibly-Olivia shook her head. 'I think he was embarrassed; you know? Said it was nothing, some bragging in a pub that'd gone a bit over the top. So, Stacey just said these people were looking around. Nothing more.'

'CCTV footage?' Casey asked, looking up.

'There would be, but if they took the sign-in book, they'd have found a way to get that deleted, too.'

'Two men and a woman, Irish,' Tinker nodded. 'Not much to go on with.'

At this, possibly-Olivia reached into her pocket and brought out a post-it note.

'Here,' she said, passing it over. 'Jimmy's address.'

'You sure about this?' Ramsey asked. 'This is beyond your remit?'

'Three people came in and maybe killed Brian, and then shortly after definitely attacked Jimmy,' possibly-Olivia straightened as she replied. 'I might not be police, or someone with the power to prosecute or get justice, but I get the impression you people are. So, find them and make them pay.'

'What about DCI Richmond?' Tinker placed the note in her own pocket. 'You should be giving this to her.'

To Tinker's surprise, possibly-Olivia shook her head at this.

'You meet a lot of people on the docks,' she explained. 'And most of these are alright people. But then you have the other ones, the people who are trying something, pretending, and over time you get a sense of who's legit and who's trying to smuggle something through.'

She coughed, straightened her top, and then started walking back to the door.

'DCI Richmond felt like one of the others,' she said, opening the door and nodding one last time at Ramsey. 'She wasn't legit. Especially as she was around Brian's locker the day it was found open, but then pretended she didn't know anything about it when I mentioned it this morning.'

And, this stated, possibly-Olivia left the outside smoking

area, re-entering her office. Tinker looked at Casey and Ramsey.

'Thoughts?' she asked.

'I think we need to get over to Jimmy Mantel's house as quick as possible,' Ramsey replied, already moving. 'This isn't good.'

'What aren't you telling me?' Tinker asked as she caught up with him, walking over to the Defender.

At the question, Ramsey stopped, looking back at Tinker.

'I'm superb at London gangs,' he replied softly. 'You place me in an area of Central London, and I can pretty much tell you who you need to speak to when you want something done. Once you move out of that area, though, it fades a little. I know some cities, and the bigger names, but that's about it.'

'Okay, so what's making you twitch right now?'

Ramsey absently rubbed at his bandaged hand as he replied.

'This area of Kent, it's got a few Irish gangs that run things. Mostly small fry and connected to other groups, but there's one. The Maguire family. They run a lot of stuff in South Essex and North Kent, so this might be out of their area. The big boss, Frank Maguire is more interested in the area north of Southend, while his cousin, Orla controls Kent.'

'Let me guess,' Tinker almost smiled. 'She's got red hair.'

'Just like the girl from *Brave*,' Ramsey nodded. 'And if the Maguires are looking for the gold, then we definitely have a gang war on our hands.'

15

POLICE ENQUIRIES

'HE'S PROBABLY ASLEEP BY NOW.'

Tinker stared up at the two-up, two-down terraced house across the road. It was built in 1915, as proclaimed by a number and year etched into the stone under the lintel of the roof, and had been covered over at some point, likely when the whole frontage had been either painted or whitewashed in a gleaming white, a colour that, over the years had faded, tarnishing, and with areas of the frontage now peeling off, showing the pale brick underneath.

'He'll probably be asleep,' Casey repeated from the back, still working on his tablet as he spoke. 'It's almost lunchtime.'

'I don't know about that,' Tinker said as she nodded up at the front upstairs window. Through it, there was the slightest hint of a shadow moving. 'I think he's not been able to sleep recently.'

'Being beaten up and in pain does that to you,' Ramsey added, patting his arm. 'I've not slept, so I'm sure he hasn't.'

'Let's go find out,' Tinker said as she climbed out of the

Defender, already walking across the suburban street and towards the house as Ramsey reluctantly followed.

Casey looked up as he did this and rolled down the window.

'I'll stay guard out here,' he called out after them. 'I think I might have something.'

Tinker glanced back and nodded approval of this before opening the gate to the house and walking the few steps to the door. Then, with a solid thump, she banged on the door.

After a couple of seconds there was a sound of someone walking down some stairs, and then the front door opened a sliver as a bruised and battered Jimmy Mantel glared out at her.

'I'm trying to sleep,' he growled. 'I'm on nights.'

'You're not sleeping, you're pacing and watching out of the window, and you're signed off for the week,' Tinker gave her brightest smile. 'Let me in, Jimmy. Before the locals think we're police and tell the Maguires.'

At the name, Jimmy jerked back, and he opened the door reluctantly.

'I don't know no Maguires,' he said sullenly as Tinker and Ramsey moved past him, walking into the hallway. It was narrow and painted a pale green. There was a staircase in front of them, a hallway leading through to what was likely the kitchen to the side. A mirror was on the side wall, next to a coat stand, and to the right was a door, likely leading to the front living room.

'Shall we go have a chat?' Tinker waved at the door, taking charge of the situation. With a frown and then a sigh of resignation, Jimmy nodded and led the way.

The room was painted the same colour as the hallway, and Tinker had started to wonder whether Jimmy had received some kind of job lot on hideous green paint, but she kept quiet as she sat on an IKEA sofa, facing across the room at Jimmy, carefully placing himself into an armchair, far older in design than the more modern seat she was on, wincing as he did so. And, for the first time, the light showed the extent of his injuries.

His face was mottled and purple, where he'd obviously been hit repeatedly, and he had stitches across his temple, most likely from where his skin had split open after a particularly vicious attack. His right eye, under the stitches, was red from where the capillaries had burst; he looked like he'd gone ten rounds with Tyson Fury.

And, judging by the way he gingerly stroked at his chest, the face hadn't been the only area they'd aimed for.

Taking her attention from him, so as not to stare, Tinker glanced around the living room. It was thin but long, with flowery curtains next to a bookcase held within a recess. A TV and satellite box were in front, on a glass cabinet, and a gas fire was within the fireplace. Around the wall were prints by Quentin Blake, and there was a table beside the sofa that held a box full of remotes.

In general, the room seemed placed together in a kind of hotchpotch randomness, and Tinker knew, without a smattering of a doubt, the man sitting in front of her had designed it with no actual plan of attack.

'Your reception called us in,' Tinker said, omitting the part where possibly-Olivia had actually brought them back because of Brian's death. 'Said you had quite a beating last night. Said the bottle of Lumetta Oil you'd been given was taken.'

Jimmy didn't reply; instead, he sullenly stared at the floor.

'You've heard about your cousin, I take it?' Ramsey asked.

'I don't know you,' Jimmy looked up defiantly. 'I know her, but not you.'

'I'm Ramsey Allen, I work with Tinker,' Ramsey smiled, indicating the bruises. 'Did the Lumetta family do that?'

'Did they do *that?*' Jimmy retaliated angrily, nodding at the bandaged arm.

'Why yes, thanks for noticing,' Ramsey forced a smile as he cheerfully replied. 'They attacked my hand with a meat cleaver, because I took a piece of paper that wasn't mine. I'm guessing they do more for stolen bottles.'

Jimmy stared at Ramsey for a good few seconds, almost open-mouthed, before shaking his head.

'It wasn't the Lumettas,' he whispered. 'It was the Maguires.'

Tinker went to speak, but a slight nudge from Ramsey, and an almost imperceptible shake of the head, stopped her. She got the message.

Now was not the time for "I told you so" crowing.

'So, what happened?' she altered her question to be more sympathetic.

'I was on shift,' Jimmy, now having decided to tell the story, ever-so-slowly leant back into his armchair, still wincing as he did so. 'Around two in the morning, maybe a little later. We were in a slack point of the night, as the ferries were now in, and it was mainly drivers leaving the UK, the eager ones, turning up too early for the first ferry. Anyway, I get a buzz from the girl at the office, apparently there are friends of Brian looking for me. Two guys and a girl. Woman. I don't remember what they said. Two males and a female.'

'Was the female Orla Maguire?' Ramsey added. 'Long red hair, small knife scar on the cheek, slim, late forties in age?'

Jimmy seemed surprised at the exactness of the description.

'Yeah,' he said. 'That's the one.'

'So, Orla Maguire and her men turned up at your place of work,' Tinker rubbed her chin as she considered this. 'Have you met them before? Seen them around?'

Jimmy nodded.

'Not personally,' he admitted. 'But I've seen them. With Brian.'

Tinker straightened on the sofa.

'Was it a day or two after Paulo Moretti would arrive?'

Jimmy shook his head, stopped, frowned, and then pursed his lips.

'Actually, maybe,' he replied. 'I never dealt with Moretti, but it was after Brian had changed shifts one day, so it could have been around the same time. Why?'

Tinker considered her next move.

Should she tell Jimmy the truth about his cousin?

'We'll come back to that in a minute,' she said. 'What did they want?'

'The olive oil I was given,' Jimmy almost sulked. 'I said it was in the staff room, but they didn't believe me. Said it was stolen goods, and I needed to bring it out to them. I said they needed to speak to Brian, and they laughed.'

Tinker felt an icy wind blow down her spine at this.

'This was after he'd been attacked and killed?'

'At the time, I didn't know,' Jimmy shrugged. 'But I reckon so.'

'Carry on,' Ramsey leant closer now. 'What did they do?'

'Well, I went and got the bottle, showed it to them, and the woman, she lost her bloody mind. Said I was screwing around. I said Brian had the other bottle, I was getting real scared by now as I knew who they were.'

'But you were in a Customs dock,' Tinker frowned. 'Surely you were safe there?'

'People like Maguires? They *own* docks,' Jimmy moaned. 'It was stupid o'clock in the morning, and nobody was around. They could have killed me and nobody would have seen.'

He winced.

'Instead, they decided to kick the living shit out of me for screwing them around,' he whispered. 'They said Brian didn't have his bottle, so he must have given it to me, and then when I showed it, they started roughing me up, saying they didn't have the time for jokes. Eventually they said I had to be telling the truth, because nobody was that stupid to lie to them. And then they walked off, pretty pissed off, I'll tell ya.'

'Did you tell anyone?' Ramsey asked.

'What, and get another kicking?' Jimmy shook his head. 'I was found later, sitting on the floor, my face a mess, I made up a story of kids getting over the fence and attacking me when I went for them, looking for me because of something I said down the pub. Easier than saying the Maguires were around. Especially as I was told there was no footage of them entering or exiting, and the visitors' book was gone.'

'And this is why you're watching out the window?' Tinker added. 'You think they're coming after you?'

'I got to the hospital and phoned Brian while there. No answer,' Jimmy carried on. 'When they'd patched me up, I went over there, but the police were everywhere. Said someone had broken in. When I said I was looking for Brian, a uniform told me he'd been killed in a mugging in town. I knew that weren't no mugging, so I ran back here and locked the door.'

He stopped, watching Tinker warily.

'You saw Brian, didn't you?' he asked, now suspicious, backing into the armchair. 'After you saw me.'

Tinker nodded.

'I did.'

'Did you take the bottle?' Jimmy asked. 'The 2021 labelled one? Is that why Orla killed him?'

'Brian poured it down his sink,' Tinker lied, well, it was partially a lie, anyway. 'He thought the police were coming.'

'What was it?' Jimmy asked. 'Drugs or something?'

'Or something,' Tinker rose, nodding at Ramsey to follow her. 'Sorry for interrupting your sleep, Jimmy.'

'You said you'd tell me,' Jimmy rose to face them, his face reddening in anger. Or, it could have been the face injuries swelling more.

Tinker sighed.

'Your cousin was taking contraband items, all stolen from the Lumetta family,' she said. 'Fifteen times over the last few months. He'd made the deal with Paulo Moretti, and a couple of days after each pass through, when he received a couple of bottles from Paulo, someone would turn up and pay him five hundred pounds for them. He didn't know who they were, and he was happy to keep making the money.'

'Do you know how much each bottle was worth?' Jimmy asked, his face paling.

'Just under four grand a bottle,' Ramsey interjected.

'Oh, Brian, you bloody idiot,' Jimmy placed his head into his hands as he started to softly weep. 'You bloody, bloody idiot.'

He shook his head.

'Did Brian kill the driver? Moretti?'

'No, we don't think so,' Tinker placed a hand on Jimmy's shoulder. 'From what we can see, the men who killed Mister Moretti had a way to bring him to them, a circuit board they placed in his van. It looks like Brian's only crime was to take the bottle.'

Jimmy sniffled, groaning as he tried to take this in.

'Sorry for your loss,' Tinker passed Jimmy a card with her number on. 'Anything you think of, let us know.'

Jimmy was silent at this, nodding softly as he walked them to the door, and Tinker got the feeling he was sleep-walking as he did this, one foot after the other, on autopilot while his mind tried to make sense of what was truly going on. She'd seen people like this in the army, ones who survived but couldn't understand how, their eyes blank and staring as they went through their daily tasks.

Now on the doorstep, Tinker looked back.

'Lock all the doors, and if anyone comes back—'

'Call you, yeah, I get it.'

'No, you bloody fool. Call the police,' Tinker shook her head. 'And then find somewhere to bloody hide.'

Jimmy stopped, looked up at Tinker as if waking from a dream, and shook, as if shaking himself into consciousness.

'Brian did it,' he said, suddenly.

Tinker looked at him, cocking her head slightly.

'Did what?'

'The circuit thing,' Jimmy was looking past them, as if trying to recall a memory. 'It was found on the driver's side, right? When Mister Moretti was showing me the items in the back, Brian stayed behind, beside the driver's door. A couple of minutes later, he walked to the back, but he looked furtive.

Suspicious. And I was sure I saw him, or at least a shadow of him, in the driver's area.'

'Have you told anyone of this?' Tinker asked slowly. 'If you're wrong ...'

'I know,' Jimmy nodded. 'And no, I wouldn't tell anyone. They'd think I was involved for a start. I just thought you should know.'

And with that, he moved back into the shadows, Tinker and Ramsey left the other side of the threshold.

The door now shutting behind them, Tinker and Ramsey walked down the drive, stepping onto the pavement, across the road from Casey and the Defender.

Casey, who was watching them, started motioning to their right with his eyes.

Looking in the direction suggested, Tinker saw a woman walking towards her. She was alone, but had the look of someone who didn't expect to need anyone; she was muscled, possibly a weightlifter or rugby player in her spare time, her short black hair giving her an androgynous look.

'DCI Richmond,' the woman smiled, pulling out and holding up a warrant card. 'I'm guessing the pair of you work with Ellie Reckless?'

Before Tinker could confirm or deny this, Richmond nodded over at Casey in the car.

'I recognise the child,' she said. 'So, there's no point denying it.'

'You're a bit out of your area,' Tinker replied instead.

Richmond clicked her tongue against the top of her mouth as she smiled slightly.

'Maidstone's closer than London,' she waved around. 'And this is connected to a murder enquiry run from up there.'

She paused, raising an eyebrow.

'And you are?' she offered, looking at Ramsey rather than Tinker.

Tinker sighed at this, looking at Ramsey. *Once more, the old man gets the preferential treatment.*

'I'm Ramsey Allen, Finders Corporation,' he said, putting on his best plummy accent. 'This is Tinker Jones, my driver.'

'I don't think ex-Corporal Jones here is anyone's driver, Mister Allen,' DCI Richmond replied, her smile widening. 'Especially for an ex-convict like yourself. Or do you mean because you have a bad hand?'

Tinker inwardly groaned. When Richmond had called Whitehouse and Delgado to get the skinny on Ellie, they must have told her everything.

'Have we met before?' Ramsey frowned.

'No, but I know all about you. When I was at Stratford, DCI Sheridan mentioned you a lot.'

Ramsey actually guffawed with delight at this.

'I bet he did,' he said after recovering himself. 'If you see Guy Sheridan around, send him my regards.'

Casey, as if guessing something was wrong, climbed out of the Defender, standing to the side of the two women.

'Can I help you, DCI Richmond?' Tinker asked coolly.

'Probably,' Richmond smiled. 'I believe you were going to share what you found with me?'

'I heard it was a mutual swap,' Ramsey matched Richmond's smile, stepping forward as he did so. 'But we have been lax. I apologise. I will make sure Finders send you a full report when we get back.'

'Or you could tell me what you have right now?' Richmond offered, her smile fixed, but her eyes now cold.

'Paulo Moretti was killed when his van was hacked into,'

Casey stated. 'They made his sat nav think he was on a short-cut, and they directed him to his death.'

'"Directed him to his death". My, you must read some incredible books for an imagination like that,' Richmond turned to face Casey now. 'And how do you know that?'

Casey paled, realising he was about to give away his theft from a crime scene.

'Confidential informant,' Tinker interrupted. 'We have a couple of people who know these sorts of things.'

Interestingly, Richmond accepted this without a question.

'Okay, well, that's good to know,' she said, finally noting Ramsey's hand. 'What happened to you, anyway?'

'Tommaso Lumetta tried to cut my fingers off with a meat cleaver for working the case for his mother,' Ramsey replied, completely straight faced. 'He didn't manage it, but they currently hurt like buggery.'

'He's a right prick,' Richmond's face softened a little at this. 'Want us to arrest him for it?'

'I'm fine,' Ramsey shook his head.

'Want us to make his life hell, anyway?' Richmond gave a dark smile. 'He threw us out of a crime scene. Bastard's guilty of something.'

'Oh, I'm sure he's guilty of a lot of things,' Ramsey flashed a smile now. 'But I'm good.'

Richmond looked up at the house.

'Is he up?' she asked.

Tinker knew she couldn't lie here, especially with Richmond having seen her walk out of the door, so she nodded.

'He's a little twitchy,' she said, deciding that a little over sharing wasn't too bad. 'If it helps, he was roughed up last night by Orla Maguire.'

Richmond's blank look wasn't surprising to Tinker; not

everyone had the knowledge of criminal families that Ramsey did.

'Irish gun runners and gangsters, links to Essex and Kent,' she added. 'Nasty bastards as well.'

'This case gets better and better,' Richmond replied as she nodded thanks and started towards the door.

'Anything for us?' Tinker asked.

At this, Richmond turned and smiled.

'Interesting thing,' she said. 'We had a call from a forensics in London. Said he'd helped with your investigation, found a lump of gold in some olive oil. He's sending us the details now, but apparently it's already been taken back to the owners of Lumetta Oils.'

Tinker kept her expression emotionless; she'd hoped Rajesh would have taken his time.

'Sounds like something above my pay grade,' she smiled, tipping her head at Ramsey. 'And they wouldn't place gold anywhere near this one.'

DCI Richmond's mouth moved to the side as she first pondered and then silently agreed with the statement.

'Well, get them to send us what they have,' she said, almost as an order as she turned and walked to the door.

Realising they had a brief respite to escape, Casey, Ramsey and Tinker all climbed into the Defender, Tinker starting it up and driving away from the house, heading as far from DCI Richmond and her questions as she could.

Tinker paused, hands on the wheel.

'It wasn't your fault,' Ramsey said.

Casey, frowning, looked up.

'What's not her fault?'

'Tinker's thinking Orla Maguire killed Brian Watson because he didn't have her bottles,' Ramsey watched Tinker as he spoke, noting her eyes tightening. 'She's blaming herself, because he poured the bottle away, so he didn't have it to pass on.'

'Am I wrong to do so?' Tinker muttered, her hands tightening on the steering wheel.

'No,' Ramsey replied honestly. 'But with Paulo dead and the bottles unlikely to be continuing, Brian was a loose thread she'd be cutting soon, anyway. It was only a matter of time. And if he'd told us everything? Then you could have saved him. He didn't. This is on him.'

Tinker's hands relaxed their grip slightly as she considered this.

'Right then,' she said. 'Back to London?'

'DCI Richmond's at Jimmy's, which means she won't be at Brian's house now,' Ramsey suggested. 'We could take a quick peek, see if anything comes up.'

'We could,' Tinker nodded. 'And then home. Anything from the back seat?'

Casey looked up, but his face wasn't his usual smiling self.

'I think I know how someone got into your email account,' he said. 'It was all the talk about holding companies. I thought about whether this was similar, and I checked through your army emails. Just name searches, I wasn't reading through or anything.'

'And?' Tinker leant around now, facing Casey.

'And a year ago you had a reunion Christmas meal,' Casey said. 'You all sent money through to a central email address, created so anyone working on the meal's planning could check the figures and all that. A holding company, but in email form.'

'And?' Tinker repeated, and her tone was darkening as her patience was thinning.

'And one of the people who had access was Staff Sergeant Aaron Meyers. Who died two years ago, and a year before this meal happened.'

Tinker went to speak, but then frowned.

'How?'

Casey spun the tablet to show her.

'He was still alive when you all first discussed it, and he was one of the people that created the email,' he said, pointing at the list. 'And, when he died, the email access was left, because, well, he wasn't going to be passing it around anywhere, was he?'

'Could someone have hacked into it?' Ramsey asked. 'And yes, I want points for understanding what hacking is.'

'Oh, they could have. And also, they did,' Casey pointed at several lines of code on another screen. 'These are the times and dates they accessed the account. And one of them was exactly a week before the blackmail message.'

He tapped on the screen once more.

'I've tracked the IP address, but you're not going to like it,' he said.

'Why?' Tinker continued her series of one-word answers.

'Because it's an IP address from Aldershot, where the Rifle Battalion your – well, friend – went to is based,' Casey held up a hand. 'And before you kick off against an entire battalion of soldiers, I've narrowed it down even more. It's the personal IP ...'

He stopped, unable to continue, or more likely scared of what'd happen once he spoke.

'Go on.'

'Don't kill the messenger, right?'

'Please,' Tinker pleaded. 'Tell me.'

Casey sighed, took another deep breath and steadied himself.

'It's the IP of Captain Jemima Fowler,' he said. 'And yeah, I know it sounds stupid, but basically the code doesn't lie. She used her own account details to hack into his old and unused email, purely to use this to gain information from you.'

16

HOUSING PRICES

AFTER VISITING MAMA LUMETTA, ELLIE HAD RETURNED TO THE Finders' offices to wait for the others, but as she arrived, she was greeted by an excited Robert Lewis, entering her small, corner office waving a piece of paper.

'Why are you so bloody cheerful?' Ellie asked. 'I don't like it when you're cheerful.'

'I might have something,' Robert replied with a salacious wink. 'I've been looking into Lumetta Oils financials, and also that Whipcrack Holdings entity young Casey found on his Speak and Spell, and I think I know why Matteo Lumetta's so interested in London.'

He placed the sheet on the desk, turning it around to show a website printout of a small, East London house, the plans and photos on an estate agent's webpage, a banner across the image stating it was SOLD.

'I think I've found Matteo Lumetta's dirty little secret,' he said.

Ellie picked up the paper, looking at it.

'A house?' she asked. 'So, he bought property. Lots of people do that.'

'Not through shell corporations and holding companies they don't,' Robert said, pausing as he looked up, working the phrase back through his head. 'Okay, some do, but not the lease Matteo Lumetta's in. This is a house so off the books, nobody knows where it is. And from what I can work out, nobody lives there.'

'He doesn't rent it out?'

'Nope,' Robert wore a smug expression now. 'And he bought the property in cash. Untraceable cash.'

'Probably in gold bars,' Ellie looked down at the sheet. 'North London, six hundred grand. Why buy a house and leave it empty?'

'Indeed,' Robert leant on the desk. 'What if Matteo has a fancy woman there?'

Ellie considered this, leaning back on her chair, and glancing at Millie to make sure she was okay on her bed.

'Matteo is in London now,' she said. 'If he's got someone on the side, he'd spend time with her, or him, whatever, while he's here, right?'

She started tapping on her phone.

'I'll get Casey to see if Matteo's checked into any hotels recently,' she said, sending the message and placing the phone back. 'But if he hasn't, then it's just a London residence. If he has, however, then we still have an empty house mystery. Especially at a time when people are hiding bottles of gold.'

'Any news from Casey and the others yet?' Robert straightened; the moment of excitement now passed.

'They're on their way back, and they have some information on the case,' Ellie said, and there was the slightest twitch to her eye as she spoke. 'Orla Maguire looks to be involved.'

'Didn't you arrest her brother once?' Robert frowned. 'I'm sure we mentioned it in the trial, to show why you wouldn't consort with criminals, because—'

'Because I'd done enough to screw every one of them over in my time on the force,' Ellie gave a wry smile. 'Yeah, that's right. And yeah, I arrested her brother. I think he's still in Swaleside, doing five to ten.'

'Well, that'll be a fun conversation, then,' Robert sighed. 'Just once, could one of your favour quests be an easy one?'

'I seem to recall you brought me this one,' Ellie said, rising and grabbing her coat. 'I'll get Sara to look after Millie, and we can go look at this house of yours.'

THE HOUSE, IT SEEMED WAS A SMALL THREE-BEDROOM HOME ON a side street off the Caledonian Road, just north of Kings Cross. And, after parking a little way up the street, so as not to spook anyone, Ellie and Robert made their way to the door. The area was a mishmash of beautiful, Edwardian three-storey houses or claustrophobic, concrete housing estates, but this seemed to be in the middle of these, a row of five, battered-looking red-bricked houses in a small terrace, windows placed in the seventies looking down onto a gated, bare park, the opposite side of a tiny service road that led to some garages.

Not all the houses were battered, however; several of them had been double glazed, and the faded, green-painted frontages had been given a fresh lick of paint, the foliage in the front tidied.

Matteo's house was held between the two. The windows weren't the more modern double glazing of the house next door, but it wasn't the single-pane seventies style of two doors down. The door itself was in a little alcove, a couple of feet deep, enough to stand under shelter on a rainy day while fiddling for your front-door keys without getting wet.

And, after Ellie had rung the doorbell enough to decide there was nobody in, it was deep enough to hide her as she knelt by the door, pulling out a lock-pick set given to her by Ramsey, and, using the skills he'd also taught her, it was deep enough to hide her picking the front-door's lock and pushing it open.

The house was empty as they entered the hallway; it was bare walled, with simple white paint the colour of choice. There were stairs ahead of them, running along the right-hand wall, and to the left was a small kitchen, a reception room next to it, with double patio doors that led to the back garden; a postage stamp of grass surrounded by high walls in every direction.

The house wasn't empty of life, however. In the reception room there were scattered cans and takeaway boxes, likely from the previous night; not cleared up, but placed to the side of a small, black coffee table in front of an enormous, four-seater sofa, a foot or so in front of the side wall. Opposite it was a mantlepiece with a fifty-inch television set secured to the wall, and a beanbag was placed haphazardly to the side.

On the table, next to the containers were remotes for the TV and the sound bar above it, and a selection of car magazines.

'Good god, look at that,' Robert said, pointing off to the left of the room, to a table placed against the divider wall between kitchen and reception. 'It's a dial phone. I haven't seen one of them for years.'

Ellie was about to point out she hadn't seen a land line in a house for years, let alone a rotary dial phone, when there was a rustle of keys at the front door.

'Shit,' she muttered, looking around. There wasn't anywhere to hide in the room, and there were definitely no understairs closets or cupboards to hide within.

They were trapped.

'Quick,' she said, bundling Robert to the sofa beside the wall. 'Over it.'

'You're kidding!' Robert almost didn't follow the order, but a muffled conversation from outside – a man's voice, obviously talking into a phone – spurred him into action, and he combat-rolled over the sofa like John McClane in *Die Hard*, landing with a painful sounding thud the other side. Ellie followed suit, but her landing was softer, mainly because she landed on Robert.

Who was about to reply angrily at this when Ellie clamped a hand over his mouth...

Because the door had opened, and someone had walked into the house.

The sofa was almost against the wall but was slightly angled backwards, which meant although there was a foot wide gap at the top, there was a little more room where they were currently hiding, and the length meant nobody would see them unless the person looking actively looked over it – and, to do that meant they'd heard something suspicious from behind it – so Ellie slowly and silently slid her way off Robert and along the edge, peering out from the end of the sofa. The door had rather kindly swung to a stop beside the left-hand side of the sofa, resting against the slightly protruding arm of it, which gave her some cover as she watched ...

As Lorenzo the driver walked into the room, pulling his gloves off and tossing them onto the sofa.

He looked at the cartons on the table and sucked some air in through his teeth, but then stopped as the rotary phone rang.

He walked over and picked it up, listening for a moment, but not stating his name or any form of welcome comment. *He knew the phone call was happening, and who it'd be from.*

'Yeah,' he said. 'I know I couldn't say anything, but you know what she's like, dad. She watches everything I do.'

There was a muffled speaking from down the phone; Ellie struggled to concentrate on it, but it was too soft.

'Nobody knows,' Lorenzo shook his head as he spoke, even though his father, on the other end of the phone couldn't see it. 'I made sure of it. And it's safe until we decide.'

Another pause, listening.

'Ah come on!' Lorenzo exclaimed. 'I only just got in! I gotta shower and change into a suit for the old bat—'

Another pause, and from his expression, Lorenzo was being shouted at.

'Okay, okay, I mean Mama Lumetta,' he replied. 'Jesus, dad. I'll do better. I promise. And if I hear anything about his actions, you'll be the first to know.'

This stated, Lorenzo slammed the phone down onto the cradle without even saying goodbye to his father, and pulled out his own phone. Dialling a number, he held it to his ear.

'It's me,' he said after a few moments. There was a little more pausing, and then Lorenzo continued. 'Dad's getting suspicious, and I can't keep him in the cold much longer. I'll pop around the Vaults tomorrow, check the stock's still there, and then we need to get moving on this before my family decide they want a special discount.'

He pulled the phone back, looking at a message on the screen, or maybe a diary entry.

'I'll be passing through Haggerston tomorrow,' he continued. 'She's having lunch with someone nearby, so I'll drop the old bat off, check everything's okay, and then come back.'

Another pause.

'But tomorrow, we need to sort this,' he finished. 'I can't keep hiding it from him. Everyone's hunting for it, and if they find it, we're dead.'

Pause.

'Yeah, I love you too.'

This done, he disconnected the call and, phone in hand, stormed out of the room. There were the echoed footsteps as he stomped up the stairs.

Ellie looked at Robert, only inches from her face.

'We gotta stop meeting like this,' she joked in a Texas drawl. 'People will talk, rumours will spread.'

She shifted and paused as she rubbed against Robert.

'Is that a phone in your pocket, or are you just pleased to see me?' she joked.

'It's a phone. You bloody *know* it's a phone,' Robert said, his voice stressed. 'Can we please just leave now?'

'Not until we know he's not coming down,' Ellie purred, enjoying Robert's discomfort. 'We may have to stay here all night.'

'You remember when I got you off—'

'You got me off?' Ellie almost laughed as Robert now reddened. 'I think I would remember that.'

'When I got you off those murder charges?' Robert

carried on, his voice now monotone and frantic. 'I never expected to be thrown into a cell beside you.'

Ellie grinned, and was about to make some kind of joke about being cellmates, when from upstairs, the sound of a shower could be heard.

'Oh, thank God. We need to go now,' Robert said, now straightening his clothing and forcing the redness from his cheeks by what seemed to be a sheer force of will, and already rising from behind the sofa. 'Men don't take as long in the shower as women. We have a couple of minutes, tops.'

They clambered as quickly and quietly as they could over the sofa, but as they went to leave the room, Ellie paused.

'Landline,' she whispered, running back to the phone.

'Ellie!' Robert hissed, but Ellie was already dialling on the phone, listening to it.

'One-four-seven-one,' she said triumphantly. 'Tells you who called you last.'

Listening carefully, and with the number of the last person to call now in her head, she placed the phone down carefully and, as the shower continued to drown out the upstairs bathroom from all other noise, Robert, leading the way slipped out of the house and exited back into the terraced street, while Ellie checked a jacket, now hanging on the coat rack – one that hadn't been there when they arrived – before closing the door quietly behind them, hurrying away after Robert in case Lorenzo looked out of his bedroom window.

'What is it?' Robert asked. 'You have that look.'

'The number, the last one dialled?' Ellie said as they stopped on a corner, now far enough away from the house not to be seen. 'Ended in seven-three-six. I'm sure I've seen it somewhere ...'

She froze as realisation stopped her.

'Oh, bloody hell,' she said. 'He sodding well told me.'

'Who told you? What did he tell you?' Robert persisted.

'Matteo Lumetta,' Ellie was walking back to her car now. 'When I talked to Ramsey earlier, he mentioned Matteo had made a statement, that "sometimes the bastards of the family were given the keys to the kingdom, and sometimes they were just the driver". We thought he meant Paulo Moretti being his bastard half-brother, but it wasn't.'

She pulled out the business card Matteo Lumetta had given her earlier that day, turning it to show the phone number.

It too ended in *seven-three-six*.

'It's the number that called, the one Lorenzo answered and said "dad" to,' she muttered, opening the door and climbing in as she spoke. 'I thought there was something odd when I saw him, he was watching Lorenzo, as if expecting him to speak. And now that comment means a bit more sense. Lorenzo is Matteo's son.'

'The records show he doesn't have children,' Robert was looking at a file on his phone to confirm this.

'That's because he's illegitimate, like Paulo was,' Ellie leant back into the driver's seat as she tried to get her head around this. 'Probably unknown to most of the family, too, going on how his mama acts around bastards. Matteo wants him to succeed. Pays for a house for him. Gets him into the family business. But Mama Lumetta? She makes him her chauffeur.'

'But if that's the case, why stand with her against his brother?' Robert frowned as he secured his seatbelt. 'Surely he'd want to work for the betterment of his son?'

'Maybe Tommaso would be worse? I just wish we could

find out who he called. What's the "vaults", and who does he love?' Ellie pulled out onto the street. 'Call the troops. I know it's getting on now, but we need a council of war before we go any further. If Lorenzo's playing for his own team, then he's been privy to everything his grandmother's been doing.'

'One question,' Robert asked. 'If Matteo's his dad, where's his mum? *Who's* his mum?'

'That's something we'll have to get answered in time,' Ellie rummaged in her jacket, pulling out a clear evidence baggie, with two hair follicles held within. 'I took these off Lorenzo's jacket. With luck, Rajesh can do a DNA test.'

'Christ,' Robert groaned. 'I'm too pretty to go to prison for this. Breaking and entering, illegally obtaining DNA samples without a warrant ...'

'You know your problem, Robbie?' Ellie grinned. 'You need to smile more. I think we're about to break this whole damn case.'

'We're definitely breaking something,' Robert sulked, as the car headed south, towards Farringdon and the city. 'A whole load of them.'

17

WAR COURT

IT WAS SEVEN BY THE TIME TINKER, CASEY AND RAMSEY HAD returned to the City; Caesar's Diner had closed for the day, and Ellie had suggested everyone come to the Finders' building, where she'd ordered in some late-night takeaway pizza.

Casey had called his mum, lying to her about some kind of skateboard video he was getting involved in, and had guaranteed himself a pass until nine pm. So, pretty much everyone was sitting in the boardroom by seven thirty, eating pizza and discussing what they'd learned.

'I don't see why we can't do this in your office,' Robert grumbled as he ate a slice of pepperoni pizza. 'And Millie keeps tapping my leg with her paw.'

'That's because you haven't given her any of the pepperoni,' Ellie replied officiously, looking down her nose at him. 'And I don't know if I can work for someone who doesn't give a poor, starving Cocker Spaniel meat from their pizza,' she smiled. 'Also, you won't give me a proper sofa for my office, so I wouldn't be able to get everyone in unless they were sitting on the floor, and that becomes fair game for spaniels on the pizza-stealing front. And do you want me to have a fat spaniel?'

Robert sighed and leant down, passing his last sliver of greasy pepperoni off his pizza to Millie, who ate it happily, watched him for a moment, and then sauntered off to hassle Casey.

'So, let's see what we have chronologically,' Ellie said, looking at Tinker. 'Why the long face?'

'I'll tell you after the briefing,' Tinker snapped. 'When Ramsey gives me back my phone.'

'It's for her own good, I swear,' Ramsey replied. 'I'm stopping a killing spree.'

Ellie wanted to ask what he meant, but decided it was better to just plough on forwards.

'Okay, so we're in Italy, and Paulo is getting his van ready,' she said. 'He knows what he has, he's delivered it fourteen times before, and he's made a little bit on the side from it.'

'Mama Lumetta decides, no matter what Tommaso says, the psychopathic man-child,' Ramsey muttered. 'So, she brought a lot more money in this time. Like ten times the amount. Why, we don't know, but Paulo has to notice this. Maybe he realises this could be the last delivery he has like this?'

'Possibly. But now Paulo drives to Dover, and while there he gives Brian Watson and Jimmy Mantel two bottles of olive oil as a bribe,' Ellie continued. 'One we know is gold, the other ...'

'Just olive oil,' Tinker nodded. 'Jimmy confirmed this. Also said Brian was expecting two bottles but Paulo only gave him one.'

'So now we need to know why that was,' Ellie noted this

down. 'Maybe someone was paying more attention, or maybe he used it somewhere at the start.'

'Maybe it was kept for something else?' Casey asked. 'You said Richmond mentioned a woman?'

'Yeah, she said at the crime scene they believed Moretti had a woman on the side, and at the time that was a plausible reason for his death, but we're not seeing anything that corroborates this,' Ellie replied.

'Maybe Richmond wanted us looking the wrong way?' Ramsey asked. 'Maybe it helped her somehow?'

'Let's come back to that in a minute,' Ellie nodded, writing it down.

'We also know Brian may have placed the sat nav circuit into the van,' Tinker added. 'But it's hearsay, and only from what Jimmy thought he saw. Brian was definitely dodgy though. He also tells Paulo to carry on travelling rather than stopping, because of unconfirmed attacks.'

'And who told him this?'

'A Lumetta Oils driver going back,' Tinker replied, 'but that could be bollocks. Especially with who he was working for.'

'Let's follow Brian for a moment,' Ellie nodded. 'He gets the bottle, goes home. He's expecting someone to pick it up, the same person Paulo usually gets to pick these up. And this, surprise, turns out to be Orla Maguire.'

'If she knew about the shipment, she might have told Brian to place the circuit,' Ramsey mused. 'The Maguires steal the bottles, and the gold. Meanwhile, the Lumettas all turn on each other.'

'Possible,' Ellie nodded. 'But, I think there's more here. I think she's working with Paulo, and I think somehow, this is connected to Matteo and Lorenzo.'

'I can answer that,' Casey looked up from a Finders' laptop he was using. 'Carl Fredricks was a bit of a wheeler dealer in the day, from what I can find. And he was arrested back in 2005 for dealing in smuggled goods.'

'Let me guess, goods that came from Orla?'

'Well, it came from Dublin, but not through Matteo,' Casey was reading the screen. 'There was a Paddy McCarthy arrested with him and he was a Maguire enforcer.'

'So, there's every chance they knew each other through that,' Ellie thought back to her conversation with Matteo. 'He said Carl Fredricks was a nice guy, and an old friend of the family. Had legal problems a while back, came to Matteo for help.'

'So far I've only found this one time,' Casey was scrolling as he spoke.

'Matteo said he sorted it and Fredricks was working for them ever since, but that he died a week back.'

'Convenient,' Ramsey replied, eating a slice of garlic bread.

'Very,' Ellie nodded. 'We need to look into ... are you okay?'

Ramsey, realising she was speaking to him, frowned.

'Why wouldn't I be?'

'Because you're only eating the garlic bread.'

Ramsey shrugged, waving his bandaged hand.

'Can't use a knife and fork,' he explained. 'And I'll be damned if I'm eating pizza with my hand, like you philistines.'

'I could cut it up for you?' Tinker suggested.

'Oh, could you?' Ramsey's face brightened, and he leant back, allowing Tinker access to his plate.

Tinker, however, paused.

'I don't trust you not to try to stab me,' she muttered.

'Your instincts serve you right, Tinkerbelle,' Ramsey smiled coldly. 'I'll look into Fredricks, Elisa. I know someone who might help there.'

'Good,' Ellie nodded. 'So now Orla arrives to take her cut, but Brian doesn't have the bottle anymore, as he poured it away.'

'If Orla turns up to pick up the bottle, could she also be the person who killed Paulo and stole the bottles?' Robert, still feeding Millie looked up. 'I mean, she has eleven hundred of them now. Why lose her cool over one bottle?'

'Fair point,' Ramsey puffed his cheeks out. 'This feels more like Orla's pissed she missed out on something. She knows what's in the bottles, she hears the others have been hijacked, she immediately goes to Brian to get what he has, only to find he doesn't have it anymore. She might even have been alerted to Brian after he checks the shipping addresses, after Tinker sends them to him.'

He glanced at Tinker, now paused, mid-pizza slice.

'Or not,' he added hastily. 'It was most likely the time he was supposed to be there, but he skipped the house, deciding to go somewhere public. But she finds him, gets him out on the street somehow. He tells her Jimmy has a bottle, and she goes for him too, but learns it's just, well, olive oil.'

'So, she kills Brian because she doesn't want him telling the police she's involved,' Casey added.

'No, that doesn't work,' Ellie shook her head. 'Jimmy's told us, even if he doesn't tell DCI Richmond. It's out there. I can't see any reason for Orla to kill Brian unless there's something we're missing.'

'Okay, so did you find anything in the house?' Robert asked.

'Is this where you tell us off for breaking in?' Ramsey replied with a half-smile.

'I think you'll find Robert is a little more lax when it comes to breaking and entering these days,' Ellie grinned, waving off Ramsey as he went to speak. 'All things in their time. Go on.'

'The whole place had been turned over,' Ramsey sighed. 'Someone was looking very hard for something that wasn't there, because it'd been poured down the sink.'

'The bins were upturned, the drinks cabinet emptied, anywhere a bottle could have been placed to blend in with others,' Tinker added. 'The problem was, I'd already taken the bottle by that point. There was a call from Jimmy at around nine in the evening, which was stuck on the answerphone, just asking if he was okay, and there was a call from a withheld number around midnight that just did nothing for thirty seconds before disconnecting.'

'Maybe they were waiting for him to pick the phone up?' Ellie asked.

'They'd have a long wait,' Casey replied. 'By that point, he was drinking in the clubs.'

'There was one thing,' Tinker added, pulling out a clear bag with an envelope inside. It was a thin, padded one with Brian's name and address on it, but no stamp. 'They did a good job, but they weren't sure what they were looking for. In a pile of old papers, I found this.'

'No stamp, so it was hand delivered,' Ellie took the bag, turning it in her hand. 'Someone was given it, who didn't know the address. And this here—' she pointed at the back of the envelope, where the words *USE IT ON THE VAN* were written in what looked to be a sharpie pen '—looks to be an order.'

'I thought we might get fingerprints,' Tinker suggested. 'I haven't seen Rajesh yet.'

'This should be with the police,' Ellie muttered as she placed it carefully on the boardroom table, keeping it away from the food.

'Why, because Richmond's sniffing around?' Casey looked up. 'Oh, yeah, right, because Richmond's sniffing around.'

'This is connected to her murder case, so you should take it to her,' Ellie said to Robert, who stared down at the bag as if it was about to attack. 'We might need to send the circuit with it, too.'

'It'll show we took evidence,' Robert replied.

'That's why I'm sending the solicitor with it,' Ellie smiled winningly. 'You can arrange an amnesty before you pass it across. Tell her we didn't know what it was.'

Sighing, Robert placed the bag into his jacket pocket, muttering under his breath.

'I don't trust her,' Tinker muttered. 'And neither does possibly-Olivia.'

Ellie frowned at this.

'Look, possibly-Olivia said Richmond turned up the day of the murder looking for clues, but was found by Brian's locker, and it was open. Brian told her later he'd locked it, but it probably clicked open by accident. And she was back there the following day.'

'Maybe she was looking for clues?' Ellie said. 'And I'd just like to point out, I also feel the same way. As I said about being aimed at Moretti's mysterious woman, I think she'd rather we weren't around. I just really hope she's not dodgy.'

'Lorenzo?' Ramsey asked. 'Could he have dropped it off?'

'He was driving Mama Lumetta on the day of the hijack,

but that doesn't mean he couldn't have done it a while before,' Tinker said.

'And he knew about the broken bottles before we went public,' Ellie suddenly remembered, straightening quickly, a move that threw Millie into alert mode, growling at whatever it was affecting Ellie without knowing exactly what it was. 'When I saw him at Mama Lumetta's, I mentioned someone cut himself at the hijack, and asked him to remove his gloves. He did, and he said "I didn't cut my hands on a broken bottle. No wounds". But I never mentioned it was a bottle.'

'Could have been a guess,' Robert suggested. 'As a lawyer, I think we need a little more here before we grab the pitchforks.'

'Yeah, fair point,' nodding at this, Ellie dipped a crust into some garlic and herb dip, shaking her head at the expectant Millie. 'But I think we can safely say for the moment Brian wasn't part of the murder, even if the people taking the bottles from him, possibly the Maguires, might have been.'

'So, the circuit hacks the van and takes him to the middle of nowhere, and he's killed as the gold is stolen,' Casey said, leaning back from the chair. 'The gold disappears here, someone was cut but we don't know who, and any evidence in the van was set fire to.'

'Only suspects so far are Matteo and Tommaso, maybe the Maguires, maybe Lorenzo,' Ellie counted off on her fingers. 'Bodies so far include Paulo Moretti, Brian Watson and Carl Fredricks.'

'You think he was murdered?' Tinker didn't sound surprised. 'I have to admit, the thought crossed my mind, too.'

'We need to find out how he died,' Ellie reached across,

taking a fallen pepperoni piece from the cardboard pizza box and passing it to Millie.

'Heart attack,' Casey replied to this, turning the laptop around. 'I've been looking into it. Papers say it was natural causes.'

'Wait,' Ramsey sat up suddenly. 'What if we're looking at this the wrong way? What if Carl dying wasn't connected to the heist, but was the actual instigator? The catalyst for everything?'

'I asked Mama Lumetta whether Carl Fredricks was the man who turned the solution back into gold,' Ellie nodded. 'She refused to answer.'

'Okay, so let's do a hypothetical,' Ramsey stood up now, pacing as he spoke. 'Carl takes the smaller shipments, melts the solution like Rajesh's mate did, but instead of tiny nuggets, he's making gold bars. And then he dies. Natural causes. A week later, Mama Lumetta ignores tradition and goes full *Italian Job*, raising the contraband from half a pallet to almost ten times the amount. But she knows Carl is gone, so he can't transform this anymore. Why does she do this now?'

'Because Carl was keeping the gold a secret?' Ellie suggested. 'Maybe with him gone, it was about to be outed to the whole family?'

'Maybe,' Ramsey nodded. 'In the same week, Matteo's making doe-eyes at Nicky Simpson and Tommaso's trying to work out how to do some family pruning. If you look at it from the outside, these are knee-jerk reactions. Matteo teaming with Nicky? After never being involved with him at all? Tommaso deciding that now is the time to make his move? The gold is more important than we thought, not just because it funds something. I don't think either brother knew where the gold was.'

'We need Rajesh to find out whose blood was on the bottle,' Robert said from the side. 'That would make it much easier.'

'I thought it could be Lorenzo,' Ellie nodded, 'but he has his own secrets.'

Quickly, and doing her best to gloss over the part where she lay with Robert on the floor behind a sofa, Ellie explained what she'd seen and heard that evening. When she'd finished, Casey whistled.

'Matteo and Lorenzo, I didn't see that coming,' he said. 'I'll look into him, but it'll take a while.'

'Tell us again what he said on the phone,' Ramsey was frowning to himself as he looked up.

'To his dad, or to the other person?'

'The one we don't know about.'

Ellie considered this.

'He said his dad was getting suspicious, and that he would "pop around the Vaults tomorrow, check the stock's still there",' she replied.

'He then said he'd be passing through Haggerston,' Robert added. 'He was dropping Mama Lumetta off somewhere, so he would go to this place, check, and then come back.'

'He also said he couldn't keep hiding this, and he needed it moved tomorrow,' Ellie continued. 'Which, if it's the gold, doesn't give us long.'

'Twenty-seven,' Casey proclaimed loudly, looking up. 'Sorry, didn't mean to interrupt. Lorenzo is twenty-seven.'

'How old's Matteo?' Ellie looked back at Ramsey.

'Forty-six, I think,' Ramsey was counting back. 'Which

means Matteo was around eighteen when Lorenzo was born in ninety-five, so conceived in ninety-four ... I was working for Mama at the time, but I wasn't that close, as she kept her distance after the, well, you know. I don't recall what was happening ...'

He smiled, looking back at Ellie.

'But I know someone who would. He was active in the nineties, and he'd know what the Vaults was, as he knows most of what happens in East London.'

'No,' Ellie shook her head. 'I refuse.'

'Sorry,' Ramsey shrugged. 'Matteo worked closely with him back in the day. He'd know for sure what was going on. And we know he hates Nicky.'

'Fine,' Ellie sighed, leaning back in her chair. 'Robert, you're on babysitting duties. Millie and Tinker.'

'Why do I need to be babysat?' Tinker exclaimed.

'Because you want to kill someone in Aldershot,' Ellie reminded her. 'Yeah, I was told. I suggest you hold fire on that. We might need you tonight. Especially if we only have until morning.'

'And me?' Casey asked.

'You're going home to your mother,' Ellie said, looking at her watch. 'You've got an hour before your curfew. But—' she held up a hand to stop his complaining, '—I'll need you to get working on this once you're in your bedroom, yes?'

'Aye aye, Cap'n,' Casey grinned. 'And what will you be doing?'

Ellie almost glared at the apologetic Ramsey.

'I'm off to Globe Town, it seems,' she said. 'To have a word with Johnny Lucas.'

18

PEOPLE'S CANDIDATE

To be honest, Ellie hadn't known what to expect when she arrived at Globe Town, in particular Bullard's Place and the Globe Town Boxing Club. As she walked towards the main doors to the building, she paused.

'Can you hear applause?' she asked, checking her watch. It read eight-fifteen. 'Why are people applauding?'

Before Ramsey could reply, Ellie walked through the doors and into the boxing club. It had been renovated a few months earlier, the spit-and-sawdust look now gone, replaced by state-of-the-art equipment, shiny weight and running machines that lined the walls, and equally new leather heavy bags surrounding the boxing ring itself, positioned in the centre of the room. In the back were the offices of Johnny Lucas, and by the door was a recently created CrossFit corner, including chin up poles and kettle bells.

But this wasn't what Ellie was taken by as she entered; the whole area was filled with chairs, ten deep and fifteen wide, on them sat locals, sitting and applauding Johnny Lucas as, in his sixties, his salt-and-pepper greying hair blow-dried back, giving it volume, he straightened his tie and held his hands up, waving for the noise to calm down. He was suited, but no longer wore his trademark black or navy-blue shirts, for there was no need to. The Twins were, for all intents and purposes, gone. And so, he wore a pale-blue shirt and burgundy tie, as he spoke to his captive locals.

'I know it's still a matter of months away,' he carried on, having obviously been mid-flow when his audience had interrupted his speech, 'but I don't want to wait until the By-Election. I want to do the things the current MP for Bethnal Green and Bow is failing to complete. To be here for you, whatever you need, both night and day. And, if not for myself, then for Mickey "The Fist", who gave his life for this place. And if not for him, then for you, and every other down-trodden resident who's been forgotten by this government!'

More applause broke out, and even a couple of people stood up at this. Johnny, to his credit seemed to shy away from showboating here, but as he looked to the doors, and saw Ellie and Ramsey, his eyes glittered with either malice, or some kind of mischievous energy.

'We might not be angels, but we're still here,' he said, pointing over at Ellie. 'A place where onetime cops and criminals they hunted now work together as allies, for the betterment of us all.'

The crowd, not knowing who the two new people were, clapped a little more politely at this, although a few of the older women in the audience seemed to know Ramsey, as shown by either their wolf whistles, or boos, depending on what their history with him probably was. Ellie wondered if some of the boos were for her, too – after all, she'd cut her teeth in the Mile End crime unit under DCI Monroe only a few years earlier, and the people around here had long memories.

'In three months, we'll prove the people of London haven't lost their spirit,' Johnny finished, nodding to the side where Pete, one of the track-suited trainers of the club offered a cardboard box, passing it up the middle, like the reverse of a church donation box, with the people instead taking out shiny metal badges and passing them along the rows.

'Wear them proudly!' Johnny said, pulling a badge out and pinning it to his own chest. 'Let's show those fat cats the common folk can't be trampled down!'

Ellie took a badge from Pete, who winked as he passed her. Both Ellie and Ramsey had known Pete for years, and the irony of the position he was in wasn't wasted on him; not more than six months back, he was head enforcer to the king of East London, when he wasn't training boxers. And now he seemed to be head of marketing for an election campaign.

The badge was simple; it was a boxing glove, a logical choice considering the history the club had in the community. On it were the words "*Johnny Lucas – fighting for Bethnal Green and Bow*" in big red letters. Ellie wanted to ask who Johnny was fighting, but she knew this was a tangent she needed to back away from. Instead, she stepped to the side as the audience rose, some walking past her as they left, while others availed themselves of the free tea and biscuits laid out on a table hastily placed above the weight rack.

Johnny was shaking hands with a queue of locals as they did this, but while smiling, his eyes didn't leave her own.

He knew this wasn't a social call.

'Ellie, Ramsey,' he said across the crowd to them. 'I'm a little busy for social calls.'

'But you literally just said you were here for us, whatever

we needed, both night and day,' Ellie smiled warmly in response, almost enjoying the uncertainty on Johnny Lucas's face. 'We can wait in the back office if you want?'

'No, no, you can wait there, but I might be awhile,' Johnny turned and thanked another attendee as they shook his hand enthusiastically.

'Fine by me, we can work on the heavy bags,' Ellie said, and then winced as she looked at Ramsey. 'Well, maybe not both of us.'

Walking over to Pete, now having given up his role as "badge giver", and returning to the more subtle role of "enforcer in the shadows", Ellie turned, leaning against the ring, matching Pete as she watched the crowd.

'Can you believe this?' she asked with a half-smile. 'A few years ago, I was trying to nick him. Now he's going for Parliament.'

'Actually, yeah,' Pete replied, still watching Johnny. 'He's always had this certain something, you know? It's what pushed him to the top of the East London food chain. We always said he could have made something of himself no matter where he was thrown. He could make it to Prime Minister.'

'I wouldn't go putting too many bets down on that,' Ellie replied and was about to make another joke, when she quickly glanced at the boxing trainer-cum-enforcer, and realised he was completely serious.

'I hope he's doing this for the right reasons,' she settled on saying, watching Johnny finish his circle of hand shaking, leaving the milling audience to their biscuits and paper cups of tea as he eventually walked over to Ellie.

'Here to cash in your favour?' he asked.

'No, but we could use your advice,' Ellie replied. 'If you're not too busy? It involves the Lumettas.'

At the name, Johnny's entire posture changed.

'I'm a legitimate businessman and candidate for the Bethnal Green and Bow upcoming By-Election,' he breathed. 'I don't converse with criminals.'

'Anymore,' Ramsey mumbled. As Johnny looked at him, he gave an innocent look, holding up his bandaged hand.

'Did I say something?' Ramsey asked innocently. 'I apologise. The pain medication. It just comes out sometimes. No idea what I say.'

'I heard about that,' Johnny nodded at the hand. 'Tommaso was out of line. But desperate people do desperate things in desperate times.'

'That's a lot of desperates,' Ellie responded. 'Looks like you know more than you're letting on, anyway.'

Johnny Lucas stared at Ellie for a good few seconds before replying.

'And you won't use the favour?'

Ellie shook her head.

'Then you'll owe me a fee for the information,' Johnny replied. 'Don't worry, what's the line you say? It's something you can afford.'

'Go on,' Ellie said. She'd expected to have to pay something; she just hoped the cost wasn't too high.

'The hijack, a couple of nights ago,' Johnny started. 'It wasn't just olive oil, was it? You tell me, honestly, what was stolen, and I'll answer any and all questions you have.'

He looked at his watch.

'It's just gone eight-forty,' he said. 'I have to be out of here before nine, so you have, let's say, fifteen minutes. If you're honest.'

'You'll answer honestly?' Ellie asked.

At this, Johnny scoffed.

'When have I ever not been honest with you?' he replied. 'You're one of the few people around – the both of you are – that have that honour.'

Ellie nodded, mulling this over.

'Four million pounds of contraband gold,' she said. 'Hidden in the bottles.'

Johnny whistled.

'No wonder they're running around like headless chickens,' he said. 'No candidates yet?'

'That's the problem,' Ramsey replied. 'For four million, they're all blasted candidates.'

'Four million,' Johnny was still whistling. 'You're lucky I've gone legit, or I might consider throwing my hat into the ring on this one. How did they smuggle it?'

'You said to tell you what was stolen, not how it was smuggled,' Ellie snapped back, keeping the smile plastered on her face so the locals in the boxing club didn't think anything was awry. 'But I'll promise to tell you everything once we've sorted it. Deal?'

'Deal,' Johnny spit into the palm of his hand and held it out to shake. Sighing, Ellie did the same, shaking Johnny's hand before wiping it on her coat. She was actually a little put out to see Johnny immediately place some antibacterial hand gel onto his own hands, wiping them down.

'Don't take it personally,' he said, nodding at the locals at the biscuit table. 'I shook hands with all of them, God knows what was on my hands.'

'Which you just shook mine with,' Ellie now stared at her own palm as if it was about to attack, but then Ramsey politely coughed, and as she looked at him, he squirted some of his own hand gel into her hand.

'I can't believe you don't have your own,' he said, genuinely surprised. 'With the amount of dodgy places we end up rooting through.'

'I wear latex gloves,' Ellie muttered. 'And when it's terrible rooting about, I send you.'

'Right then, what do you want to know?' Johnny asked.

'A couple of things,' Ellie rubbed her hands together as she spoke. 'But first, I want to know about Matteo's illegitimate son.'

If Johnny had been expecting anything here, this was not the question. He stepped back, more in stunned silence, before regathering his thoughts.

'He's rumoured to have a few,' he smiled. 'You'll have to be specific.'

'A boy, around the mid-nineties,' Ramsey said, carefully omitting the name of the child. 'Matteo would have been eighteen back then.'

'Ah, the Dublin babe,' Johnny nodded now. 'It was an interesting time in London during the early nineties, Major and the Tories were on the way out, the Kemp brothers had done that movie on the Kray Twins, and it'd revitalised the East London gang community, with every old bugger in Whitechapel suddenly claiming they were "good old boys" the Krays used to know, because everyone wanted the rub from the movie press. I wasn't bothered by that, and by then I was on my own, rebuilding my empire after the Turk tried to destroy it a couple of years earlier. Anyway, around this time, Matteo Lumetta comes into my life. He's what, maybe fifteen at this point, pissed off at his dad and his older brother, and he's dropped out of school and wants to be his own man.

And, knowing I'm good at what I do, he turns up here, in this very boxing club.'

He looked around, imagining it back in the day.

'I said I'd teach him boxing, nothing more. The Lumettas were connected to Dublin and the mountain routes into Northern Ireland, and this was before the Good Friday Agreement; we were still getting IRA attacks over here. That's not to say the Lumettas were IRA, but they probably knew people who could really screw you up. People gave them a wide berth, allowed them to do what they wanted. And all they really wanted to do was bugger around with the Micks in Boston, so we were fine with that. They didn't want to muscle in on us, so we allowed them to do their own thing.'

'So how long was he here?'

'He turned up twice a week for two years. And, during that time, he hung out with some of my younger ... well, employees. He got a street's-eye view of London; one his family never showed him. He put together his own crew, did a few minor jobs, just pocket money stuff, and of course I knew nothing about this.'

'Of course,' Ellie smiled.

'Anyhow, he gets into a scrap in Soho,' Johnny continued. 'Bad one. Papa Lumetta turns up here with a face of thunder, and I tell him I'm nothing to do with it. Papa tells me he's banning Matteo, who's now almost seventeen, from coming back. I agree to abide by this, but point out that even with me not around, Matteo's got the bit between his teeth now, has a taste for blood, and the police are asking questions. So, they decide to send him back home.'

'To Italy?' Ramsey was surprised at this. 'Sounds more like *The Godfather* every day.'

'No, you fool, to Dublin,' Johnny shook his head. 'Anyway,

this is done to tame him, and he buckles down. However, we then hear stories of him sleeping with one of the daughters of a rival family, and now she's up the duff. The Irish contingent send him straight back to London, and from what I hear the baby was put up for adoption, with neither family knowing who took it in.'

He smiled.

'I didn't even know it was a boy until you said "son", so I'm guessing you know who it is?' he asked. 'Go on, I won't tell.'

Ellie sighed.

'We think it's Mama Lumetta's driver, Lorenzo,' she said. 'He called Matteo, and in the call, he used "dad" to identify him.'

'Maybe he's like a step-dad?' Johnny suggested.

'Maybe, actually. Thanks, Johnny, you've explained a lot here,' Ellie nodded. 'Also, do you know who the daughter of the rival family was?'

'Yeah, I do that, and so do you, as you nicked her enough,' Johnny grinned. 'It was Orla Maguire.'

At this, Ramsey and Ellie glanced at each other.

'You're sure?' she asked.

'As sure as one can be when there's no baby to prove it,' Johnny shrugged. 'It was well known around then she was sent to some family near Derry for a few months. She returned a lot darker, and a lot slimmer, if you know what I mean.'

Ellie did. She couldn't know how it'd feel to have your child taken from you, but she guessed it'd take you to a pretty dark place.

'I'm guessing this was a catalyst in making her the woman she is now,' she said.

'That and the insane grandparents she lived with,' Johnny

shrugged, eager to get back to his glad-handing and baby kissing. 'Now, was that it?'

'One more thing,' Ellie held up a hand. 'Storage units in a place called the Vaults. Do you know it?'

At this, Johnny looked over at Ramsey.

'You haven't told her?' he asked.

'I felt it spoke to a part of my past I don't talk about anymore,' Ramsey shrugged. 'And if I recall, you have a better connection to it, anyway.'

At this, Johnny nodded, accepting the comment.

'The Vaults is the name for a storage unit building near London Fields on the Blackstone Estate,' he said to Ellie. 'Probably mid-way between you and me if you diverted via Hackney. It's off the books, known by people, well ...'

He grinned.

'The people who owe you favours, let's just say.'

'So, it's a place to store stolen goods?' Ellie asked.

'That and things you don't want your rivals or the police finding,' Johnny replied, lowering his voice as he continued. 'They used to be one of those Acorn self-storage places, or the one that has the lock as a logo, I forget. Corridors of garage doors, each one locked and rising when opened, no questions asked to the contents inside. You pay a yearly fee, regardless, and you can come in and out as you need. No CCTV, either, for obvious reasons.'

'What if someone steals from there?' Ellie frowned.

'Well, then they probably call you, don't they?' Johnny waved across the room. 'There's a three-year waiting list to get in, so if Lorenzo has a stash there, according to the conversation you heard, he's had it a while, or he's using someone ...'

He stopped.

'Danny Martin,' he said. 'He used to have a spot there, I even sorted it for him. Been in prison for almost a year now though, I wonder if he's let someone use his keys?'

Danny Martin. That was a name Ellie hadn't heard for a while. One of Johnny Lucas's most trusted advisors and right-hand man at one point. Around a year back, he'd gone against Johnny, attempting power after the bodies of his daughters, both murdered years earlier, were found. He'd been caught by Ellie's old mentor, DCI Monroe and his team, and Ellie still held a little piece of bitterness about this. If she'd not been framed for Bryan Noyce's murder, she would have most likely moved into his new City of London unit, and *she* would have been the one taking Martin down, rather than his new protégé DI Declan Walsh.

But Danny Martin was close to Johnny Lucas. If he allowed Lorenzo use of it, could this have been while looking to take down his master, or while he was looking to protect him?

'Would he know Lorenzo?' she asked, coming out of her thoughts.

'He knew Mama Lumetta, and he was close with Matteo back in the day, so quite possibly,' Johnny nodded. 'I'll get Pete to check into it, send you the number. Maybe it can help you somehow.'

Ellie nodded thanks and then stepped back as Johnny suddenly found himself surrounded by eager locals who, unable to wait any longer, had decided to crash the conversation.

'Appreciated,' she said, motioning for Ramsey to leave with her.

'Reckless,' Johnny said, halting her. 'You still have membership here, but I haven't seen you in the ring lately.'

'Got a dog now,' Ellie smiled. 'Makes it more difficult.'

'Bring the pupper along,' Johnny replied, distracted now by the others. 'We're pet friendly.'

As Ellie and Ramsey walked out into the evening air, Ellie looked sideways at Ramsey, currently fiddling with his hand.

'Did you have a storage lockup there?' she asked.

'I did,' Ramsey replied. 'It's why I felt a little bad mentioning it. I gave it up, though.'

Ellie smiled.

'You mean you moved everything elsewhere, right?'

Ramsey smiled back in response as they walked to her car.

'Nicky Simpson bought out an entire floor,' he explained. 'I didn't enjoy having anything of mine so close to ... well, him.'

'Understandable,' Ellie said as she entered her side of the car. 'Come on, let's go look at the Vaults.'

19

VAULTED

ROBERT WASN'T SURE HOW "BABYSITTING DUTIES" WITH TINKER and a Cocker Spaniel turned into a night-time walk into Shoreditch, but here he was, at close to nine at night, walking into an East End pub with Tinker in the lead, hoping he'd made the right choice, and that he wasn't just enabling her to kill random squaddies in connection with her own private issues.

The *Crown and Thistle*, nestled into a street crossroads somewhere between Shoreditch and Brick Lane was a small, out of the way "boozer" that looked like it'd been built during the Industrial Revolution, with the top two external floors of the three-storey building blank and nothing more than plaster, while the bottom level was completed by green tiles, seven small windows and an ornate black sign which explained, in gold writing, how there'd been a pub here since 1792.

The inside looked little better; a long bar ran around the middle as the drinking area seemed to be more of a U-shape, with pale cream walls covered in old *Punch* sketches, secured in as varied a collection of frames as you could find, and mahogany furniture placed on a deep red carpet, many of which were occupied by lone drinkers or furtive groups, whispering to each other. The bar was filled with as many pumps as could humanly be placed on a bar, and behind one of them a burly man in his fifties looked up at Tinker, Millie and Robert as they entered.

'Oi,' he said, the pub instantly going quiet as he looked at the new arrivals. Robert almost turned there and then and left, leaving Tinker to whatever plans she had.

'Yes?' Tinker replied defiantly.

The barman nodded to Millie.

'Does she need a bowl of water?' he asked, as the pub returned to life.

'That'd be nice,' Robert let out a long breath as he followed Tinker around the bar, eventually stopping at the end where a man, in his late-thirties, with short black hair and curated stubble under a navy pea-coat and jeans sat, nursing a pint. She stopped beside him, waiting patiently until he looked up, noticing her for the first time.

'Erik,' she said, through introduction. It wasn't posed as a question, a confirmation on whether the man actually was named thus, but more a statement. She spoke as if she knew this man.

Or, at least, she gave the *impression* of knowing him.

The call had come through while they finished pizza in the office; Tinker had bemoaned the fact she wasn't allowed out on her own, but accepted she probably would have driven straight to Aldershot. And, as they munched on the last slices, feeling a little left out from all the other adventures, a message had come through from one of her contacts. Carl Fredricks had a brother, Erik, and he was in town for the funeral. Well, the funeral and then the closing up of the business, anyway. And, she'd been given the address of one of his usual haunts, an old "spit and sawdust" pub, one of the last remaining ones, it seemed, in the run-down area between Brick Lane to the west, and Shoreditch to the east, nestled within an area of pop-up shops and bars, colourful graffiti'd walls and music management companies.

And somehow, and Robert still didn't know how, Tinker Jones had convinced him to go with her there.

Erik Fredricks looked up from his half-filled pint, glancing at Tinker.

'I don't know you,' he said, his gaze moving across to Robert, and then down to Millie, where they suddenly sparkled with delight.

'Well, hello *you*,' he said, leaning down and stroking the smiling Millie. 'You're a beauty.'

Robert now knew why Tinker had insisted he brought Millie along; when they checked Erik on social media, they'd seen in several photos that Erik Fredricks owned Cocker Spaniels.

'Her name's Millie,' Robert explained. 'She's five.'

'She's wonderful,' Erik smiled, and it was genuine, as he passed Millie a pork scratching nugget from the bag he'd been eating from, now forgotten on the bar. 'So, what do you want?'

'You're right, we've never met you,' Tinker continued. 'But we knew your brother Carl. I wanted to pay my respects.'

Erik had warmed up, but there was still the slightest hint of suspicion in his eyes.

'You weren't at the funeral,' he said.

'A lot of us weren't,' Tinker replied. It was a calculated

guess, something she hoped couldn't be corroborated. 'You know, the people he knew in the shadows.'

She waved at the barman.

'Same again, make that two, and a—'

'And a Coke with ice,' Robert made a smile, pointing at Millie. 'I'm the designated driver.'

'So,' Erik leant back now, watching Tinker. 'You were one of *those*.'

'I'm not sure what that means, exactly,' Tinker kept her face emotionless. This was a dangerous game she was playing, as they still weren't a hundred percent convinced Carl had been the man who smelted the gold back into bars. But it was too late to back off.

'You're with the *Lumettas*.'

Erik filled the words with venom, and Tinker quickly shook her head, instantly re-evaluating the situation. There was no love lost here, so there was a chance she could create an asset rather than an enemy.

'Do we look like them?' she said, making light of the accusation. 'We were, shall we say, more of a side hustle.'

'My brother was exclusive,' Erik replied.

'Even exclusives have time for personal projects,' Tinker grinned. 'I'm Tinker, this is Robert.'

'What sort of projects?'

'Smelting projects.'

Erik nodded, looking back to the bar as his new pint arrived.

'Well, I hope you have all your projects finished,' he said softly, 'because the smelting's stopping. I'm a legitimate businessman. I'm not my brother, and I don't have his ... problems. We're closing the process down, and I'm moving it closer to home, which is way up north.'

Tinker picked up her drink, sipping it as she took this in. It was known Carl had some kind of financial issues, as he'd been arrested for smuggling items in 2005, and Matteo had apparently bailed him out, likely paying the legal fees.

'I didn't come here to ask if we could continue,' she said, raising her glass in salute. 'I came to toast Carl.'

Erik looked surprised at this, but clinked glasses.

'You'll go elsewhere?'

'He wasn't the only one in town who did what he did,' Tinker said, deciding once more to play a card. 'And I got the impression he hated doing it, anyway.'

'Yeah,' Erik muttered, and it was more of a growl than a reply. 'He didn't enjoy the family business, you know? Came to London to make his name. Then about fifteen, twenty years ago he had some problems—'

'You mean when he was arrested with the Irish lad?' Tinker interrupted, hoping the knowledge would show a little more of his cards. 'He spoke of that once to us. It was accidental, and I don't think he even realised he'd spoken it, but he gave the impression he was bound to the Lumettas or something?'

'Yeah, he owed Matteo, that's the son, for getting him out,' Erik sipped at his drink. 'And for about ten years, he was their gopher, doing whatever they wanted. Sickened me, it did. Told him to come home so many times, but he never would. Then one day he turns up, says he wants to go into business with me, and tells me to bring my equipment, or at least some of it, down south. Says he thinks we can make a go of it in London, or at least with a London warehouse. Sold me on all the arty metalworkers around here. And I agreed, as I'd actually been considering it.'

'So, you went into business with Carl?' Robert asked,

forgetting to mask his surprise at this, considering they were already supposed to know. However, Erik took it as a question to his own intentions, and shrugged.

'We did it as a joint venture, and he put up some of the money, but it was my company, equipment, all that. And we made some money, enough to keep profit. And then the Italians came with their insulting company.'

'Insulting?' Now it was Tinker's turn to be confused.

'Whipcrack Holdings,' Erik snapped. 'They made Carl the director, gave him twenty or thirty grand a year for the privilege, but it was a front for a dozen dodgy things. He was there to take the blame when it all fell through. And the name? A message. Telling him they still cracked the whip. And once this started, the special jobs began.'

'The olive oil,' Tinker said softly.

Erik's eyes widened slightly.

'He really did tell you everything, didn't he?' he whispered, and Tinker actually felt a twinge of shame for leading this obviously innocent man on.

'As I said, we were close,' she lied. 'Well, as close as you could be with him.'

'Yeah, I get that. Anyway, they started bringing these bottles to him around two, three years ago. Pretty much after he got involved with the company. They knew we had the chemical knowledge, or at least knew people with the knowledge to do all the things needed to make the liquids into solids, and then smelt it back into bars. But he wasn't proficient in it, so I came down a couple of times a year to do this with him.'

He leant back on his stool, sighing.

'That's how I saw the way they treated him,' he added. 'And I swore I'd find a way to stop it. But his debt was too great, and he was now making money on the side from this, and he didn't want to stop.'

Tinker was about to take a sip of her pint, but stopped, the lip of the glass beside her mouth.

'Money on the side?'

'Oh, don't worry, I wasn't meaning you. I didn't even know you existed,' Erik smiled, but it quickly faded. 'I think he would siphon off some of the gold from each batch, and send it to Whipcrack. He could claim it was from the process, that some of the gold solution would evaporate out as steam, even saying the people in Italy who'd turned it into liquid had done it wrong and wasted the product, but for every hundred grand or so he'd gain, he was pulling around ten percent off for his friends. And the Lumettas, annoyed at the loss, still found it more palatable than the forty to fifty percent they'd lose going through Customs.'

Tinker wasn't the best at maths, but even she could see what Carl and Whipcrack Holdings were taking here. If every "special" delivery had half a pallet, that was approximately a hundred and ten bottles. At three and a half grand each, that was around four hundred grand each time. And if Carl was removing, say, forty grand a go? Then, in fourteen deliveries, he'd skimmed over half a million in two, maybe three years.

If someone outside of the Whipcrack cabal learnt this, that would be reason enough for Carl to be killed.

'Who did you deal with in Whipcrack?' she asked.

'You don't want to be dealing with them,' Erik's voice soured. 'They're death.'

'No no, I was thinking we'd make sure we could avoid them,' Tinker shook her head. 'I don't need hassle like that.'

'Never met them all,' Erik thought about this for a moment. 'I met the Italian—'

'Matteo?'

'No, the driver. Paulo something. He was part of this. Would tip them the nod or something whenever there was a big-time delivery coming. I never asked too much. And then there was Matteo, and the Irish woman, never got her name.'

'Red hair?'

Erik smiled weakly.

'Don't they all have red hair?' he asked. 'Anyway, she's why I'm here still.'

'How so?' Robert was feeding Millie a biscuit treat as he looked up.

'So, Carl passed a week back,' Erik explained. 'Accidental causes, found in the warehouse, they think he just had a heart attack and died. He was only forty-two. Shite way to go. Anyway, a couple of days after, I let Matteo know I'm closing up shop. But he then says Mama Lumetta has one last big job, and then, after that, all debts are squared. It was already coming in, so I agreed we'd do that and move on, as the last thing I wanted was Carl's debt still hanging over my bloody head. Then I hear Paulo's dead, the stock's gone, and the smelting isn't needed. But then I get a message from someone else this might still happen, and the bottles will be brought to me tomorrow. So, here I sit, waiting like an idiot.'

'What time tomorrow?' Tinker asked, remembering Ellie's comment about Lorenzo, stating he'd check the "Vaults" the following day. 'I just ask because it'd be nice to come in and look at the place one last time.'

'I'll be there all day, but I don't think they'll arrive until lunchtime,' Erik replied, 'and I don't think this will be a quick job. It'll probably take the rest of the week to finish it.'

Tinker nodded.

'Well, we might see you again,' she said, motioning

slightly with her head to Robert; it was time to get out of there before Erik started suspecting. 'Stay safe, yeah?'

'I always do,' Erik smiled.

'One last thing,' Tinker stopped. 'Who told you the last shipment was coming?'

Erik turned to face Tinker now, examining her again.

'You didn't know my brother, did you?' he asked.

Tinker thought about lying again, but instead shook her head.

'Sorry, but no,' she replied. 'But if it helps, we're looking to gain justice for his death.'

'You think it wasn't an accident?'

'I don't know, Erik, and I wish I could answer that better,' Tinker stated. 'But know this, if he was killed, the people who did it will suffer.'

'Why?' Erik frowned, shaking his head. 'What was Carl to you?'

'A piece of a puzzle,' Tinker explained, her face ice cold. 'One that, when we finally put together, we're going to light up and burn into ash.'

Erik smiled, and it was a dark, bitter one.

'It was a woman,' he said. 'I never heard the Irish bitch speak, so I assume it's her. But her accent was weak, almost non-existent. She told me to wait for a call from someone called Lorenzo. Does that help?'

'It does,' Tinker nodded. 'Sorry for lying to you.'

'Whether or not he died naturally, those bastards made his life hell,' Erik replied coldly. 'You can pay me back by destroying each and every one of them.'

And with this demand made, Erik Fredricks gave Millie one more ruffle of the head and then turned away, the conversation over.

With Robert already leading, Tinker left the pub, feeling the cold air on her face as she emerged out into the London night.

'Do you think Carl was murdered?' Robert asked.

'I think stealing a half a million is enough for anyone to be murdered,' Tinker shoved her hands into her jacket pockets to keep them warm. 'But if that's the case, it's likely Mama Lumetta was the one who called the hit.'

'I really hate this gig,' Robert muttered as they walked back to Finders, and the remains of cold pizza waiting for them.

20

OPEN SESAME

JOHNNY HAD BEEN AS GOOD AS HIS WORD, AND BY THE TIME Ellie and Ramsey reached London Fields, a text had come through not only giving the number of Danny Martin's old storage area, but the name of someone to ask for, who was still loyal to Johnny Lucas and his empire, even if he was moving into politics.

Which, frankly, was still terrifying.

The Vaults were a warehouse at the back of an industrial estate, surrounded by *Screwfix* stores, courier warehouses and what looked to be a pole dancing school, although Ellie hadn't really paid attention while driving, and it was only Ramsey's excited yelps that even pointed the location out. They parked out the front of what was effectively an enormous, three-storey high, red-bricked building, maybe fifteen years old, with a large roller door to the side, large enough to drive a Luton van into, and a door to the right of it. Ellie guessed the people who used this place often needed to bring in vans, so the roller door probably led to an area where things could be removed, maybe even with a forklift truck.

If the van had been hijacked, and the product brought here, Ellie wondered why they simply hadn't driven it in, rather than burning it. She supposed it was a fear of the ANPR cameras catching them, or even a confusion about what to do with it afterwards.

After all, places like the Vaults made their reputations on people not shitting on their doorsteps, she considered.

The door, an A4 sign on the other side of the wired glass stating the location was "Open 24 Hours" was locked, which meant that even though the location was open, the door wasn't. There was a buzzer on the side, and Ellie pressed it, aware the CCTV camera on the wall above them had rotated slightly and was now aimed at them.

They were being watched.

'Yes?' A male voice spoke through the speaker.

'We're here to speak to Squeaky,' Ellie said, really hoping Johnny Lucas wasn't pissing around.

'Squeaky's not here,' the voice continued, a hint of suspicion in it. 'You have a storage unit?'

'We're here on behalf of Johnny Lucas,' Ramsey leant in. 'It's his unit.'

There was a click, and a moment of silence.

'Squeaky said he doesn't know you.'

'I thought you said Squeaky wasn't there—' Ellie started, but a warning shake of his head from Ramsey stopped her. *Confrontations wouldn't help here.* '—Johnny said to tell Squeaky he still owed him for the Vaseline.'

Ellie didn't know what this meant or why there was a debt, but after a moment the door buzzed, and Ellie could pull it open. Walking through, they faced a staircase leading up to what looked to be a fire door.

'Up we go, then,' Ramsey said cheerfully, and Ellie

wondered if this was because he found himself in a warehouse filled with stolen items, and this was powering his criminal side up, like caffeine, on a tough morning.

Walking through the door, they found themselves in a bare white reception room. There was a small, no bigger than A2-sized window at the other end, a high table in front of it that looked through into another office, just as bare, and the whole thing reminded Ellie of a post office or bank, and she had no doubt the glass was bulletproof.

And, if someone came in to steal something, they'd have a tough job getting through the door, and the many likely weapons the other side of it.

'I'm Squeaky,' a man said, as he appeared in the window; he was in his sixties, slim and wore a dirty blue overall, wiping his greasy hands with a rag. 'I'm fixing the forklift, so apologies for the look.'

He squinted as he stared at Ramsey.

'You'd better be on your best behaviour, Allen,' he said with what seemed to be recognition. 'We audit the lockers, so we *will* know.'

Ramsey frowned, walking closer, and then his eyes widened in utter delight.

'Willie James!' he exclaimed. 'Bloody hell, I heard you were in Belmarsh!'

'I was,' Squeaky replied. 'But it was only a two-year stint. Got out a couple of years back and walked straight back into this job.'

'Why Squeaky?' Ellie couldn't help herself.

'I got caught burgling a house a few years back,' Squeaky shrugged. 'Door squeaked open. I'd used WD40 on it, but it hadn't worked. Anyway, when I got out six months later,

Johnny, or maybe Jackie, I could never tell them apart, sent me a tub of Vaseline in the post. Said it was better to rub into hinges, as the jelly acts as a lubricant, and doesn't get WD40 all over you. But I was called it ever since. Which is fine, as I'd got sick of being called "Willy" by the younger generation of wannabe Twokers.'

'Yeah, I see that,' Ramsey smiled, looking at Ellie. 'Twoker is slang for thieves who take items without the owner's consent. When they're arrested, they have TWOC written on their charge sheets. Hence, Twokers.'

'Wow, thanks for letting me know that,' Ellie deadpanned. 'I mean, having been a copper for many years, I'd never have known such a thing.'

Ramsey's face darkened as Ellie grinned.

'Good to see you're still working for Johnny Lucas, although I heard he'd gone legit.' Squeaky sniffed at the thought. 'Still, I'm guessing those wankers in Parliament aren't exactly squeaky clean.'

He laughed at his own joke.

'You get it? Squeaky clean!' he exclaimed before suddenly becoming all serious, pulling out a book.

'Right then, what number?' he asked.

'You don't have it on computers?' Ellie was surprised at this.

'All analogue, no chance of being hacked,' Squeaky explained, reaching to the side, and pulling out a sawn-off shotgun. 'And anyone who tries the more traditional way gets this.'

'Sixty-two,' Ramsey said quickly. 'It's storage sixty-two.'

Squeaky smiled as he placed the shotgun back out of sight, running his hand down the list.

'Busy box,' he said, marking next to it. 'You're the second people this week to visit. Well, second group, rather.'

'Who was the first group?' Ramsey asked and then winced. 'Sorry. You can't say, can you?'

'Only to the owner, and that's not you,' Squeaky replied, almost apologetically. 'I'm guessing you were given a key?'

Ramsey patted his thigh.

'Right here,' he said.

'Can I see it?'

'No,' Ramsey looked horrified. 'I remember you, Willie. You could make a bump key from one glance at twenty metres. I'm not allowing you a look at this one.'

Squeaky smiled.

'Busted,' he said. 'Go on, piss off, do what you need to do. And if you need anything else, I'll be trying to fix the forklift. Bugger's got some kind of brake-seizing issue.'

Gratefully nodding, Ramsey and Ellie left the reception through a second door that buzzed open as Squeaky walked off, and made their way down some black-painted metal stairs, and through another grey fire door at the end. Now, on the ground floor, they followed the almost garage-width roller shutter doors, along one corridor and then turning right to continue on down a second, until they reached a black roller shutter with the number "62" written on it. On the side was a padlock, a chunky one with some real heft.

'This is it?' Ellie asked, surprised. 'All these criminals and the things they steal, and they hold their items safe with a padlock?'

'There's no CCTV, and no record of people coming in and out, and the padlocks aren't great,' Ramsey replied, already examining the lock. 'But this is also because they don't expect anyone to be stupid enough to burgle this place. It's not just the honour among thieves bollocks, or Willie and his shotgun, there's an unspoken rule. If you shit here, they find you. As I said before, Simpson owns the third floor, and you don't want to get on his radar.'

'How many floors are there?'

'Just three,' Ramsey was pulling out his lock pick set now with his good hand, staring down at it in confusion as he realised he wouldn't be able to do what he wanted. 'And there's a basement too, I think. I had a small locker at the back, didn't need one of these big buggers. Could you do me a favour and hold this tension rod for me? I'm doing this one handed.'

Ellie took the lock picks from Ramsey and moved him aside.

'I think I can do a padlock,' she said. 'I had a good teacher, after all.'

'You had the best teacher,' Ramsey watched down the corridor. 'But hurry, yes? They might not have CCTV, but if Willie comes down here to check on us and finds us picking the lock, we'll be in trouble.'

The padlock clicked open, and Ellie looked at Ramsey triumphantly.

'Well, it's only a padlock,' he muttered sullenly and, with a smile, Ellie passed him back his tools, now back in their case. And, with the padlock removed, she pulled the roller shutter up.

'Shit,' she said as she looked inside.

The light wasn't even needed to be turned on; in the middle of what was almost a double garage-sized area were pallets of extra-virgin olive oil, stacked five rows high.

Turning on the light switch, Ramsey entered the space, motioning for Ellie to pull the shutter down behind her.

'We don't want anyone seeing this,' he said as he examined the towers of bottles. 'Lumetta Oils, 2022. And here, on this one, I can see 2021 on the label.'

'They stole the whole bloody thing,' Ellie whispered. 'I thought they'd just keep the gold.'

Ramsey was already walking around the lockup, examining what else Danny Martin had left there.

'Good Lord, he's got a Banksy,' he muttered. 'Danny Martin has a bloody Banksy. No, actually, that sounds about right.'

'Ramsey, focus,' Ellie waved her hand to regain his attention. 'We're not here for Danny's things, we're here for this.'

'Lorenzo's things,' Ramsey finished, staring up at the bottles. 'How do you think they knew each other?'

'Who?'

'Lorenzo and Danny,' Ramsey looked across at her. 'He had to know him, to know of this place. It's not connected in any way to the Lumettas, so nobody in the family would know. Maybe Nicky told Matteo, and he told his son?'

'I got the impression Matteo doesn't know about this either. But Lorenzo used Simpson's Health Clubs, so maybe this was a more direct connection between the two of them?' Ellie shook her head as her phone beeped. Opening it, she saw a message from Tinker.

Spoke to Carl Fredricks's brother. Carl was skimming 10% off all jobs, took over half a million from Lumettas before he died.

'I thought I told Tinker to wait at the office?' Ellie grumbled.

'Looks like she has the same healthy respect for you the rest of us have,' Ramsey gave a winning smile as he looked at the message. 'But if they killed Carl for stealing ten percent, they'll blood eagle Lorenzo for taking all of this.'

Ellie didn't know what a "blood eagle" was, nor did she want to know, as she leant back against a pile of boxes, staring up at the pallets.

'So, what now?' Ramsey said, watching her carefully. 'You go tell Mama Lumetta you've found her missing sheep?'

Ellie didn't reply.

'Seriously, Elisa, you were hired to find the bottles, and you've found them,' Ramsey pressed harder. 'You have to tell her. The job is done.'

'Three people have died for these,' Ellie spoke softly, barely a whisper.

'You don't know that,' Ramsey added. 'And if they did, every one of the deaths was connected to them probably going off script.'

'And they should be killed for that?' Ellie spun to face the elderly thief, who instantly stepped back from her anger.

'That's not what I said and you know it,' he replied, keeping his voice calm. 'But the fact of the matter is, you're either solving the bottle theft or solving the murder. And, last I heard, it was the police doing the latter.'

Ellie went to reply, but stopped, her body deflating as she slumped against the boxes.

'But they're bad people,' she replied simply.

'Last I saw, that was a sliding scale, and one we're both on,' Ramsey spoke softly now. 'What do you want to do, boss? We'll follow you, no matter what you decide.'

Ellie looked up at the ceiling and then took out her phone.

'We pass what we have to Richmond, and we let her do her job,' she said. 'Meanwhile, we complete our job.'

She dialled a number, placing it on to speakerphone for Ramsey's benefit. After a couple of rings, it answered.

'Mrs Lumetta?' Ellie spoke into the phone. 'It's Ellie Reckless and Ramsey Allen on the line. We have an update for you.'

'Really? I'd be happy to hear it,' the voice of Tommaso Lumetta spoke.

Ellie glanced across the storage locker at Ramsey, seeing him jerk back from the phone instinctively.

'After what you did to one of my people, Mister Lumetta, you'll understand I'd rather speak to your mother,' she said, holding her voice steady.

'And that'll be a problem,' Tommaso said happily. 'She retired today.'

'If you've hurt her—' Ramsey started, but stopped as the sound of Tommaso's laughter echoed around the room.

'You'll what, attack them with your good hand?' he said. 'I'm not a monster, and she's still my mama. But we had a long chat this evening, and she's decided to hand over all power to me. So, if you have anything new to say before I fire you, once again, from this case, let me know.'

Ellie looked at the pallets, considering her options.

'We learned that Carl Fredricks had been stealing from the gold,' she said. 'Possibly mid-six figures worth over the years.'

'Is that it?' Tommaso's voice sneered. 'You called up to grass on a dead man?'

'You don't sound surprised.'

'Of course, I'm not,' Tommaso laughed. 'Why do you think he's singing with the choir eternal?'

'You killed him?' Ramsey asked.

'Didn't you hear, old man?' Tommaso was enjoying this call way too much. 'He had a heart attack. Purely natural.'

At that moment, Ellie knew without a doubt it was far from that.

'So now you work for me,' Tommaso said. 'And I want my gold.'

'Will you honour the deal your mother gave us?' Ellie asked, waving a suddenly protesting Ramsey silent.

'Hell no,' Tommaso chuckled. 'A stupid bloody favour? That's for children. No, I'll just incentivise you by saying if you don't find my gold, then I'll do what I did to your thief to all of you – but I'll use the other edge.'

Ellie kept silent.

'Do you know where my gold is?' Tommaso asked.

'Actually, yes,' Ellie replied, as Ramsey almost exploded in silent frustration.

'And will you tell me where it is before I have to come find you?'

'You know what?' Ellie smiled now. 'You were rude to me at the crime scene, and I get that. But you hurt one of my friends. And for that, you can go *fuck* yourself, Mister Lumetta.'

And that done, she disconnected the call.

'I've never heard you say that word before,' Ramsey was in shock.

'I've never been that angry before,' Ellie replied, already typing another number into the phone. 'And I'll be damned if I'm giving him the gold. And if we can't give it to Mama Lumetta, we might as well solve the whole damn case.'

She paused, speaking into the phone's mouthpiece.

'Johnny,' she said, her voice now light, as she hatched her

plan in her head. 'Change of plan from what I said earlier. It's time to pay your debt. And to be honest, I think you're going to like this one.'

21

CLUB RULES

Casey had received the text early that morning; he wasn't to go to Finders or Caesars for their breakfast meeting, but wait for further instructions where to meet later, and in travelling to it, to make damn sure he wasn't followed.

Tinker had also received the text, but hers had come the night before, while still at Finders. And her text had been more detailed, telling her to make sure Millie and Robert got somewhere safe and hunkered down, as Tommaso Lumetta was likely to be on the rampage. Ellie had also ended this with "Plan Z", which both Robert and Tinker understood. She also understood the lack of any alternate location to meet yet wasn't because Ellie didn't have one in mind, but more because she was making absolutely sure nobody could find it if they grabbed the phone from Tinker and read the message.

Which meant she was also expecting someone to try to take the phone. Which wasn't good.

However, rather than find a place to hide, they both decided that a high floor of a building with built-in security was a good start, and crashed out for the night; Robert on his sofa, with a long coat he had as a blanket, and Tinker on the inflatable roll and sleeping bag she always kept in the coat wardrobe in Ellie's office; only waking around seven in the morning when the faint sounds of the office cleaners could be heard, and her face was suddenly wet with the licks from a confused and hungry Cocker Spaniel, who'd spent the night asleep on the bed in the corner. But, before using the corporate showers (or, rather the one shower that was in the ladies' toilets), she walked down to the underground car park where her Land Rover Defender was, aiming to grab her "go" bag from the back.

Plan Z was a failsafe Ellie had set up after the Danny Flynn case; if everything went pear-shaped, or if they pissed off some underworld kingpin so badly they needed to lie low for a day or two, they'd need a change of clothing, some cash and anything else to help them close to hand. Ellie and Robert had these in their offices, while Ramsey and Tinker kept bags in their cars.

Or, in Ramsey's case, a full-on suit-protector.

Interestingly, even though he hadn't taken it with him when he went out the previous day, his inability to currently drive leaving his hideous old Rover benched in the car park, someone had been in his car during the night, as Tinker could see fingerprints on the back of the boot, where hands would have pushed when closing it down. Walking over and checking it, she saw that there were a clear set of fingerprints in the dirt on the right-hand side, while the left was a little more scuffed. As if a man with a bandage on his left hand had returned, during the night, and taken something out.

So, Ramsey returned to get his go bag too, Tinker thought to herself. *But he didn't come and find us. Probably didn't realise we were upstairs.*

However, as she walked back to the elevator, she paused.

There was a man watching from the main entrance to the car park.

He was young, in a black leather jacket and deep-blue T-shirt, and when Tinker turned to face him, he disappeared as quickly as he'd arrived.

They were being watched. What the hell had Ellie done now?

Walking back to the offices, Tinker saw Robbie had already showered and changed into his own set of new clothing, and was currently using an electric shaver to remove the remnants of the previous night off his chin.

'Millie needs a walk,' he said, nodding over to Ellie's office, where Millie glared at them through the glass. 'I would have taken her, but I know you've both bonded.'

'Let me clean myself up and change into some new clothes, and I'll do it,' Tinker smiled. 'I need an excuse to check outside, anyway.'

Before Robert could ask what she meant, Tinker took her go bag into the women's toilets. And, after a quick shower and change, with her wet hair pulled back and under her baseball cap, she placed the lead on Millie, gave her a quick cuddle, and took her out of the building.

By now it was almost eight in the morning, and London was coming to life. And, as Tinker took Millie around the block, aiming for a grassed residential area she knew nearby, she monitored the glass windows of the buildings beside her. Or, more accurately, *behind* her, using every opportunity, usually when Millie paused to have a sniff of something, to glance down the street.

The young man was still following her.

He didn't look familiar, but that meant nothing in the grand scheme of things. Because he was unknown made him even more of a potential threat. Was he connected to the *Screaming Angels?* Was he something to do with the reason Plan Z had been called?

Tinker pulled out her phone as it buzzed – it was a message from Casey.

On my way to you at office. I have news and I think someone's watching my house.

Tinker swore under her breath. She'd hoped Casey would have been enough on the fringes to avoid whatever this was, and had been clever enough to hunker down. Of course, if someone was following him, she'd rather he was nearby, where she could kick the living crap out of whoever it was.

Now dialling the phone, she placed it to her ear.

'You okay?' It was the voice of Ellie answering the call. She sounded tired.

'I should ask you that,' Tinker said. 'Why are we being followed exactly?'

'I might have told Tommaso Lumetta to go f— um, to make sweet, sweet love to himself last night,' Ellie admitted awkwardly. 'Judging from how he reacted with Ramsey, I thought it best to warn you all.'

'So why isn't he going all psycho on us?' Tinker stopped as Millie decided that here, in the middle of the street, was where she wanted to poop. 'He's not the cautious, waiting kind.'

'He is when he believes I know where the gold is,' Ellie replied. 'And he'll follow you to find me, so lose them before you come to me.'

'And when exactly are you going to tell me where you—' Tinker started, but Ellie had already disconnected the phone. Muttering an obscenity, Tinker pulled out a poop bag and cleaned up Millie's mess, tying the top and placing it into an appropriate bin.

The man behind was finding it harder to have a reason not to pass, and was now staring into a window. Tinker, having had enough, started walking towards him.

The man, seeing this, went to move, but Tinker held up a hand, pointing directly at him.

'You move, and I scream blue murder,' she said loud enough for him to hear, as she continued on. 'I want words.'

The man, now visibly only a teenager looked flustered as Tinker stopped beside him.

'We don't know where it is,' Tinker hissed. 'Tell Tommaso that. You can follow us all you want, but we can't help you. Ellie's in the wind, probably spooked by your boss. Got it?'

Nervously, the young man nodded.

'Good, now piss off because I've gotta give this one her breakfast,' Tinker replied, walking past the man and continuing back to Finders. She'd put on a brave face, but she was concerned. Something had obviously happened last night. *But what was it? Had Ellie and Ramsey found the storage locker? And if so, was the gold in it?*

Arriving back at Finders, Tinker saw Robert had called in a takeaway breakfast.

'We still have cold pizza,' she said as she picked up a bag of kibble, already prepared by Ellie in advance for Millie, in case she wasn't able to get home in time to feed her there, and filled the bowl with it. As Millie hungrily started on it, Ellie noticed Robert shaking his head.

'Cold pizza,' he said. 'Philistine.'

'You can microwave it,' Tinker replied, taking a bacon sandwich. 'We're being followed. Apparently Ellie told Tommaso Lumetta where to go last night, and he's hunting answers.'

'Answers to what?'

'Answers I think involve the location of the gold.'

Robert bit his lip rather than cursing. After gathering his thoughts, he walked to the window.

'She should have told the client if they found the gold,' he said. 'Get it done and dusted. We wouldn't be hiding out in the office for a start. What if the Lumettas come in here guns blazing? I could lose my job.'

Tinker grinned at the concern of employment rather than death.

'They wouldn't do that,' she replied knowledgeably.

'How do you know?' Robert looked back at her.

'Because we're not in a Michael Mann movie?' Tinker suggested innocently as, through the glass wall of the office, she saw Casey enter the floor from the elevator, running down the corridor at a sprint.

'Are you okay?' she asked as Casey half-tumbled into the room.

'No, I'm bloody not,' he panted in reply. 'There's a bloody guy following me. Stopped as I got here. Is mum gonna be okay? Are they going after my family?'

'They're just doing a shit job of following us to Ellie,' Tinker faked a smile for the teenager. 'Don't worry about it.'

'Oh,' Casey seemed a little crestfallen about this. 'I thought it was like—'

'A Michael Mann movie?' Tinker enquired.

Casey, however, had moved on, and was opening his laptop on Robert's desk.

'Is Ellie okay?' he asked as he pulled up lists of data. 'I have something.'

'We're about to go to her, so tell us what you have while we wait for a location,' Robert moved his keyboard aside so Casey could sit at the desk. He had no ego where the teenager was involved, mainly because he knew what Casey could do to his credit rating if he was pissed off.

'I was checking into Whipcrack,' Casey said as he was typing. 'Did you know they've made around half a million in undeclared earnings over the last two years? Crazy. But that's not the big thing. I was searching for stuff on Lorenzo, found him on HOLMES 2.'

'Are you sure you should be hacking into the police main computer network?' Robert asked sarcastically.

Casey looked up from the screen.

'Oh, no mate, it's completely illegal,' he said, straight faced. 'You should totally not allow me to do stuff like that. However ...'

He typed in some numbers and a screen appeared; Lorenzo's face, a slightly more bruised and battered one than what they'd seen before, stared out at them, wrapped into a police report.

'Lorenzo Lamas,' Casey explained. 'His adopted parents' surname. Six months ago, he got into a fight in West Ham, was arrested and placed in a cell overnight. He was never charged, though.'

'Let me guess, it was a simple breach of the peace issue?' Tinker replied, kneeling beside Millie. 'Make him stay the night in a cell, then dump him out?'

'No, he really attacked someone,' Casey shook his head. 'Broke a pint glass and slashed open their cheek.'

'Charges should have been pressed,' Robert now walked

around, peering at the screen. 'Who was the arresting officer?'

'That's not what you should be looking at,' Casey tapped the screen. 'You need to be looking here at who released him.'

Robert puffed out his cheeks and whistled as he saw the name.

DCI LUCY RICHMOND, STRATFORD

'This was before she was transferred to Maidstone.' Casey spun the laptop around so Tinker could also see it. 'DCI Richmond knew Lorenzo well enough to get him off a rather vicious assault charge. Look here.'

Another screen – this time it was a scan of a handwritten note.

Lorenzo Lamas is crucial to a case we're on, please drop all charges for the moment and release him into my care. DCI Lucy Richmond.

'Why does that look familiar?' Tinker frowned, not really expecting an answer.

'Is there any way we can find out if they knew each other outside of this?' Robert continued, but stopped as Tinker's phone dinged.

She read the message, nodded, and then rose from her crouched, dog-nuzzling position.

'Ellie sent me her address,' she said. 'And yeah, she's in trouble if she's there. We need to go now.'

'How come she didn't send me it?' Robert was already closing up his computer.

'Probably because she doesn't trust us all to make it,' Casey replied ominously.

'Right then,' Tinker pulled her army coat, currently tossed on Robert's sofa, back on. 'We'll go in the Defender.'

'My car would be quicker,' Robert suggested, before looking at Millie. 'Although one of you would have to hold Millie on your lap.'

'I know your car would be better, but my car is sturdier,' Tinker said, already rummaging in her go bag, and pulling out a Glock 17 pistol, tucking it into her jacket and ignoring the look of horror from Robert. 'And if people are out there hunting us, *chasing* us, I want a fighting chance. And I'm way more comfortable slamming my Defender into an enemy vehicle than I would be your hairdresser's car.'

'Enemy vehicle?' Casey was placing his laptop back into his own bag. 'You make it sound like we're at war.'

Tinker didn't reply, and Casey wasn't sure if that was scarier than any kind of response.

ONCE THEY WERE BACK IN THE DEFENDER, TINKER EXPLAINED where they were going, ignoring Robert's inevitable tantrum on why Johnny Lucas was back on the scene, instead politely reminding him that there was a Cocker Spaniel sitting next to him, and he should keep his voice down.

She'd also told everyone to place their seatbelts on, clicking Millie's harness to one as well, demanding Robert also shield the dog with his life, if needed. And then, slamming the Defender into gear, she screeched out of the car park, swerving onto the street outside to the annoyance and irritation of the passing traffic forced to stop rather than slam into the side of her, and started eastwards out of the City.

Immediately, she saw the SUV at the corner move into the street behind them.

'Hold on tight,' she said. 'This is going to get a little hectic.'

Before anyone in the Defender could comment on this, she slammed the brakes on and spun the Defender northwards, heading up to the Clerkenwell Road, the SUV following. Pulling out onto the road itself she forced traffic on either side to stop once more and hitting the accelerator, she ignored the approaching lights as she hurtled towards the five-way crossroads at the junction of Old Street and Goswell Road.

'Red lights! *Red lights!*' Casey cried out as Tinker sped up more, ignoring his cries and the traffic crossing as the Defender slammed across the crossroads, the SUV following and failing to match them, clipping the back of a Ford Focus and spinning slightly before righting itself, carrying on. It had, however, lost ground on Tinker who, now speeding down Old Street, slammed the brakes on and spun the steering wheel to the right.

'Hold on!' she said as, behind her, Robert held the struggling Millie tightly. Now heading south on Golden Lane, she whistled a flat tune.

'This reminds me of army training,' she said happily as she wrenched the wheel again, the Defender now turning left into Banner Road.

'Did army training talk about driving down one-way streets in the wrong direction?' Robert yelled from behind. '*Because that's what you're doing!*'

Tinker wasn't listening, mounting the pavement to avoid

an Amazon van travelling in the correct direction, crossing Whitecross Street as she continued. Behind her, way in the back now, she could see the SUV attempting to follow her, but lagging as they tried to thread the needle of oncoming traffic, already thrown off kilter by the maniac in the Defender. And, as she finally turned left onto Bunhill Row, a road going the right direction for a change, she immediately screeched to an almost-stop, as she took a very sharp turn through a parking entrance nestled between two shops, following it around and, as soon as she was out of sight, stopping the Defender in a parking spot as she leapt out of the car, running back to the entrance.

A moment later she returned with a smile on her face.

'They carried on,' she said as she climbed back into the car. 'They'll hit Old Street roundabout in a moment, and they won't have a clue which way we went. We'll backtrack on ourselves, and then carry on to Globe Town.'

'Cool,' Casey said queasily. 'Do you think we can stop somewhere with a toilet? I need to throw up my breakfast.'

Tinker patted Casey on the shoulder and looked back at Robert and Millie.

'Brave soldiers, good dog,' she said as, starting the engine up again, she exited the car park and this time headed south.

22

UNDER THE TARPAULIN

THEY ARRIVED AT THE GLOBE TOWN BOXING CLUB AROUND thirty minutes later, parking around the corner of the building in the middle of a selection of British Gas vans, hoping they would mask the Defender from anyone passing. With Millie now sniffing everything excitedly as she led them without actually knowing where she was going, they entered the club.

Ellie and Ramsey were there; both had changed, probably using the club's changing rooms and showers to freshen up in the process. Ellie knelt down and hugged Millie tightly in front of the boxing ring.

'Did you save them from the nasty villains?' she asked, ruffling the smiling dog's hair. 'And did Auntie Tinker feed you yummies for breakfast?'

'Can someone please tell us what the hell's going on?' Robert, frustrated, asked. 'And why are we in a gangster's—'

He stopped as Johnny Lucas emerged from the back of the club wearing an unusual collection of jogging bottoms and hoodie.

Robert swallowed.

'I mean a *potential Parliamentary candidate's* boxing club?' he finished.

'I needed a favour, and Johnny owed me,' Ellie said, looking back at Johnny.

'I shouldn't have taken the call,' he muttered. 'I've got the press coming in half an hour and I'm going to be standing on stolen property.'

'Only if they pull up the tarpaulin,' Ellie smiled, doing just that to show the newcomers the pallets of olive oil, now pushed under the boxing ring. 'And they'll want to see you, not this.'

'Christ, Ellie!' Robert exclaimed. 'You found it... and *stole* it?'

'It's more complicated than it seems,' Ramsey spoke now, and he looked dog-tired, most likely from helping move all this contraband through the night. 'Ellie found it in the lockup and called Mama Lumetta. But Tommaso answered. Said he'd forcibly taken over the family.'

'That'd make the job null and void,' Robert mused. 'And I'd rather he didn't have the bottles, but why here? And don't give me "he owed a favour". Half of London owes you a bloody favour.'

'The storage locker Lorenzo used was owned by Danny Martin,' Ellie explained. 'And Danny gained it through his then boss, Johnny Lucas. So, everything in the locker ...'

'Was technically Mister Lucas's,' Casey grinned. 'Nice.'

'I like the kid,' Johnny said as he checked his phone. 'He has manners.'

'He's sucking up so you give him the Wi-Fi password,' Ellie replied. 'I'd suggest you don't if you want to keep any of your secrets.'

'Secrets like four million in liquid gold under my bloody boxing ring?' Johnny shook his head. 'You're lucky my brother's gone; he might have something to say about this.'

There was movement near the door, and everyone froze but it was only Pete the trainer, leaning in.

'Film crew's turning up,' he said. 'Thought you might want your friends and their dog to, like, you know, piss off out the way.'

'Go in the back, please,' Johnny smiled, waving towards the back office. 'This'll only take half an hour.'

'Leave you out here with all these bottles? I don't think so,' Ramsey spoke light-heartedly, as if joking, but the intent was deadly serious.

'Ramsey, I'm about to have three local papers, a student news crew and a guy making a documentary on me and filming me sparring with one of Pete's lads for ten minutes while I tell them why I should be an MP,' Johnny was now motioning more forcefully, ushering them away. 'Even you couldn't steal the bloody things out from under their noses.'

'Flattery will get you everywhere,' Ellie replied, reluctantly moving towards the back of the club. 'Come on, we can do a briefing as I'm sure we have lots to talk about.'

ELLIE STARED AT CASEY, SHAKING HER HEAD AS SHE DID SO.

'She definitely got him out?' she asked. 'There's proof?'

'Casey showed us the screen,' Robert nodded. 'It was DCI Richmond.'

'It explains a lot,' Ramsey was examining the wrappings of his bandages. 'You said Richmond mentioned knowing Danny Martin.'

Ellie nodded.

'She said at the crime scene she'd arrested Danny Martin a couple of times,' she replied. 'She had every chance to make a connection with him during these.'

'When I was looking into Lorenzo, I couldn't find any records of him meeting with Martin in Belmarsh,' Casey was already skimming through pages. 'But maybe I was looking for the wrong person?'

'You think Richmond visited Martin?' Ramsey stroked his chin. 'That could work. Lorenzo knows Richmond – maybe they're closer than we think – she's his get out of jail free card while she's in Stratford, and then she moves to Maidstone. They keep in contact, Carl dies, Lorenzo learns Mama Lumetta is sending a massive delivery of gold, and brings Richmond into the plan.'

'That's a bit of a reach,' Tinker frowned. 'This had to be arranged in a week.'

'True, but there's a plausibility here,' Ramsey was pacing now. 'Carl dies. Lorenzo sees an opportunity. Maybe he's annoyed dad isn't cutting him into the Whipcrack money. He tells the driver going back about the alleged issues at the overnight location, maybe even pays them deliberately to tell Brian. Or maybe he just tells Brian directly.'

'Or whoever sent the circuit tells him—' Casey started, but stopped as Tinker suddenly yelped.

'That's it!' she exclaimed. 'The handwriting! Richmond's note to the police telling them to free Lorenzo – it's the same hand as the message on the envelope!'

'Makes sense, it'd be easier for Richmond to get to Dover docks than it would be for Lorenzo,' Ramsey nodded. 'Maybe that's why she was hunting in his locker, too? Looking for the envelope, making sure it disappeared?'

'You mean the one we got Rajesh to send to her with the circuit in?' Casey muttered. 'Well, that's evidence we won't see again.'

'A problem for another time,' Ellie replied, already deep in thought.

'So, Lorenzo knows the time and date of the arrival because of his position, he gets DCI Richmond involved by finding him a safe place to put the gold, as all his contacts are Lumetta based,' Robert was considering this now, looking at Tinker. 'What was it Erik said about the job he was staying behind for?'

'He said he was called by a woman. Claimed he'd never heard Orla Maguire speak, but he assumed it was her. But he added her accent was weak, almost non-existent.'

'Which would track if it was Richmond calling, instead of Orla,' Ellie clicked her tongue against the top of her mouth. 'And by placing the hit location in her jurisdiction rather than in Dover, or even London, she gets to take the case, and control the narrative.'

She slammed a fist onto the desk behind her.

'Dammit,' she muttered. 'She said she believed me, that I was innocent. I thought I had a copper in my corner.'

'You do, it's just she might be a corrupt one,' Robert shrugged. 'But they didn't kill Carl Fredricks though, right? Or Brian?'

'I asked Rajesh to have a look into Carl's death,' Ellie replied. 'As for Brian, I think that was definitely Orla.'

'You think Matteo knew about this?' Casey looked up from his laptop. 'Or Tommaso?'

'I get the impression Tommaso didn't know about anything, including Whipcrack,' Ellie almost smiled at this. 'So much for the new face of Lumetta Oils.'

'On that, are we rescuing Maureen Lumetta?' Ramsey asked, and Ellie could hear the edge of concern in the voice. 'While she's around, Tommaso will always have a reason to look over his shoulder.'

'You think he'd kill his own mother?'

Ramsey glanced down at his bandaged hand.

'You know,' he replied sadly, 'I think he would.'

Ellie's phone buzzed, and she looked down at it.

'Casey, could you?' she asked, showing him the screen. Nodding, Casey tapped on the keyboard of his laptop.

'I told Rajesh to let me know when he was ready to talk, but we'd do it over video,' Ellie explained to the others. 'I didn't want him getting involved right now, especially as he'd have to explain to DCI Farrow at Mile End why he was hanging around in Johnny Lucas's boxing club.'

Casey spun the laptop around, and on the screen Rajesh Khanna pushed his pince-nez glasses up his nose, repositioning them as he stared slightly below his own laptop's webcam.

'Are you all there?' he asked.

'We are,' Ellie said, walking into view. 'What do you have for us?'

'I spoke to a coroner friend, and he showed me the Carl Fredricks' notes,' Rajesh explained. 'As far as anyone was concerned, he died of a heart attack. However, my friend had been involved in the autopsy—'

'Why would you need an autopsy if it was a heart attack?' Casey frowned.

'He died on the way to hospital,' Rajesh replied. 'It was likely the hospital making sure they couldn't be sued for anything that happened in the ambulance. Either way, he gave the body a cursory once-over, but found nothing out of the ordinary. However, I gave him a hypothetical situation; what if Carl had suffered strain because of some kind of emotional shock?'

'What if he was literally scared to death,' Tinker said.

'Ten points to Gryffindor,' Rajesh smiled. 'This was an acute cardiac event which couldn't be diagnosed in an autopsy, but in this hypothetical situation, it could directly result from the circumstances prior to death.'

'The scare.'

'Yes. The physiological mechanisms responsible for such a demise include an increase in catecholamine levels, an increase in both blood pressure and platelet aggregation, and the kicker? It includes a delay in cardiac or vascular recovery from the stress inflicted. In layman's terms, if Carl was susceptible physiologically to suffer an amplified reaction to stress, then being held in a super stressful situation could have killed him by a lethal cardiac arrhythmia caused by that emotional stress. Which is manslaughter, or even murder, depending on intent.'

'Tommaso commented on Carl,' Ellie said softly, as she worked through the explanation. 'Said he knew Carl had been skimming, even claimed "why do you think he's singing with the choir eternal", which to me says he had a part in the death.'

She looked at Ramsey.

'What if he did the same act he did to you, but during this, Carl's heart gave out? Tommaso would have left, and Carl would have died. Probably managed to call 999 with his last breath.'

'That's a horrid visual to have,' Ramsey shuddered. 'Okay. So now we have Carl definitely killed. What else?'

'The DNA strands Ellie gave me of Lorenzo Lamas?

They're a match for Matteo Lumetta as the father,' Rajesh held up a sheet of printed numbers, but it was more for reveal purposes than actual expectation of them being able to read them. 'But the other half, the maternal side? It was a ninety-eight percent match with Orla Maguire.'

'Which we expected,' Ellie nodded.

'Did you find anything on the blood sample on the broken bottle?' Tinker asked now. 'I'm aware it's part of a police enquiry so if you can't—'

'Actually, that's an interesting one.' On the screen, Rajesh rummaged around for a moment.

'There was a DNA match, but it wasn't from the criminal database. It was from the police one.'

'It wasn't DCI Lucy Richmond by chance, was it?' Ramsey asked.

'No, she didn't have a cut on her hands,' Ellie shook her head. 'Go on, Raj.'

'Records matched a Constable James Robinson, currently based at—'

'Maidstone nick,' Ellie finished the comment. 'The bloody crime scene officer, the one by the police tape. He was wearing blue latex gloves. I didn't think anything of it, as we were all wearing gloves.'

'So, PC Robinson was there the night Paulo Moretti was killed?' Casey whistled. 'Maidstone sounds like a fun place to be arrested.'

'They're not all bad apples,' Ellie replied coldly, 'but I think it's time to prune the tree a little. Anything else?'

Rajesh shook his head.

'Only gossip, but you probably already know it,' he said. 'Tommaso Lumetta made a power play last night, claims he's the head of the company, and has his mother held for her own safety in an apartment off Islington High Street.'

'So, she's still alive then,' Ellie breathed a small smile of relief. 'Thanks Raj. I owe you.'

'Not until my debt to you is cleared you don't,' Raj nodded back, still completely emotionless. And, without a farewell, he disconnected the call.

'All work, no play, that man,' Tinker grinned. 'Okay. So now we have some interesting developments, and very little time to process them.'

'Maybe less than we thought,' Ramsey suddenly paused. 'We were going on the schedule Mama Lumetta had. That Lorenzo would check the storage location after dropping her in Haggerston. But if Tommaso's taken control, Lorenzo now works for him.'

'And, if he knows Lorenzo's heritage, that could end this real fast,' Tinker nodded.

'And if he doesn't, Lorenzo will want to get out as quick as possible,' Ellie nodded. 'Think about it. He was willing to rip off the whole Lumetta family yesterday. While they're in chaos, it makes it even easier for him to escape with the money. Or, rather, it would have been easier, before I got there.'

'What exactly did you do?' Robert asked.

'I called Johnny and called in my favour,' Ellie replied, taking a moment to stroke Millie. 'I asked for a team to come to the Vaults, using his name, and bring all the bottles, both years, to his boxing club, where they'd be held for safekeeping, while I worked out what to do. And, in their place, I left a business card. Mine. And, on the back, I wrote "call me", just in case they really didn't understand.'

'That's a pretty bloody large target you've painted on your

back,' Tinker shook her head sadly. 'You've got a lot of people coming for you. For us.'

'No, just me,' Ellie rose from Millie, who grumbled at the sudden lack of attention, laying down at Ellie's feet with a sigh. 'I've got a plan. But it's changing a little right now.'

'Why?'

'Because I was allowing the police to do their job,' Ellie hissed. 'I was listening to what you all say, and stopped trying to be a police officer, as that's not my place anymore. But when the actual police in this case are corrupt, then I reckon all bets are off.'

She looked at Robert.

'As soon as I start this in motion, you'll all be safe again,' she said. 'I intend to gather all these threads – Tommaso, Matteo and Orla, Lorenzo, even bloody DCI Lucy Richmond and her friends – and tie them all into a neat little bow. But I'll need some help.'

'Whatever you need,' Robert smiled.

'Good,' Ellie looked out of the door, seeing Johnny still play-sparring with a young boxer for the delight of the press, before turning back to Tinker.

'How good a marksman are you these days?' she asked. 'And, more urgently, do you have a sniper rifle handy?'

23

TIN CAN ALLEY

LORENZO LAMAS HADN'T HAD THE BEST OF DAYS. THE PREVIOUS night he'd gone to bed planning out the following morning driving Mama Lumetta to some business meeting with a restaurant chain; some kind of legitimate work to balance out the more criminal activities. And while she ate expensive food with them in some rubbish gastro deli, he would take the car and drive to the Vaults to check Danny Martin's storage locker and make sure everything was still okay there. After he'd locked everything back up, he'd return to driver duties and take Mama back to her office.

Once he'd done that, Lucy would bring some of her cop friends, out of uniform for the occasion, and pick up the special bottles from the lockup – he had to remember to tell the old guy with the shotgun she'd be turning up, or there might be issues – and take them to Carl Fredricks' brother to be returned into gold bars. It'd take days to do this, Lorenzo had learnt all about it while talking to him, but nobody would know it was even happening, and they could finish the job under the radar. Then, next week, he could quietly quit his job, and by that he meant just disappear with Lucy, the two of them taking their four million, minus cuts to her team, use a contact he'd gained from one of his father's business partners to cash in the gold, and start a new life somewhere abroad.

He'd liked the idea of South America. It was warm there, and they could live on the beach, maybe buy a hotel or something. Anything that moved him further from his family was good.

He'd learnt about his father when Matteo hunted him out when he was a teenager; he'd always known he was adopted, but never who from. And when Matteo arrived, it excited Lorenzo to learn a part of his past. But Matteo would never say who his mother was, claiming it was "her right to tell him", whatever the hell that meant, and so Lorenzo had to work it out himself.

When he was in his early twenties, and he'd been fired from yet another dead-end cafe job, it was Matteo who turned up with a proposal; to work with him in the Lumetta family. To learn the ropes and climb up the ladder, maybe even rule the family with his father, one day.

But on his first day there, he realised this wasn't to be the case.

Matteo still hadn't told anyone about his illegitimate son, and Lorenzo Lamas was simply the new driver, the go-to man if you wanted your dry cleaning picked up.

Matteo had sat Lorenzo down, and explained it was for his own good, as Mama Lumetta and his new Uncle Tommaso wouldn't understand, and more likely would consider Lorenzo a threat to their empire; a newcomer with a stake in the action. But, as the years went on, and Lorenzo slowly made his way from basic, standard van driver to Mama

Lumetta's personal chauffeur, he saw that this was in fact a blessing, as he could learn about the company still, see all the dirty secrets, even, but this time he didn't have to consider sharing everything with his father when he took over.

He also met Paulo Moretti, learning he was his half-uncle. Another Lumetta bastard made to drive. He'd sat in that driver's seat and listened to everything. He'd learnt what worked and what didn't, and planned to move up the moment he could.

And then he learned his father, an Irish woman named Orla and half-uncle Paulo, had been ripping the family off for years.

This was when he finally learnt about the gold in the olive oil bottles. Paulo, seeing a kindred spirit, had been complaining how he only made twenty grand a year from this while they made hundreds of thousands, and although he thought he was confiding in an ally, Lorenzo now saw him as a threat. One removed when the most recent gold delivery was intercepted.

However, when he woke he had messages waiting; Tommaso had taken over the company while he was sleeping, and now his services were no longer required. He even had to wait in his house for someone to come and pick up the company car. The chances were also that Tommaso would soon squeeze Matteo for information on the stolen money, and the house Lorenzo had been living in would be sold.

Lorenzo had a choice, to wait for the new driver to arrive and take his keys, his pass to get into the building, anything in fact that connected him to Lumetta Oils, or he could get into the car right now, before anyone appeared, drive to the Vaults and start the removal process early. So, by ten in the morning, he was parking up at the London Fields location, walking through reception, down the corridor and unlocking storage locker sixty-two with one of the two keys the newly bought padlock had come with, the other one currently in Lucy's possession.

As he opened the shutter up, however, he immediately realised something was wrong. Mainly because the space was quite empty, and missing a rather obvious selection of pallets. It didn't hit him immediately, however; he actually glanced to the sides of the storage space, as if expecting them to have been hidden beside some of the small trunks in the corner. But of course, there was nothing left here.

Someone's been here.

Of course, someone's been here, you idiot. But who?

Lorenzo's first thought was Lucy, as she had a key. But he knew she wouldn't double-cross him, as she loved him.

Maybe it was Tommaso.

But how would he have known? Could someone have followed Lorenzo?

Maybe it was Matteo, having people tail his son to find the gold.

No, neither of them knew it had been Lorenzo. If they had, he wouldn't be walking right now. So, who could it have—

It was then Lorenzo noticed the business card placed on the floor.

Picking it up, he held the card to the light, swearing as he saw the name on it. And, as he turned it over, he saw the hand-written order to call Ellie Reckless.

Bloody Ellie Reckless had taken the gold.

Taking his phone out, he dialled a number, pacing from foot to foot as he waited for it to connect.

'Now's not a good time,' Lucy Richmond's voice spoke through the earpiece.

'Is it not?' Lorenzo hissed. 'Oh, sorry to interrupt your important police work. But I wanted you to know Ellie Reckless has stolen *all the sodding gold.*'

'She *what?*' The voice was rising in anger, but still soft, as Richmond was moving out of wherever she was, looking for a place to speak privately. 'Say that again.'

'I'm at the Vaults.' Lorenzo could feel the sting of tears rising as he looked around the storage space, praying this was some kind of sick joke. 'It's empty. She cleaned it out. Even the legit bottles. And she left a card, saying to call her.'

'Have you?'

'Christ, no!' Lorenzo hissed. 'I'm gonna kill her!'

'You can't,' Richmond's voice was calm now. 'We need the gold first. She's making a statement. We need to make one back. Call her, find out what the plan is. She'll likely want to meet.'

'And then?'

'And then you tell me where it is, and I turn up as well,' Richmond replied coldly. 'I'll bring Robinson, a couple of others, and we'll bring some coke, a couple of bags' worth. We'll fit her up, then end her. We can claim she attacked, and we had to act in self-defence. But we can't do that until we know where the gold is. So, stop whining like a little bitch and phone her.'

The call disconnected, and Lorenzo glared at it. Forcing his anger down, he dialled the number.

ELLIE STOOD ON THE ROOFTOP OF THE FARRINGDON BUILDING, looked up at the sky and took a deep breath, taking in as much of the London air as she could, before breathing it out.

Glancing at her watch, she noted the time; almost noon, the time she'd arranged the meeting for. In a matter of minutes, everything they'd planned would come to fruition, for better or worse.

She could have held the meeting at the boxing club, she knew Johnny would have allowed it, but she didn't feel this was fair. She'd already placed stolen goods in his building, and no matter what he owed her, she didn't want to screw up any chance he had of going into Parliament.

That, and this was a far better location for what she had planned.

The terracotta-red rooftop was four-storeys high and flat, with air conditioning units to her right, a door to the staircase just past them, and three sides that led straight down to the pavement. And, surrounding it were city buildings, coffee shop roofs, luxury apartments, Farringdon Station itself. On top of each of the six air conditioning units was a bottle of Lumetta Oils extra-virgin olive oil, dated 2021.

Apart from that, she had nothing.

Her phone beeped – an alarm reminding her it was exactly twelve, the time she'd said on the phone to meet her here. It was exposed, but incredibly private, away from anyone else and only visible to someone on a higher floor of the surrounding buildings looking out onto the roof, still too far away to work out what was going on. As she tucked the phone back into her top jacket pocket, almost on cue, the red double doors leading back into the building opened, and Lorenzo walked out onto the rooftop.

He was in blue jeans and a long black coat, a pair of

sunglasses on, most likely to avoid recognition, although who was going to recognise him was any guess. He saw Ellie and then saw the bottles.

'Sick game you're playing,' he said coldly. 'Dangerous game.'

He nodded at the bottles.

'I'll be taking those,' he said, walking towards them.

'I wouldn't,' Ellie smiled, pausing him. 'We haven't started this yet.'

'I don't know what "this" is, and I don't really care,' Lorenzo snapped, as behind him, the door opened and DCI Richmond walked out onto the rooftop, followed by PC Robinson, both in casual clothing. 'You see, I know you said to come alone, but you had to realise I was never going to do that.'

Richmond nodded at Ellie as she walked to the side, looking over.

'Sorry it has to be like this, Reckless,' she said, turning back to face both Lorenzo and Ellie. 'Let's get this over with.'

'Not until everyone's here,' Ellie continued to force the smile, projecting an element of calm while inside, she was far from this.

'Everyone *is* here,' Lorenzo frowned. 'Unless—'

He spun to face the door.

'Oh, you silly bitch,' he said. 'Tell me you didn't.'

'Yeah, I probably did,' Ellie shrugged as the door opened and Orla Maguire walked through, followed by Matteo Lumetta. 'Oh, look, it's mum and dad.'

Matteo took in the people on the roof, and then the bottles, before looking back at his son.

'You did this?' he hissed. 'You stole the gold?'

'I only did what you've been doing for years,' Lorenzo snapped back.

'Never like this!' Matteo exclaimed, turning to Ellie. 'You said we'd be alone!'

'Yeah, I might have lied,' Ellie shrugged again, waving for them to come closer. 'And you might want to move from the door, as you're not the only ones I'm expecting. Hey, Orla. How's your brother?'

'I hope you're not expecting Mama, because she's out of business now,' Lorenzo was only just managing to hold back his anger, as Orla, equally furious, just stared at Ellie in impotent rage.

'Oh, she doesn't need to be here,' Ellie walked towards the air conditioning units now. 'In a strange way, she wasn't actually involved in any of this. Well, apart from the smuggling.'

She looked back at Matteo.

'I was thinking of inviting Nicky Simpson here, but I realised last night he wasn't a part of this, was he? I mean, he was probably part of your side hustle at Whipcrack, but not this?'

Matteo glared at Ellie, but then jerked to the side as the door to the roof slammed open, and Tommaso Lumetta marched out onto the roof as if expecting a fight.

Looking around, his face broke out into a wicked-looking grin.

'Oh, you have to be kidding,' he said. 'You said to come alone, not that it was some kind of screwed-up family picnic.'

'Yeah, I might have lied to you, too,' Ellie said.

'That's not a good thing to do to your boss,' Tommaso replied, also noticing the bottles. 'What the hell?'

'First off, I don't work for you, I signed a deal with your

mother,' Ellie said calmly. 'Unless you're saying *you* are the head of Lumetta Oils?'

'Yeah, I'm saying that,' Tommaso frowned, shaking his head. 'Are you slow or something?'

'But you're only the *recent* owner and head, right?' Ellie asked.

At this, Tommaso visibly bristled.

'That old bitch has been nothing but a figurehead for years,' he hissed. 'I've run the bloody thing while she took credit for everything I did.'

'Bullshit!' Matteo exclaimed, but Ellie held up her hand.

'No, he's the head of the house, and apparently has been for a while now, so let him have his say,' she stated. 'We'll be coming back to this later. However, first we need to talk about the four million pounds of contraband gold, smuggled in by Lumetta Oils, and hijacked by young Lorenzo there.'

'Or, we could throw you off the roof and discuss the gold ourselves,' Lorenzo finally snapped, walking over to the six bottles of olive oil, only to stumble back in shock as the first of them, closest to his hand, exploded in a shower of glistening golden liquid.

'Christ!' he snarled, backing off and looking around.

'Oh, yeah, I forgot to mention,' Ellie grinned. 'I've got a sniper on a roof, watching you all. And every time you do something stupid? She shoots a bottle. That first one, it was your warning shot, and that's what, three and a half grand gone, just to make sure you get the message. Did you get the message?'

'Yeah,' Matteo muttered. 'We got the message.'

'Good,' Ellie paced as she continued. 'So, you should also know the other five bottles are linked to each of the five pallets of contraband bottles you smuggled in. Bottles I now hold. And every time my sniper destroys a bottle? You also lose the other two hundred and twenty-four bottles of that pallet, as my associates pour them into the Thames Estuary. Or the drains. I don't know their plans, to be honest. I just know you lose just over three quarters of a million pounds *every time you piss me off.*'

Lorenzo looked at Richmond as both Matteo and Tommaso glared daggers at Ellie.

'So, what's the plan,' the DCI said to Ellie. 'I'm assuming you have one?'

'I do,' Ellie nodded. 'We discuss who really owns the gold, while we each take responsibility for our actions. Every time you go against this? Tinker Jones also shoots a bottle. And when all five are destroyed? Well, you all leave a little poorer.'

There was a long moment of silence, as everyone on the roof took in the ramifications of this. They could accept what they did, revealing everything in some kind of sick, twisted family therapy... or they could lose four million in hidden gold.

'So,' Ellie clapped her hands together. 'Who wants to go first?'

24

FAMILY THERAPY

Tommaso laughed at this.

'Family therapy,' he eventually spat, looking over at Lorenzo. 'You think you can fix us? Our family of secrets and bastards?'

'You think you can do better?' Ellie shook her head. 'No, I don't think so. And neither do they. But all I want to do right now is get some answers here. I think I know how it all worked out, but it all came from one domino, didn't it?'

'Go on then,' Richmond muttered. 'Tell us what we did.'

'Okay, but here's the thing,' Ellie pointed at the five remaining bottles. 'If you lie, and I know it's a lie? Tinker shoots another bottle.'

The others on the roof looked at each other nervously at this, but nodded agreement.

'Your sniper is shooting at a lot of bottles,' Tommaso muttered. 'If we do this, if we do that, if we lie, do nothing ...'

'Oh, is this a problem for you? Tough shit,' Ellie smiled. 'Let's get through all the backstory fast, yeah? We all know Lorenzo is the son of Orla and Matteo, right?'

'I didn't know about Orla,' Richmond glared at Lorenzo. 'But I'm sure he was going to tell me—'

Ellie wasn't expecting the lunge, as Richmond suddenly burst into action, charging at her, but Tinker was, and as Richmond started moving, the first of the five remaining bottles exploded into shiny, glinting pieces in the sun, as the second bullet went through the middle of it, shattering it into shards of golden loss.

Richmond, throwing herself to the side, thinking the bullet was for her, glared angrily up at Ellie, before looking at the others.

'I slipped,' she said, clambering back to her feet.

'Of course, you did,' Ellie said soothingly. 'And in the process cost you all another three quarters of a million. So, let's be more careful of your "slipping" in the future, yeah?'

'When you run out of bottles to shoot, I'm gonna hurl you off the building,' Tommaso hissed.

'You'd allow over three million to be burned just to kill me? I don't know whether to be flattered or scared,' Ellie flashed a smile. 'Okay, so now we know Lorenzo's parentage. Good. But at this point Lorenzo doesn't. He grows up adopted, while Matteo watches from afar, because he knows his mother's opinion on bastards. His Uncle Paulo is a constant reminder. What was it you said? Oh, yes. "Sometimes they're given the keys to the kingdom, and sometimes they're just the driver." Shame it went the wrong way.'

'I thought we were getting through this fast?' Orla muttered, lurking at the back of everyone.

'True,' Ellie replied. 'I'm terrible when I have a captive audience. So, at this point, the Lumetta family is doing well, in London, Dublin and in Italy. Mama runs things here, Matteo has Ireland, and Tommaso bounces between here and Europe. All good, until Brexit hits. Then Customs rise, you're having to make new alliances with the US and that costs money, especially as your primary contact with Boston is the woman who had Matteo's bastard.'

'You call me that again and I'll kill you,' Lorenzo hissed. 'And I don't care how many bottles get destroyed.'

Ellie nodded acceptance at this.

'But around here, Matteo gets an idea. He learns how to take all this gold you have in Italy, generations of family jewels taken as payments, or as tithes, whatever it took to get them, melt them into a solution, in the process removing all the impurities, and then re-smelting them as gold bars.'

She looked at Matteo again.

'This was Carl, wasn't it?' she asked. 'He owed you still, and suddenly he had a way to repay you. His family worked with gold, purifying it, and had the equipment to do this. And he made a deal with you. For funding provided by you, he'd convince his brother to open a London location, where you could bring the gold solution, and have it re-poured into easier to pass around gold bars. And, you could explain how to do this to Boston, or just give them gold instead, whatever helped your expansion. But you had your own plans.'

'How do I know you're not recording this?' Matteo pointed at the phone in Ellie's jacket pocket. 'Or that you're wired?'

'I'm not a copper, and unless you confess live to one, I think it's classed as entrapment anyway,' Ellie looked at Richmond. 'It's entrapment, right? Either way, I'm not recording anything. Pinkie swear.'

Matteo considered this and then nodded.

'I started Whipcrack Holdings,' he said, looking at Tommaso. 'I'd already been told I wouldn't be needed once my brother took over. I was always Mama's favourite, and that really got to him. I'd be dumped back in Dublin and given a small area to look after. Bollocks to that. I met back up with Orla, and we went into business for ourselves. We'd take over Boston and then America. To hell with family. Both of them.'

'And you brought your gold smelting deal to Mama Lumetta,' Ellie replied. 'Explained how you had everything planned, all she had to do was provide the drivers. You even had one in mind. Uncle Paulo.'

'He was always angry he'd been left out of the family,' Matteo shrugged. 'He'd been given a sympathy job driving the vans, but he had ambitions, yeah? Like all Lumetta men. So, I told Mama he would drive the van to my contact, who would then make the bars.'

'You didn't mention the cut you'd be taking, though,' Tommaso hissed. 'Ripping your own family off. Scum.'

'I wasn't ripping Mama off,' Matteo glared daggers at his brother. 'I was making sure I was ripping *you* off. With every delivery, I made sure Carl kept a small percentage of the gold aside. Our "commission", so to speak. I paid him thirty grand a year to do this, and I paid Paulo twenty grand. They were both happy with the money, it was more than they deserved.'

'And after all, each delivery was netting you and Orla, the owners of Whipcrack a cool forty grand a shot. And, over the two years you did this, you made almost half a million for yourselves, even after these pay-outs,' Ellie added, now looking at Lorenzo. 'But they never told you about this, did they? Some parents.'

'We gave him a house to live in!' Orla hissed. 'That was what we gave him!'

'Yeah, but it wasn't my house, was it?' Lorenzo snapped

back. 'It was just where I lived, rent free. It was an investment, nothing more.'

'It was a good life, though,' Ellie looked back at Matteo. 'Until Paulo's own little side deal screwed things up.'

'Side deal?' Matteo frowned. 'What do you mean?'

'Oh, I thought you'd told him,' Ellie looked at Orla. 'The extra bottles you'd taken.'

'I don't know what you mean,' Orla snapped. 'I ain't taken no—'

There was another *crash* as a bullet smashed through the second of the five remaining bottles, and everyone flinched back.

'That's a lie,' Ellie spoke calmly. 'And another three quarters of a million gone.'

'Shite!' Orla looked conflicted as she looked around the rooftop. 'Aye, I might have had a little side hustle going, then. Paulo would give one of the Customs guys a couple of bottles each time, and he'd hold them for a couple of days. Then I'd come along, grab the bottles, and give him five hundred quid for his troubles.'

'Nice little side hustle,' Ellie smiled. 'And Paulo would gain a little more spending money, while you made seven grand a shot. So that's another hundred grand off the top of the contraband.'

'I'm gonna find that guy and kill him,' Tommaso hissed.

'Too late,' Ellie spoke, and now her voice was ice cold. 'Because Orla here killed him. Thought he was holding out on her with those last two bottles, when in fact he'd only been given one, and he'd thrown it away, thinking we were police when my associate went to visit him.'

Orla paled.

'I only roughed him up,' she said. 'I didn't think he'd die.'

'We'll come back to that,' Ellie looked back at Tommaso. 'Because now, you'd realised money was missing. And you confronted Carl Fredricks.'

'I knew he was ripping us off,' Tommaso replied calmly, as if this was nothing to him. 'So, I went and had a word.'

'Was this a word like the one you had with Ramsey Allen?'

Tommaso smiled.

'Yeah, pretty much,' he said. 'You gonna shoot a bottle? No? Then you know I ain't lying.'

'What I know is your "conversation" with Carl Fredricks ended with him suffering a lethal cardiac arrhythmia caused by emotional stress. Did you know this?'

Tommaso said nothing for a moment.

'Of course, I knew,' he eventually said. 'I watched him having it.'

'You were there?' Matteo spun to face his brother, his hands balling into fists. 'You're a goddamn psycho! You could have called an ambulance for him!'

'I called the ambulance, so quit your bellyaching,' Tommaso snapped back, but then smiled. 'Maybe if I'd called earlier, he might have lived.'

'So, you deliberately let him suffer?' Ellie asked.

'I was considering my options,' Tommaso replied. 'Not my fault he was too weak to take it.'

'Okay, so now Carl Fredricks is dead. And everything changes,' Ellie, her voice cold now, continued. 'His brother, who doesn't owe you anything, arrives in town and tells you he's closing up shop. He was never the biggest fan, but he agrees to do one last session for you.'

She looked back at Matteo now.

'You realised this is *one and done* now, no more deliveries, and you convince Mama Lumetta to put everything in this time. A massive four million pay off. You're looking at almost half a million being skimmed off, easily enough for moving on money. But you hadn't figured on one thing. Your son.'

Now it was Lorenzo's turn to be singled out as Ellie turned to him.

'You'd seen everything driving for Mama Lumetta. You'd stored it all away, and you knew your dad wasn't going to give you anything. So, you took it for yourself. Or was it your girl-friend that suggested it? The one that got you off countless charges while she was at Stratford?'

Lorenzo stared angrily at Ellie, and she laughed.

'Yeah, I think Richmond there is the brains of this rela-tionship,' she said. 'You told her about this, and she decided to hijack it. You needed somewhere to hide it, so she spoke to an old contact, currently in Belmarsh, offering him a percentage for his storeroom key, perhaps. What was it, ten percent?'

'Five,' Richmond replied defiantly. 'He wasn't really in a position to negotiate.'

'So now you have somewhere to hide it, you know when it's coming in because of the conversations Matteo's having with Mama Lumetta, and you start to set things up. You pay one of the other drivers to pass the news to Paulo that his usual place to crash is compromised, and you have a little chat with Brian Watson, getting him to help.'

'Lorenzo had learnt Paulo was skimming himself, and followed the trail,' Richmond replied. 'We met Brian, and again, we convinced him it was in his best interests to help us. He put the circuit in. I gained that from a friend.'

'Shouldn't have written on it,' Ellie smiled. 'Matched your handwriting.'

'Yeah, I realised that later,' she said, not bothered about hiding the fact. 'Even went through his locker looking for it.'

Ellie looked at PC Robinson now, who, up to this point, had been skulking around the side of the group.

'At what point did you come on board?' she asked.

'I wasn't on board,' Robinson flustered. 'I-I wasn't there. Why would I be there?'

Bang. Another bottle shattered, to the sounds of vicious cursing from the others.

'That's a lie, and another three quarters of a million gone, because you left your DNA all over the crime scene,' Ellie replied. 'The blood you left on the bottle, where you slashed your hand open.'

'The bottle?' Robinson said, and then opened and shut his mouth several times, confused. 'I threw it away.'

'Not far enough,' Ellie smiled.

'The boy in the tree,' Richmond nodded, realising. 'Well played.'

'So, I'm guessing the team there was brought in by you,' Ellie said back at Richmond. 'All police?'

'A mix,' Richmond replied. 'Friends of mine; people Lorenzo knew. Nobody was supposed to find out. And we intended to keep a lid on it.'

'Especially as you were the detective placed on the case,' Ellie replied. 'Nice call, making sure it happened within your remit. But Lorenzo couldn't risk Paulo telling anyone he knew who did this, especially as they had the bond of Lumetta bastards going for them, so he shot him, and then torched the van after removing everything.'

'Paulo always treated me like shit,' Lorenzo muttered. 'Hypocritical wanker. He deserved a slower death than the one he got.'

'And now everything falls apart,' Ellie straightened as she continued. 'With the gold gone, Orla pushes for the bottles Brian should have, and kills him when he can't provide. She even takes the bottle from his cousin, which turns out to be normal olive oil. Meanwhile, everyone comes home to roost, hoping to work out where the gold is.'

'I came to London to meet with Nicky Simpson, and give my mother support,' Matteo shook his head. 'I decided I could use his criminal connections to help us into Boston. All I had to do in return was give him some land for his health club criminal fronts.'

Ellie grinned widely at this.

'We're not here to talk about Nicky Simpson,' she said. 'As far as I know, he's a businessman, and has nothing to do with this case. One which, by this point, Mama Lumetta calls me in to solve.'

'And well done,' Richmond clapped her hands. 'You solved it. Lorenzo and me, stealing money owned by gangsters.'

'Are you seriously trying to liken yourselves to Robin Hood?' Ellie exclaimed. 'Stealing from bad people to what, give to the good?'

'In a way, yes,' Richmond breathed out heavily, releasing all her pent-up anger. 'With us being the good, that is.'

Ellie stood silently for a moment, the atmosphere building up as she stared at the people in front of her.

'Tommaso Lumetta, I should arrest you for the murder of Carl Fredricks,' she said. 'Orla Maguire, I should arrest you for the murder of Brian Watson, and Lorenzo Lamas and Lucy Richmond, I should arrest you for the murder of Paulo Moretti. And this isn't even considering the amount of bullion smuggling I could charge Whipcrack and Lumetta Oils on, if I was still police.'

'Now wait a moment,' Tommaso frowned. 'Lumetta Oils was Mama's deal. Not me.'

'Yeah, about that,' Ellie smiled. 'Remember, I said we'd come back to this. What was it you said earlier? "That old bitch has been nothing but a figurehead for years, I've run the bloody thing while she took credit for everything I did." That sounds like you, pretty much claiming to be the head of the firm, Tommaso. And the police might want to have a word with you.'

In the distance now, on the roads beneath them, the faint sounds of police sirens could be heard.

'All of you? You're screwed,' Ellie said. 'But here's the deal. I'll leave right now, and you can fight over the last bottles. Each one has a location taped to the base. You get to it; you can at least gain something from this.'

'Why should we let you leave?' Lorenzo looked around, as if surprised he was the only one speaking. 'This is just hearsay! You already said you weren't recording!'

'Yeah, about that,' Ellie nodded, pulling out her phone. 'I was telling the truth, I wasn't recording ...'

She turned the phone around to show the others – now, on the screen was Ellie's face as the camera on the back aimed at her.

'But I have been live streaming this on social media since you arrived,' she continued, waving at the camera. 'In fact, I know DCI Farrow of Mile End nick has been very interested in it. Why do you think I said to meet here? Great reception.'

Tommaso made some kind of huff huff noise, and Ellie realised as she turned the phone back onto him he was hyperventilating with anger as he pulled a wicked-looking blade out of his jacket.

'I am gonna fu—' he started, but this merged into a scream of intense pain, as his fingers suddenly exploded, a gunshot echoing around the buildings. As he fell to his knees, gripping his now ruined hand, Ellie walked over to him.

'That was for Ramsey Allen,' she said icily, looking back at the others. 'Two bottles. A million and a half left. Make your choices fast.'

And, this said, Ellie continued walking, shutting the door behind her as on the roof she could hear the shouting of people, probably as they argued who should have the bottles, followed by two rapid gunshots – the type of sounds you'd hear if someone, say a woman trained in the Rifles and with a sniper rifle in her hand shot out the two remaining bottles before anyone could get to them.

With a smile, Ellie carried on down the stairs, hearing the sounds of booted feet running up towards her.

'Looks like you're just in time, boys,' she said, stepping to the side as the police carried on past. 'Go wild.'

Turning off the phone to stop filming, Ellie carried on out of the building, past the now hastily erected police cordon, and heading back to the Finders offices.

She needed a stiff drink, a couple even, and a dog to hug.

Maybe not even in that order, either.

25

ALDERSHOT

THEY'D FOUND MAMA LUMETTA IN HER ISLINGTON APARTMENT, held under lock and key by one of Tommaso's loyal goons – recognised by Ramsey, who pointed out to Tinker, beside him, that this was one of the men who held his hand down as Tommaso crushed his fingers.

Tinker hadn't taken kindly to this, and within a matter of seconds, the goon guarding the door, not expecting such a vicious attack, lay in a crumpled position on the floor, clutching at both his groin and broken and bleeding nose simultaneously as Ellie unlocked the door and entered.

'You took your time,' Mama Lumetta said, lounging on a sofa and reading a style magazine. She looked up as they walked into the living space. 'Is my idiot son arrested?'

'I think by now they both are, I'm afraid,' Ellie replied, pausing as Ramsey and Tinker joined beside. 'I hope you don't mind; I brought some friends. Thought you might need rescuing.'

'Do I look like I need rescuing?' Mama Lumetta rose from her seat now, placing the magazine back onto it as she faced the new arrivals. 'I take it you found my gold and worked out who stole it?'

Ellie nodded.

'Your driver and illegitimate grandson,' she replied. 'But to be honest, it was a bit of a group effort.'

Mama Lumetta sighed, walking to a cabinet and pouring out a generous measure of what looked like vodka.

'Did you find all the gold?'

'Yes and no,' Ellie replied. 'I know for a fact we broke six bottles while we confronted the others, and I think there may have been a few others disappearing during the collection process. But honestly? By the time you gain the gold back, you'll probably have more than you usually get—'

'Because Matteo won't be skimming off the top?' Mama Lumetta smiled, and then smiled wider at Ellie's surprised expression. 'I'm a mother. I can't blame my son for doing that. Especially as Tommaso was always intending to take over when I was gone. They're really both arrested?'

'Yes, but I don't know how long they'll be away for,' Ellie said. 'I suggest, however, you get your affairs in order, find someone to replace you and have them brought in officially.'

Mama Lumetta shook her head sadly.

'We're a family,' she replied. 'If my sons won't follow, then I'll close up shop. The olive oil side can keep going, but the rest of it? I think retirement might be a good idea after all.'

'That's your son talking,' Ramsey stepped forward now. 'And no matter what you think of him, Tommaso wasn't right to do what he did.'

'On either occasion,' Mama Lumetta nodded at Ramsey's bandaged hand. 'So, what's the deal?'

'Well, we'll send the bottles to Erik Fredricks, who'll fulfil his promise with this last order,' Ellie explained. 'He'll then pass you the bullion to do with as you will. But to be honest, you hired me to find the gold, and I found the gold. It's time to sever this business relationship.'

Mama Lumetta watched Ellie for a very long, uncomfortable moment.

'You know, *you* could be my successor,' she said. 'You have competent associates, and Ramsey's a good consigliere to have by your side. And judging from the way you came in, your friend here in the army coat is a solid muscle to control the troops.'

'Are you offering me the keys to your kingdom?' Ellie was genuinely surprised at this. 'I don't think it's really how we roll.'

'Maybe,' Mama Lumetta smiled now, and for the first time, it looked genuine. 'But you should consider it. You're owed enough favours to make good on anything. You could even unite London. You're young enough.'

'I'm saving the favours for something else,' Ellie replied, possibly a little quickly. At this, Mama Lumetta pursed her lips, took a sip of the drink, and sighed.

'Destroying Nicholas Simpson won't fix your problems,' she said, holding up a hand to stop Ellie's next question. 'I watch the streets; I know what's happening. Nicky Simpson definitely had a hand in what happened to you, but you're still trying to find out how he managed it. I get that. But you won't do it. He's too experienced in this. His covered trails have had covered trails placed over them. And going after him will lead you to nothing but pain, and maybe even death, as you learn the truth.'

'And what's that?' Ellie's face had set into an emotionless, unimpressed expression now, the face of someone not expecting a lecture, and sure as hell not wanting one right now.

'That Simpson's a facilitator,' Mama Lumetta walked over to Ellie now, facing her from only a couple of feet as she stared directly into her eyes. 'There's always someone bigger.'

'Do you know this for a fact?' Ramsey asked now, diverting her attention.

'No, but I've walked the road for many years now, and I recognise all the houses on it,' Mama Lumetta stroked his cheek tenderly. 'You recognise patterns too, after a while.'

The moment finished, she walked back to her sofa, sitting down on it.

'What do I owe you?'

Ellie looked back at the others.

'Two hundred pounds per diem each, per day,' she said. 'We started on this two days ago, so—'

'You started three days ago,' Mama Lumetta replied. 'It was morning, so you're over forty-eight hours. I'll class it as six hundred each. And then there was the thirty thousand to your company—'

She leant closer, watching Ellie.

'And two favours, freely given,' she finished. 'Is that about right?'

'That's about right,' Ellie looked at Tinker and Ramsey, checking her maths was correct. 'I'll get Robert to write up an invoice for you.'

'Or you could just keep nine of the bottles,' Mama Lumetta suggested. 'Off the books.'

'On the books, I'm afraid,' Ellie smiled, shaking her head as Ramsey went to speak. 'No matter what my thief thinks.'

With this stated, and the conversation ended, Ellie

nodded her farewells, leaving the apartment with Tinker, as Ramsey stayed behind.

'If you need anything,' he said, his sincerity obvious on his face, 'you know where I am.'

'Actually, you might be able to help,' Mama Lumetta replied. 'I was supposed to be going to a formal dinner next week with Tommaso as my escort. Would you consider being my plus one?'

'I'd be honoured,' Ramsey took Mama Lumetta's hand and kissed it gently. 'I'll see you then.'

'Ahem,' Mama Lumetta held out her hand. And Ramsey, with a grin, placed the recently gained ring back onto her palm.

'Just testing,' he said. 'You know how it is.'

And with a bow, he, too, left Mama Lumetta and her apartment.

'Do we know what'll happen to her?' he asked as they drove in the Defender away from Mama Lumetta and London. 'Will she be charged with the smuggling?'

'Probably not,' Ellie smiled. 'Tommaso claimed all the credit for himself when he spoke on the roof, so if she has a clever solicitor, they can use that to gain credible doubt on whether she even knew it was happening.'

She looked out of the window, tapping Tinker.

'Could you stop at the office before we carry on?' she asked. 'I was going to drop off Ramsey and pick up Casey beforehand.'

'Beforehand?'

'Yes,' Ellie looked at Tinker. 'Before we all drive to Aldershot, and you speak to your blackmailer.'

'That's something I'd rather do on my own,' Tinker replied sullenly.

Ellie placed a hand on the ex-soldier's shoulder.

'I've been doing things on my own for way too long,' she said. 'I've recently learned it's way better to go through things with friends.'

Tinker went to reply, but decided instead to make some kind of low-level growl as they pulled up outside the Finders Building.

'It's two pm,' Ellie said as Ramsey opened the door. 'Be back at the boxing club by seven,'

'Why not here?' Ramsey frowned, looking up at the offices. 'Or Caesars?'

'The diner isn't open then, and this isn't for Finders,' Ellie smiled. 'Seven. And if you can, try not to get collared by Nicky Simpson. I reckon he's going to be really pissed right now.'

'Being outed on a social media live stream can do this for you,' Ramsey paused. 'You think Maureen Lumetta was right? That he might not be the tip of the iceberg?'

'We'll see soon enough,' Ellie replied. 'Go take some painkillers, grab a nap on Robert's couch, and I'll see you later.'

As Ramsey left, there was a commotion and Millie jumped onto the back seat, wagging her tail, her face seemingly smiling, as Casey climbed in behind her.

'Robert said they're not a doggy day-care,' he said. 'And that you can start paying a day rate if you keep on.'

'Oh, I think he'll be okay later,' Ellie smiled. 'Now, are you ready to do your work?'

'What work?' Tinker frowned as they pulled out into the afternoon traffic.

'Casey, tell Tinker what you learned about the IP address,' Ellie said.

'We know about the IP address,' Tinker snapped. 'I don't know why, but Jemima Fowler was the one who hacked the system.'

Casey opened up his laptop.

'Not exactly,' he said, as the Defender headed west out of London, and towards Aldershot. However, Ellie wasn't listening as Casey continued, because her phone had buzzed. And, as Casey spoke while Tinker drove, Ellie looked down at the screen, reading the text from a number she didn't recognise.

I didn't appreciate being called out as a criminal.

Ellie half smiled, but at the same time half groaned; she knew Nicky Simpson would hear of the conversation on the roof. After all, she had live streamed it to the world.

I didn't do it. It was Matteo who named you.

You knew it would happen.

Ellie frowned, unsure of what to write next. Simpson was right, she had known it'd come out. She knew because Matteo and Nicky were working together, most likely because of the plans he had resulting from his stolen gold.

I didn't, and I don't appreciate being called out about something I didn't do.

Ellie stared at the message and then began to type.

If you have a problem, come and find me. We'll talk about it. Or would you prefer I waited until I had enough favours to force you to tell me what really happene_

She stopped. *Did she really want to send this?* It was giving away everything she knew.

No.

Quickly, she deleted the line, replacing it.

If you have a problem, you know where to find me. And what my office hours are.

This done, she sat back, catching the end of the Casey and Tinker conversation.

'He did what?' Tinker screamed in fury. 'I'm gonna kill him!'

At least some things didn't change, Ellie thought to herself with a smile.

———

Captain Jemima Fowler wasn't billeted in the Officers' barracks in Aldershot, instead she lived in married quarters around half-a-mile north, in a new-build estate created purely for army families, and it was here that Tinker pulled up outside a red-bricked semi-detached house that didn't look over five years old.

'Perhaps I should do the talking?' Ellie suggested, but it was to Tinker's back, as she'd already climbed out of the car and was walking up the drive. Sighing, Ellie looked at Casey as if for silent affirmation this was a good idea, and then hurried after her friend, arriving at the front door just as Tinker hammered on it.

'You have a plan?' she asked.

'Murder's not a plan, is it?' Tinker offered, before looking back at the door as it opened.

A man in his thirties, wearing jeans and a polo shirt, with short dark hair combed to the side, had opened the door, and was now staring in confusion at Tinker.

'What the hell—' was all he managed to say before Tinker stepped through the doorway and slammed a fist into his face, sending him staggering back, clutching his now exploding nose.

'What da hell!' he exclaimed as Tinker continued into the house.

'Evening, Trev,' she said conversationally, wiping her now bloody fist on a tissue she'd pulled from a box on the side table. 'Jemima in? *Jemima!*'

There was a noise from upstairs, a chair being scraped back, and after a couple of seconds a woman in army fatigues appeared at the top. She was also in her thirties, with short blonde hair.

'Jones?' she half-whispered, seeing Casey and Ellie behind her. 'What are you—'

She stopped as she saw her husband, now ramming tissues up his bleeding nose.

'What the bloody hell are you doing!' she snapped, her voice going into full "officer mode", glaring at everyone in the hall.

'Sit down,' Tinker pointed at the sofa. 'The pair of you.'

'I should call the MPs,' Captain Jemima Fowler

complained as she took her husband to the sofa and sat him down. 'You're a psycho.'

'I'm not the one hacking into emails and sending messages stating I'm looking for retribution,' Tinker said in response.

'Well, neither am I!' Jemima replied indignantly, but then looked at her husband, frowning.

'What's going on?'

Trevor said nothing, still focused on his nose.

'I was hacked, Jem,' Tinker explained. 'Someone got into my emails and downloaded the photos from the body cam.'

At this, Jemima's eyes widened, and Ellie saw she knew exactly what the implications of this meant.

'Who?' she asked.

'Well, at first I thought it was someone in the unit, because they'd come in through a group message when we did the reunion a while back, but I couldn't think of anyone who'd want to see you hurt, and there wasn't anyone who felt like I needed retribution, which they sent to me in an email, while telling me they had the photos.'

'Captain Fowler, Tinker was worried someone was trying to turn you into an asset,' Ellie explained. 'I'm a colleague of hers, and she came to me after it happened. We used our resources to find out who sent the message, and who was gaining blackmail material about you.'

'And where did it lead to?' Jemima's face was dark now as she realised the danger she'd been in.

'Here, actually,' Casey looked up from his tablet. 'The IP matches this house's Wi-Fi address. So, it was either you or Mister Bleedy there.'

There was a long moment of silence, and Jemima looked at Trevor.

'We talked about this,' she said. 'You understood the job came before family.'

'No, you decided that for me,' Trevor muttered. 'I never had a say in it.'

He looked up at Tinker.

'She used to want kids,' he said coldly. 'Until you turned up. After that, she was different.'

'Maybe you were?' Tinker offered back. 'I apologised for what happened. I took full blame. I don't know what else I could do.'

'Maybe not punch him in the face?' Ellie suggested.

Jemima rose from the sofa now, glaring down at Trevor.

'You broke into my emails?' she said. 'To find information on me?'

'I always knew the photos were there,' Trevor snapped back. 'I decided maybe if you weren't a soldier, you'd want to be a mother.'

'What I want right now is not to be a wife,' Jemima was reddening with rage. '*Your* wife.'

'You can't leave me!' Trevor rose now to face his wife, and Tinker mimicked him, ready to get between them if she needed to. 'I'll go to the top, I'll—'

'Be arrested as an enemy spy,' Ellie said calmly, and everyone stopped, looking at her.

'What?' Trevor replied in confusion.

'You broke into an army email list to gain compromising photos of a Captain in the fourth battalion of Ranger Regiment,' Ellie said as she watched Trevor. 'Now, as they're really close with the Army Special Operations Brigade, this is a bit of a sticky situation, because there are serious levels of military secrets she probably has access to. And here you are, pushing to get her to do what you say. Turn her into an asset.'

'I'm not a spy!' Trevor looked at Jemima for confirmation. 'I'm not!'

'Yeah, but a spy would totally say that,' Casey shrugged. 'Especially one with connections to North Korea and China.'

Trevor was paling now as he looked around the room from face to face.

'But ... but I don't ...'

'Oh, I know, *currently* you don't,' Casey smiled. 'But I'm very good. In an hour I can have people in the Chinese Embassy thinking you're their bestie. And how do you think that goes when they learn you're trying to blackmail your wife into turning on her country?'

'It's my country too ...' Trevor's voice was barely a whisper as Tinker moved in close.

'You lose the photos, and you forget the email password you used,' she hissed. 'You do whatever Jemima decides and you don't argue it. You tried to force her hand, and it failed. Live with it. Because if you don't—'

'You'll be on a plane to Beijing within a week, with a bag over your head,' Ellie finished.

Tinker looked over at Jemima.

'What do you want to do?' she asked.

'I'll have a chat with my husband,' Jemima said icily. 'It's between us. I'll make sure he never contacts you again, Jones.'

Tinker nodded.

'Then I'll leave you to it,' she said, turning and walking out of the door without another word, Casey following.

Ellie, however, watched Jemima.

'Tink means a lot to me,' she explained. 'And she loves you. Like "take a bullet" levels of love. You treated her like shit, after whatever you had. And now? She went to war for you and you couldn't even say thanks?'

Ellie turned and walked to the door.

'I don't know what the hell she saw in you,' she finished, closing the door behind her.

Tinker was already starting the Defender.

'You good?' Ellie asked as she climbed into the passenger door. Tinker, however, stayed quiet, only showing any emotion when the door to the house opened again, and Jemima walked out.

'Tinker,' she said, walking to the Defender. 'This was a shock. I didn't thank you for what you did. That was remiss of me.'

'Not a problem,' Tinker forced a smile. 'I'll always help the Rifles.'

'You threw away your career for me, and I left you in the cold,' Jemima nodded at this. 'Maybe we could have a coffee sometime, regain the friendship we once had?'

Tinker stared at Jemima for a good few seconds before smiling; this time a little more genuine.

'Nah, I'm good,' she said, looking back to the road as she placed the Defender into gear. 'You take care of yourself now, Captain.'

And, this last request given, Tinker Jones drove Ellie and Casey out of Aldershot, and back towards London, as Captain Jemima Fowler stared after them in what could only be seen as abject confusion as to what had just happened.

26

BONUSES

It was just before seven in the evening when Ellie and the others arrived at the boxing club. A hastily positioned sign was on the door as they walked up to it.

CLOSED – PRIVATE FUNCTION

'Are we the private function?' Casey asked as they entered, and Ellie smiled.

'I think we might be,' she replied as they walked into the boxing club to see Ramsey, Robert, and Millie waiting for them beside the ring. At the back of the club, Johnny Lucas was counting bottles of olive oil with Pete, arranging for them to be moved.

'What's going on?' she asked Robert, nodding over at Johnny before kneeling down and hugging the now super-excited spaniel.

'Johnny's arranging the delivery to Mama Lumetta,' Robert explained. 'He's counting the stock right now to make sure it's accurate. And, of course, he's making sure Mama

Lumetta owes him. I think he learned from you about the power of being owed a favour.'

Ellie smiled as she walked over to the gangster-turned-wannabe politician.

'You good here?' she asked, looking over the pallets. 'She's taking everything?'

'Minus a couple of bottles of the genuine stuff,' Johnny said, nodding at a couple of olive oil bottles on the side of a table beside the door. 'I do like a good bit of olive oil to dip my focaccia in, after all. Want some?'

Ellie nodded at a bag on the boxing ring, a bag she'd gotten Robert to bring.

'We have one each in there,' she smiled. 'At one point, I worried it was my only payment.'

'What year are they?' Johnny almost started walking over to check.

'2022,' Ellie said. 'Go check them if you want. I've had enough of gold solution to last a lifetime.'

She looked at a five-pallet tall tower of 2021 labelled olive oil.

'How many are we short?' she asked.

'Well, your mate with the rifle blew up six of them on a roof,' Johnny replied, 'and somewhere between the hijack and the arrival here we seem to be out another twelve. For all we know, they were taken by Lorenzo, or Richmond, or—'

'Or you,' Ellie didn't smile as she spoke, observing Johnny. 'You don't think we didn't count them while we brought the bottles here? You're nicking twelve bottles for yourself. And you know? I'm fine with that.'

She paused, looked away, and then returned her gaze to Johnny.

'That's what, forty grand?' she counted on her fingers.

'And whatever Mama Lumetta gives you for helping. You've done well here.'

Johnny watched Ellie carefully.

'Go on then,' he eventually sighed. 'Another favour for the bottles.'

Ellie grinned.

'Thought hadn't even crossed my mind,' she said. 'But I'll accept the favour. And as for the bottles … what bottles?'

Johnny smiled, nodded to Ellie and then walked off to the back rooms with Pete, most likely to find a truck to take the bottles across.

This done, Ellie walked to the others, picking up the bag of bottles as she did so.

'Here you go,' she said, pulling out the bottles and passing one to Ramsey, Tinker, Casey, and Robert. 'I'll keep mine in the bag. Class these as a little bonus.'

'A bottle of olive oil,' Casey smiled, checking the label and seeing it was 2022. 'Mum will be pleased.'

'Mum will be more pleased when she realises it's not oil,' Ramsey smiled. 'These are the six bottles of gold Tommaso and the others believed were shot on the roof. As of right now, they're untraceable.'

'We took six of each and swapped bottles, a bit like PC Robinson did with the broken bottle you found,' Ellie explained to Casey. 'So, the bottles were the gold ones, but the contents were normal olive oil. The sheen was the remnants of the gold on the insides of the bottles.'

'And that's why you shot them all at the end,' Casey nodded, understanding now. 'You couldn't let them open one and realise.'

'Give the boy a sweetie,' Ramsey said. 'Each bottle still

has a little over three grand in them, and Rajesh has a friend who can smelt these down, for a ten percent cut.'

'That's why Rajesh isn't getting a bottle,' Ellie explained. 'That and the fact the moment he gained three grand in smelted illegal gold he could lose his career.'

'So, who's getting the last bottle?' Casey asked, looking at the second bottle left in the bag. 'Millie getting a lot of dog treats?'

'Actually, it's a donation,' Ellie looked at Tinker. 'I'll be sending the contents, when smelted, to the *Screaming Angels*. The money should cover any issues they may have with Tinker.'

'Thanks,' Tinker smiled. 'I was going to give them my one—'

'Oh, in that case we'll do that, and I can buy some dog treats with this one!' Ellie exclaimed, leaning over and ruffling Millie's head. The spaniel, having no clue what was going on but getting attention, wagged her tail and smiled up at everyone.

'So, what happens now?' Casey asked. 'I mean, you uploaded everything online. There's no getting out of this, even if the police don't charge them, they're damned by public opinion.'

'I think there's enough to get Richmond, Robinson and anyone else they had connected kicked off the force.' Ellie pursed her lips. 'Which is a win. Matteo has enough distance to get out, but will head back to Ireland as soon as he can. Tommaso will be charged with Carl's death, but heart attacks are tricky things. At best, he'll get manslaughter. Orla's more likely to get time because of Brian, but that'll only be if Jimmy testifies, and I can't see that happening, so Lorenzo's the only one looking at serious years. Although, as the Lumetta driver, he'd have heard enough things to give him leeway for a deal, maybe even witness relocation.'

'Even though he killed Paulo?'

'We don't know what happened, and neither do the police. It'll be based on the evidence found.'

Ellie held her bottle of olive oil, turning it in her hands.

'The Lumetta family is pretty much done; they'll have to stick to the legitimate business for a while. But they'll find a way to continue. Their type always does.'

'And Nicky Simpson?' Ramsey asked. 'He was at my house when I got back earlier. Didn't say anything, was unimpressed he'd been spoken about, but as it was Matteo who named him, he couldn't kick off.'

He smiled.

'What he did mention, however, was that he's had to pull out of the health club deal, as he can't be seen to be working with criminals. So, we might not have him yet, but he's lost out because of this, and that's not a bad thing.'

'Did he say anything else?'

Ramsey shook his head.

'I think he was embarrassed about being a part of this injury,' he replied, waving his bandaged hand. 'Something I'll make damn sure to continually remind him about.'

There was movement at the door, and Ellie saw DI Mark Whitehouse and DS Kate Delgado enter, the latter of whom looked a little sheepish.

At their appearance, Millie growled.

'Your dog is an excellent judge of character,' Ramsey said as the two detectives walked over.

'Could we have a quick word?' Whitehouse asked, looking nervously at the others.

'No,' Ellie replied. 'You have something to say, you can do it here. What do you want, Mark?'

'We wanted to say you did a good job today,' Whitehouse said, nudging the obviously unhappy to be there Delgado. 'Isn't that right?'

'Yeah,' Delgado said, looking at the floor. 'When I saw you were working for the Lumettas, I ... that is we ... thought you'd embraced the dark side. But the live stream you did showed we were wrong. So, um, yeah. Sorry.'

'Thanks, Kate,' Ellie said, but although she smiled and looked genuine, there was an element of sarcasm in the tone. 'Maybe now you might actually believe me when I tell you I was framed.'

Delgado's eyes snapped up.

'One win doesn't make a season,' she said coldly, now looking back at Whitehouse. 'Are we done here? Being close to criminals makes me itch.'

The last line was either aimed at Ramsey, or at Johnny Lucas, now returning to the boxing ring.

'No police, you know the score,' he said, ushering them off with a wave. 'Come back with a warrant if you want anything else.'

Whitehouse looked at the pallets of oil at the back, glanced at Ellie, and then nodded.

'Don't be a stranger,' he said, following Delgado out of the door.

After a moment, it was Johnny who vocalised the question almost everyone had been thinking.

'So, was it the bloke or the bitch who grassed you up?' he asked.

'Could be either, but my money's on the bitch,' Ellie smiled. 'We good?'

'We are, but it's almost half-past-seven and I have a function I need to get to,' Johnny pointed at the door. 'So, all of you be lovely and piss off, yeah? So, I can close up?'

'I'll be confirming the amount of bottles that arrive,' Ellie rose from the leaning position against the ring she'd taken, stretching as she did so. 'So be honest.'

'I'm standing as a Member of Parliament,' Johnny looked horrified that Ellie could consider him doing anything else. 'Of course, I will!'

Laughing, Ellie gathered up her things and, as the others left, all in conversation, Johnny grabbed Ellie's arm, halting her for a moment.

'He'll come for you now,' he whispered. 'Simpson's been exposed. And I've seen his bad side. You don't want to be on it.'

'I can handle Nicky Simpson,' Ellie shrugged. 'I appreciate the—'

'I don't mean the man,' Johnny replied. 'I mean the person controlling him.'

He leant in.

'We all know he bundled his father off when he took over, and he learnt from his grandad, but Nicky couldn't do that on his own. He had to have help. Someone in the shadows, who's gaining from Simpson's success. And you gave him a body blow today. Be careful.'

Silently nodding, and swallowing as she considered this, Ellie grabbed her bag and, motioning for Millie to follow, left the boxing club.

Outside, the others were saying their goodbyes, already moving on. Tinker was planning on how to apologise to the *Screaming Angels,* while also forcing Jemima Fowler from her mind.

Ramsey was still playing the rakish cad, but Ellie could see his recent beating had made him nervous about returning home on his own; the London nightlife forever twisted in his soul by one man and a meat cleaver. Robert had agreed to drop Ramsey home before returning to the office, while Casey was already pulling his skateboard out on his way home to his mother.

Looking down at Millie, Ellie considered Johnny's last words, ones that had echoed Mama Lumetta, as well. Everything she'd done was to gain enough favours to take down Nicky Simpson and prove her innocence.

But what if there was someone else in the background? What if they came for her?

Taking a deep breath to force down the sudden panic that was threatening to take over, Ellie straightened, told everyone she'd see them in the morning and then, with Millie beside her, took the scenic route home to Shoreditch.

She could deal with Nicky and whomever was behind him tomorrow.

Yeah. Tomorrow.

IN A CAR PARKED ON A SIDE STREET JUST OFF BULLARD'S PLACE, Nicky Simpson watched the team as they left, his eyes lingering on Ellie Reckless.

'You want me to follow them?' his bodyguard, a well-suited bald driver asked, his eyes locked on the group as well.

'No, Saleh,' Nicky leant back against his seat now, a slight smile on his lips. 'We know where they're all going.'

He watched Ellie and her dog walk out of sight before continuing.

'We know everything,' he finished, mostly to himself. 'Come on, let's get back and see how many sponsors have pulled out now.'

And, as the team of Finders went their own ways, so did Nicky Simpson, heading deep into the London night.

Ellie Reckless and her team
will return in their next thriller

Released May 7th 2023

Gain up-to-the-moment information on the release by
signing up to the Jack Gatland VIP Reader's Club!

Join at www.subscribepage.com/jackgatland

ACKNOWLEDGEMENTS

When you write a series of books, you find that there are a ton of people out there who help you, sometimes without even realising, and so I wanted to do a little acknowledgement to some of them.

There are people I need to thank, and they know who they are.

People who patiently gave advice when I started this back in 2020, the people on various Facebook groups who encouraged me when I didn't know if I could even do this, the designers who gave advice on cover design and on book formatting, all the way to my friends and family, who saw what I was doing not as mad folly, but as something good.

Editing wise, I owe a ton of thanks to my brother Chris Lee, who I truly believe could make a fortune as a post-retirement copy editor, if not a solid writing career of his own, Jacqueline Beard MBE, who has copyedited all my books since the very beginning, and editor Sian Phillips, all of whom have made my books way better than they have every right to be.

Also, I couldn't have done this without my growing army of ARC and beta readers, who not only show me where I falter, but also raise awareness of me in the social media world, ensuring that other people learn of my books.

But mainly, I tip my hat and thank you. *The reader.* Who once took a chance on an unknown author in a pile of Kindle books, and thought you'd give them a go, and who has carried on this far with them.

I write Ellie Reckless for you. She (and her team) gains favours for you. And with luck, she'll keep on gaining these favours for a very long time.

Jack Gatland / Tony Lee,
London, October 2022

ABOUT THE AUTHOR

Jack Gatland is the pen name of *#1 New York Times Bestselling Author* Tony Lee, who has been writing in all media for thirty-five years, including comics, graphic novels, middle grade books, audio drama, TV and film for *DC Comics, Marvel, BBC, ITV, Random House, Penguin USA, Hachette* and a ton of other publishers and broadcasters.

These have included licenses such as *Doctor Who, Spider Man, X-Men, Star Trek, Battlestar Galactica, MacGyver,* BBC's *Doctors, Wallace and Gromit* and *Shrek*, as well as work created with musicians such as *Ozzy Osbourne, Joe Satriani, Beartooth* and *Megadeth.*

As Tony, he's toured the world talking to reluctant readers with his 'Change The Channel' school tours, and lectures on screenwriting and comic scripting for *Raindance* in London.

As *Jack Gatland*, he's written thirteen books so far in the *DI Declan Walsh* procedural crime series, two books in the *Tom Marlowe* spy series, two books in the *Ellie Reckless* procedural crime series and one book in the *Damian Lucas* adventure thrillers series. He doesn't intend to stop any time soon.

An introvert West Londoner by heart, he lives with his wife Tracy and dog Fosco, just outside London.

www.jackgatland.com
www.hoodemanmedia.com

Subscribe to my Readers List:
www.subscribepage.com/jackgatland

www.facebook.com/jackgatlandbooks
www.twitter.com/jackgatlandbook
ww.instagram.com/jackgatland

Want more books by Jack Gatland? Turn the page...

LETTER FROM THE DEAD

"BY THE TIME YOU READ THIS, I WILL BE DEAD..."

A TWENTY YEAR OLD MURDER...
A PRIME MINISTER LEADERSHIP BATTLE...
A PARANOID, HOMELESS EX-MINISTER...
AN EVANGELICAL PREACHER WITH A SECRET...

DI DECLAN WALSH HAS HAD BETTER FIRST DAYS...

AVAILABLE ON AMAZON / KINDLEUNLIMITED

THEY TRIED TO KILL HIM...
NOW HE'S OUT FOR **REVENGE.**

NEW YORK TIMES #1 BESTSELLER **TONY LEE** WRITING AS

JACK GATLAND

THE MURDER OF AN **MI5 AGENT**...
A BURNED SPY **ON THE RUN** FROM HIS OWN PEOPLE...
AN ENEMY OUT TO **STOP HIM** AT ANY COST...
AND A **PRESIDENT** ABOUT TO BE **ASSASSINATED**...

SLEEPING
SOLDIERS

A **TOM MARLOWE** THRILLER

BOOK 1 IN A NEW SERIES OF THRILLERS IN THE STYLE OF
JASON BOURNE, JOHN MILTON OR **BURN NOTICE,** AND
SPINNING OUT OF THE **DECLAN WALSH** SERIES OF BOOKS

AVAILABLE ON AMAZON / KINDLE UNLIMITED

JACK GATLAND

THE LIONHEART CURSE

HUNT THE GREATEST TREASURES
PAY THE GREATEST PRICE

BOOK 1 IN A NEW SERIES OF ADVENTURES
IN THE STYLE OF 'THE DA VINCI CODE'
FROM THE CREATOR OF DECLAN WALSH

AVAILABLE ON AMAZON / KINDLEUNLIMITED

Printed in Great Britain
by Amazon

10901907R00187